I0658677

Typewriter Pub, an imprint of Blvnp Incorporated
A Nevada Corporation
1887 Whitney Mesa DR #2002
Henderson, NV 89014
www.typewriterpub.com/info@typewriterpub.com

ISBN: 978-1-64434-233-6

DISCLAIMER
This book is a work of fiction. The characters, incidents, and dialogue are drawn from the author's imagination and are not to be construed as real. While references might be made to actual historical events or existing locations, the names, characters, places, and incidents are either products of the author's imagination or are used fictitiously, and any resemblance to actual persons living or dead, business establishments, events or locales is entirely coincidental.

HER FINAL SORROW

FLORA MCCONNELL

type
writer
pub

My grandparents,
for reading my stories when they were about a monster grandma.

PROLOGUE

She runs towards me, fear in her eyes.
I know what I need to do.
I do what I should have done all along.
I lift my gun and I pull the trigger.
Death is a small price to pay for happiness.
And now, I finally am free.

ONE

Ava Milberry did not like to consider herself a divorcee. It was something that had never appealed to her, and as much as her seventeen-year-old self had believed in happily ever after, the divorce happened anyway. It wasn't as if it had come as a surprise to her, or that she had been cast aside by her husband after he had an affair with the young nanny. Her story wasn't dramatic, sad, or surprising. It was just a simple divorce. Mutual. Papers signed. House sold. *Simple.*

Ava certainly did not look back at her marriage with regret. How could she? Patrick brought her Mia, and she would never change that for the world. The one thing she did regret was selling her life away to her husband. Leaving her fun, single, university friends was a bad idea. Moving into Patrick's hometown was a bad idea. Becoming friends with Patrick's sister, Lily, was a bad idea. Selling her life to Patrick meant that now she no longer belonged to Patrick—that life was non-existent. They were Patrick's friends. It was Patrick's home. Lily was Patrick's sister, not Ava's best friend.

And so, she was lonely. Ava knew loneliness would be the first thing to creep in when the whole thing was said and done. Even when the marriage was on the rocks and she and Pat slept in different rooms, she was still married. She had someone to cook for. Someone to watch the evening news with. And now . . . she was divorced.

Being divorced put you in a whole new category of mothers. When Ava attended parent meetings, she would hear the question, "Will Mr. Milberry be joining us?"

She'd have to ruefully tell them that there was no Mr. Milberry. In fact, she was a single mother.

Despite that, Ava did not want to be married to Patrick anymore, she also did not want to be single. She couldn't remember what it was like to be single. Her last glimpse of being single was Freshers Week of university—where she managed to kiss a new boy every night. She doubted that single life in your late twenties was the same. A week into university and she met Pat. Her friends were envious; why wouldn't they be? She managed to tame Patrick Jules because he fell in love with her.

And now she was single. She often caught herself wishing she could go back in time and tell her twenty-year-old self to end the relationship while she still could. Immediately, she'd feel guilty because no Patrick meant no Mia.

And so, Patrick got to carry on living in Grennly with Ava's friends—ex-friends, it now seemed—who hadn't spoken to her since the divorce. She was now the ex-wife of the gorgeous and amazing Dr. Jules. Who would divorce such a man?

There wasn't anything wrong with Patrick. He was gorgeous, smart, funny, and an amazing father. But something had changed in him a year ago. It was as if he'd just fallen out of love with Ava, just like that.

Whilst Patrick's life had remained unchanged—apart from the fact the mothers from Grennly Park School for Infants would be fussing over the single, hot dad in town—Ava had to find a new town to settle into. There was no way Ava was going to stay in Grennly. She was going to find a new town and make new friends. She was going to start a new life.

It had been six months since the divorce was finalized. Six months since she left her life in Grennly. Six months living with her parents. And now there she was, sitting in her parents' sitting room,

3

which smelled faintly of cigarettes even though her mother had sworn to give them up.

"There's no rush for you to move away, sweetie." Ava's mother, Carol, poked her head into the bathroom. Ava looked up from the bath where Mia squirmed about in the bubbles.

"Mia is turning five soon. Five means primary school," Ava told her mother bluntly. She had fond memories of her childhood home, but ever since returning, she could not wait to get her own life again. Having her parents around twenty-four-seven was far from ideal. Initially, it meant she had this newfound freedom. Now she felt constricted by their smothering and constant reminders that she *will* find another man.

"You could send her to school here. You've met some lovely women at the gym, haven't you? It isn't like you don't have friends here, sweetie," Carol insisted. Ava cast a bored look to her mother.

"Mum, I've found a house. Let me go live in it." Ava felt herself becoming irritated with her mother. She knew that she didn't visit her parents often when she was with Patrick, but things were different now.

"I'm just trying to help you, Ava." Carol's voice became sterner. Ava felt anger creeping up her spine. Her mother was acting as if she was a teenager again, telling her what to do. She seemed reluctant to accept that Ava had grown up and had a child—a child that needed a steady home.

"I know, Mum." She pushed the anger away. "But I don't want Mia to grow up in London. Plus, Tansbury is only an hour by train."

Tansbury was the town she had decided to reside in. It was a small town with one of the top primary schools in England. It was only short train ride to London. It sounded perfect.

Carol kneeled next to Ava and poured some shampoo into her hands. She gently applied it to Mia's wispy hair before speaking

4

again, "Are you sure Tansbury is for you, Ava? It sounds remarkably similar to Grennly."

Ava knew this. She knew the sort of town she had landed herself into. Yummy mummies who were married to wealthy men, living in large houses that look like they should be in Beverly Hills. She loved her life in Grennly. She loved the people, the atmosphere, everything. So the fact that Tansbury was a clone of her ex-husband's town was some sort of victory.

"It's better for Mia that way," Ava said stubbornly before taking over Mia's bath time ritual. Carol looked slightly offended, because she knew this was the most she was ever going to be able to see her grandchild.

Carol didn't speak much more, and Ava was grateful. She was moving out to start her new life tomorrow. She had been given a clean slate and she sure as hell wasn't going to screw it up this time.

*　　　*　　　*

The next morning was how Ava expected it to be: stressful. She seemed to have had accumulated more clothes ever since staying with her parents. Mia wouldn't stop crying, Carol kept getting in the way, and Ava had to do all she could to not tell her to leave her alone. Her father, Oliver, was bumbling around with no direction, unsure of what to do with himself.

"Oliver, honey, have you put Mia's suitcase in the car?" Carol pestered her forgetful husband. Oliver looked blankly at his wife before shuffling to Mia's room to collect the fifth thing he had forgotten that morning.

"Mia, what's wrong?" Ava's daughter could not have picked a worse time to start crying.

"Mama, I want to see Daddy," she wept. Ava felt her stomach drop. The last time she had seen Patrick was a couple of weeks ago when he had dropped Mia off after their day at the zoo.

Patrick and Ava didn't speak much during the exchange, and she had felt as if she was involved in some sort of drug deal.

"Mama and Daddy are spending a little time apart. Okay, darling?" Ava used the same phrase she always used when Mia began to ask questions.

"I want to go home," Mia sobbed and Ava felt a pang of guilt. Why had she and Patrick not managed to sort out their differences? Why did they argue over everything?

"We're going to a new house, and you're having a Barbie room!" Ava tried to sound excited through her guilt. This idea seemed to perk Mia up, so much so that the crying stopped. This was a little victory for Ava, so she continued her packing of the car.

"Honey, are you sure about this?" Carol met her daughter at the car as she loaded the last suitcase into the boot. Ava inwardly rolled her eyes, but since she was leaving her mother for good, she decided not to treat her with tough love.

"I know this is hard for you, Mum. But I need to move on. I need a new life, okay? And I can't start one living under your roof." She placed her hand on Carol's arm. "You can come to visit whenever you want. I won't have my controlling husband there to stop you."

That comment made Carol laugh. She had never been particularly keen on her daughter's choice of husband, so when the divorce happened, she was secretly happy. She was not a fan of smug men, and Patrick was very smug indeed.

"I'm only a train ride away, sweetie. If you hate it—" she began, but Ava cut her off.

"I will be back in an instant. But Mum, I really think this is going to be good for me. I think I'm going to love it there." She pulled Carol into a hug and gave her a kiss on the cheek. Her father's goodbye was quiet and humble. She loved that about him; he knew what she wanted and always seemed to agree with her.

"Mia, let's get you strapped in." She placed her daughter in her booster seat and strapped her in. After double checking that she was safe, she bid her parents one last farewell before driving off to start her new life.

Ava was not used to driving in London; she and Patrick rarely visited since he was always busy in the hospital. She often wondered that if Patrick hadn't been a doctor, they might not have gotten divorced. But she cast away those thoughts because Patrick was a doctor and that wasn't going to change.

London was busy and the traffic made her grateful she wasn't staying with her mother any longer. This thought became especially prominent as she escaped the hustle and bustle of the city and entered the countryside.

"Where are we going, Mama?" Mia asked thoughtfully. Ava was relieved that her daughter had received her own personality traits rather than Patrick's. Patrick was charming, yes, but he was very arrogant. Her mother loved to point that feature out.

"To the Barbie house," Ava told her daughter happily. She *was* happy. She was going to live in a lovely white house in a lovely town with lovely people. She even allowed herself to think of the possibility of meeting someone new.

"Yay!" Mia had cheered up dramatically since their departure. She seemed to love being in the car, which Ava found very strange. Mia must have inherited that trait from her father.

As the miles on the road signs began to reduce, Ava felt herself becoming nervous to arrive in the new town. She began to worry about what the other mothers would think of her lifestyle. She wondered who, if any, the other single mothers would be. Would she be shunted to the side?

As the attempted to cast her negative thoughts aside, Ava nearly missed the turning. *Tansbury 2 miles.* Her heart leaped as the spun the steering wheel and turned onto the narrow road.

"We're nearly there, Mia!" Ava said, trying to push her anxiety away. Mia let out a little squeal excitedly. Within five minutes, the sat nav was telling Ava to turn into her new home. As they pulled onto the road, Ava spotted the house. She let out a little squeal herself. It was small, but perfect for the two of them.

"Here we are!" She pointed at the white house. Her daughter raised her sleepy eyes to the house, and they widened immediately.

"Barbie!" the little blonde girl yelped, and Ava let herself admire the house. For the first time in six months, she *let* herself be happy. The crushing pain from the divorce has lessened. No longer did she feel inadequate.

"Shall we go inside?"

*   *   *

> *Zoe: You there?*
> *Louise: Yes.*
> *Zoe: Do you think she did it?*
> *Louise: Did who do it?*
> *Zoe: You know who.*
> *Louise: No, I don't. It must have been some sort of accident;*
> *let's leave it at that.*
> *Zoe: That was not an accident, Lou.*
> *Louise: Could have been. If it was her, she would be crazy.*
> *I know she's not crazy.*

TWO

Louise Jones tapped her pen on the table, as she often did when she was stressed. Zoe Maxwell sat opposite her, soaking in the last August sun rays.

"Are you going to help me?" Louise stopped her pen tapping and gave her friend a malicious glare. Zoe pulled her sunglasses off her eyes and gave Louise a look. The latter often got like this before the year started. Organising, organising, organising. Non-stop. It was a children's party for god sake.

"How would you like my help, oh dear friend?" Zoe raised her eyebrows, which only seemed to make Louise angrier.

"I can't find the contact number for this new mum." Louise skimmed through her large contact book furiously. Zoe leaned forward to look at the list of names on the sheet.

"Ava, huh. Cool name." Zoe paused. "I bet she's one of those really cool mums. The ones that let their child do anything," she speculated. Zoe loved it when new families moved into Tansbury. The shiny new toy to play with. The adults were almost as bad as the children.

"You can't tell that from just a name," Louise pointed out. Louise was the sensible one out of the two. She made plans and she stuck to them. Zoe, on the other hand, was . . . less organised.

"Oh! And I bet she does yoga. Lots of yoga." Zoe ignored her friend's comment. "She's totally going to show us up."

Louise rolled her eyes. "Speculating about whether Ava is a cool mum or not won't help me in my search for her mobile number."

Zoe wasn't sure why Louise was putting in so much effort. Louise held an annual barbeque at the end of summer so that the children had a chance to see each other before school started. Zoe doubted this new mum, Ava, would want to come. Especially if she was a *cool mum*. She'd probably be busy practicing meditation.

"Maybe she doesn't have a phone. She's probably against all social media." A thought struck Zoe. "And I *bet* she's a vegan."

"I hope she's not. Because I'm putting chicken on the barbeque," Louise snapped, causing a startled expression from Zoe. Zoe liked being friends with Louise because she seemed to have a lot of control over the other mothers. They seemed to respect her. But she often felt that Louise resented her because she was happily married. Louise, on the other hand, was walked out on before her son, Luca, was even born. Zoe often wondered if that was the reason that she was so uptight, but she knew she was wrong to think that

"Just go to her house and invite her in person," Zoe suggested, although she was still confused to why Louise wanted her at the party so badly.

"Good idea. I don't know why I didn't think of that." And with that she snapped her book shut. "I'll do the rest of this at home."

As Zoe watched her friends retreating behind, she tilted her head to one side, and one single thought popped into her head. That woman needs to get laid.

Zoe continued to sunbathe since she had been granted the day off looking after the children. Her husband, Dave, had taken the children to the beach. She was looking forward to her children going back to school; catering for three young boys everyday was exhausting her.

And like that the peaceful serenity was over. The door opened to the patio and within an instant, three boys surrounded her.

"Mum, guess what I found on the beach!" yelled her middle son, Sam. He gave her a goofy smile, one of his teeth missing. She quickly reminded herself to pay a visit to his room tonight to be the tooth fairy.

"A mermaid?" She put her best mum voice on. "A dolphin?"

"No, mermaids are for girls!" Sam cried in a babyish voice. "Look at my rock!" He presented a large grey rock to her. It was covered in green algae and had a salty stench. Zoe was confused to why Sam was so excited about a rock.

"No, Mum, I found it! Sam stole it from me," Wren, her oldest child, protested. Wren often felt entitled to everything since he was the oldest by four years. "I found it *in* the sea. I was brave enough to go in and find it!"

"Very brave. Sounds very exciting." Zoe nodded. This comment made Sam start crying, and she immediately wished she hadn't said anything.

"But mum, I found it on the beach!" he sobbed. "Wren just left it!" And just like that, her two eldest sons began to squabble.

"Good day, milady," came the voice of her husband, tinted with his Californian accent. "How was your afternoon?" He placed a kiss on her lips, which (of course) repulsed their sons. Dave had their youngest child, Callum, on his hip. Zoe immediately noticed a red lump on his arm.

"Dave! What happened to his arm?" Her motherly instincts set in and she began to examine her youngest son's arm.

"I stung, Muma," Callum told her. "I was brave." She let out a breath of relief. Being a mum, whenever something bad happened, Zoe would find herself picturing the worst-case scenario.

11

"Did you put any cream on it?" Zoe turned her attention to her husband. He nodded hastily before raising his finger to his lips.

"It's not cream, is it Cal?" Dave turned to the little boy on his hip. Callum shook his head.

"Magic lotion! For brave heroes!" the little boy cried. Zoe gave him a small smile. She could just picture what had happened; Callum got stung, he cried a lot, so Dave persuaded him that he could be a hero if he wore the magic lotion.

Sometimes, Zoe believed that Dave was a better mum than she was. Despite working most of the time, he had managed to be around for all three of his children's first steps, going to school, and everything in between. Dave was a miracle husband.

Zoe often felt guilty about this—not that she should. Louise was very unhappy and had a large hatred for the male population. She felt as if she couldn't even speak about Dave in front of her friend. She found herself only inviting Louise around when Dave was at work or out of the house.

"Shall I put the supper on?" Dave asked her. Again, he was being the miracle husband. Zoe shook her head. It was her turn to be the perfect parent.

*   *   *

"This is your room, sweetie!" Ava showed Mia into her large room. She was faintly aware that she was ever so slightly spoiling her child, but she didn't care. She was almost competing with Patrick—nicer house, bigger room for Mia, hotter rebound. Two of the three had been checked off.

Ava knew that Patrick would have no problem moving on and finding a rebound. All the mothers at Mia's old school absolutely adored him. Come to think of it, there could have been another woman. Ava would have had no idea if Patrick was having an affair. It was very likely; they never spent time with each other.

Despite wanting to compete with Patrick, Ava knew that moving on was going to be difficult. If Tansbury was anything like Grennly, everyone would be happily married. But the move wasn't about finding a body to cuddle up with—it was for finding a new start.

With that, she turned her insistent thoughts off and placed Mia's suitcases in her large room. Patrick had offered to split their furniture, but Ava was so keen on a fresh slate that she didn't want anything from her old life. Plus, the landlady had furnished the house beautifully, so she didn't need Patrick's poorly chosen furniture.

Ding dong.

Ava sat upright in a flash. Who would be ringing her doorbell? She didn't know anyone here. Had Patrick decided he loved her after all, and was here to beg on his knees for her forgiveness?

Fat chance, thought Ava. She quickly scuttled down the stairs and opened the front door. In front of her stood a tall woman, around her age. She had a broad jaw and short, caramel hair. Pretty in a distinctive way.

"Hello, sorry to come barging in like this," said the woman. Ava noticed that she was posh—like all the mothers in Grennly.

"How can I help you?" Ava gave her a smile and crossed her arms over her chest. The woman pulled out a piece of paper.

"You're new to town, yes?" The woman handed the paper to Ava. It was a beautifully decorated invitation to a barbeque. "I'm Louise. I'm head of the mother's council at Tansbury View." She stuck her hand out.

This is all very formal, thought Ava. She shook Louise's hand and introduced herself.

"I'm Ava. My daughter and I have just moved in."

"It's always nice to have a new face in Tansbury," Louise told her enthusiastically. "What's the reason for the move?" She paused. "If you don't mind me asking."

13

Ava shook her head hastily. "Oh, not at all. My husband and I separated. Long story short, I moved away to distance myself from him," she explained, impressed at her own ability to open up to this stranger.

Louise looked somewhat happy at Ava's statement. "Another single mother. Rejoice!" She clapped her hands together. Ava immediately realised that her joy meant that she was a single mother too. This lifted a weight off her chest.

"Are you a fellow divorcee?" Ava immediately loosened up. "In fact, come in, we can have some coffee."

Louise followed her into the house. The house was furnished with in a modern style. Sleek marble surfaces, and large blue paintings. Louise sat down at the round table.

"How do you like your coffee?" Ava asked as the started the Nespresso machine. It was the one thing she took from Patrick, since he despised coffee. Sometimes, she wondered whether she bought it just to annoy him.

"Milk and one sugar please," Louise asked politely.

"Same as me," Ava noted; she found herself immediately warming up to the woman. Ava brought the coffees to the table and settled down opposite of Louise.

"In answer to your question, I am single, but not divorced. I was walked out on," Louise said. Ava noticed that her answer was robotic, as if she had practiced her answer millions of times before. Ava nodded slowly. At least Patrick hadn't walked out on her when she got pregnant.

"Oh." Ava wasn't sure what to say. "I'm so sorry."

Louise shook her head instantly. "Don't be. He was an arsehole, excuse my language." Louise tapped herself on the wrist as if to tell herself off. Ava could instantly tell what kind of mother she was: organised, strict, and sensible. The opposite of herself.

"Hear hear." Ava rose her coffee as if it were some toast to all the men out there who weren't adequate fathers. She silently reminded herself that Patrick was a very good father.

14

"If you don't mind my asking . . ." Louise took a sip of coffee. "What was the reason you and your husband divorced?" Ava started to notice Louise's personality traits emerging more. She was reserved, careful not to say anything wrong. *A people pleaser.*

"I think he just . . . fell out of love with me. And I didn't recognise the man he became. Simple as that," Ava told Louise. She, too, had practised what she was going to say to new people. Louise pouted a little as if to say: what a shame! Ava wanted to tell her that it was not a shame at all.

"Thank you for the coffee, Ava." Louise put her finger up. "Am I pronouncing it right? *Ay-va?*" Louise was a control freak; Ava knew this now.

"Yes. Just like its spelt." She paused and realised she should probably be polite. "Thank you for the invitation. Mia and I would love to come." Louise looked pleased at this revelation and stood up hastily.

"I must dash. Do you have a mobile number?" Louise pulled her phone out. A blackberry. Ava nodded and pulled out an iPhone. Patrick bought it for her, insisting it was the best phone to have. Ava was fine with a simpler phone, but Patrick got his way.

"Yeah. Put your number in," Ava told Louise, before her new organised friend bustled out of the house.

*   *   *

Kelly has joined the chat.
Kelly: You two are gossiping about the murder, aren't you?
Louise: It was an accident.
Zoe: Lou is being self-righteous as per usual.
We all know it was a murder.
Kelly: I agree. I also think this is a sign.
Louise: A sign? Someone is dead, Kelly.
Kelly: A sign that husbands should never get involved.
They cause too much drama.

15

Zoe: I disagree with you on that, Kelly. Dave never causes drama.

Louise: Oh, shut up both of you. It was a tragedy and husbands had nothing to do with it.

THREE

Louise was excited about the barbeque. Even more so now that she had a new friend. Ava was the polar opposite of Louise, which was exactly why she liked her so much. Many of the mothers at school disliked Louise, with one in particular whose mission was to be Louise's rival.

She distinctly remembered the day she met Nancy Gilbert. Nancy was a fellow mother; she was outspoken, feisty, and argumentative. No one was quite sure what Nancy did—all they knew was that she was a 'big name in the city'. Other mothers often gossiped about her in awe: what *must* it be like to work every day? Louise was also in awe of Nancy—not that she'd ever admit it—since she had managed to marry a gorgeous man who had become a stay-at-home dad.

All the mothers were obsessed with Jake Gilbert. He had devastatingly good looks and was very kind. Zoe believed that Nancy abused Jake, and that's why he stayed with her. Louise would tell her to not joke about such things; but she secretly agreed. How *did* Nancy tie down Jake? Nancy was attractive, yes, but in a cosmetic way; bleach-blonde hair, bright-blue eyes—they *must* be contacts—and a lot of . . . adjustments. Nancy did certainly *not* seem like Jake's type. Carefree, relaxed Jake. Louise even thought she might be a tiny bit in love with him.

The day Louise met Nancy was a very strange day indeed. Nancy's daughter, Melissa, and Louise's son, Luca, became friends at school instantly. Luca was boyish and charming; and Melissa was quiet and beautiful. The recipe for a young romance. Louise had taken Luca to Nancy's house for a play date. Louise had expected to be met by Jake—she was immediately taken by him—but it was Nancy who opened the door.

"You must be Louisa," she had proclaimed loudly. "I'm Nancy, Melissa's mother."

"Louise," Louise had firmly corrected. She immediately disliked this woman. "This is Luca." Louise's dislike for Nancy had been confirmed by her look of distaste when she looked at Luca. Nancy observed him like he was a zoo animal.

"Nice to meet you." Nancy had a look as if there was a bad smell under her nose, "I would invite you in for a coffee, but I'm terribly busy."

"No worries. I'll come to get Luca in a couple of hours," Louise had said and Nancy scrunched her nose.

"If you could just come back after one hour, that would be fab. I'm worried Luca is a bad influence on Melissa, that's all." Nancy smiled. "you understand, don't you?"

And from that moment onwards, Nancy and Louise did not get along. Luca and Melissa had drifted apart too.

Louise bustled around her kitchen, making sure the potato salad was ready for the mums, and the chips were in the oven for the kids. The chicken was on the barbeque and the sun was out. It was due to begin in an hour. Louise was on top of everything.

"Mummy, when are the other children getting here?" Her youngest daughter, Issie tugged on her skirt. Issie was the product of a sperm donor. She had never wanted Luca to be an only child, and so when he was four, she was pregnant again.

"An hour, cupcake," Louise stroked Issie's face. Issie often asked where her father was, but she didn't want to explain that Luca wasn't her proper brother, or that Mummy had selected Daddy out of a brochure.

18

"Is Callum coming?" Issie asked. Issie and Callum got along very well, much to Louise's happiness.

"And a new friend for you. Her name is Mia," Louise told her daughter. She hoped that Mia would become friends with Issie, meaning that they too would stay friends. She highly suspected that Nancy would try to take Ava under her wing.

"I like that name," Issie burst out, and Louise agreed.

*   *   *

Ava couldn't decide whether to bail on the barbeque or not. She knew that going was the right option. She would meet new people; Mia could make friends. But a part of her was too scared to go. Going meant she was accepting her new life. A new life without Patrick.

And life with Patrick used to be good. Their university years were amazing. When they first moved to Grennly, it had been amazing. But then something happened. Something changed in Patrick. Something changed in her.

"We'll go," Ava said, not really talking to anyone in particular. Mia sat on the stairs, playing with her Barbie dolls. She claimed they were on a mission up the stairs.

"Where are we going?" asked Mia, being the inquisitive child she was. At this moment, one of her Barbie's fell off the step. "Oh no, Ken save me!" Mia put on her best Barbie voice. This made Ava chuckle.

"To a barbeque, sweetie. You're going to make some new friends from your new school. Isn't that exciting?!" Ava tried to make herself sound excited. She *was* excited, but there was a part of her that was nervous. All her old friends were Patrick's friends, and so she hadn't had to *make* new friends since her university days.

"Honey, are you ready to go?" Ava called out to Mia in attempt to distract her daughter from her current game. Mia looked up and dropped her dolls.

"Yes mama." She skipped over and took Ava's hand. Ava felt a surge of butterfly's flutter in her stomach, but she was determined to be brave. The only way to get over Patrick was to move on.

*　　*　　*

As Ava pulled up to Louise's house, she was surprised by the size. Louise seemed like the type to be living in a small cottage where not much could go wrong. But this house was definitely on the larger side. Ava calmed her nerves and climbed out of the car with Mia in tow.

Immediately voices of chattering mothers could be heard from behind a gate leading into the garden. Thank goodness it was a nice day. Ava opened the gate to see twenty or so people, mainly women, and children playing on the grass.

"Ava!" She recognized the voice as Louise called her over. Ava smiled in relief; Louise had come to her rescue. Louise tottered over in wedges and a sundress—Ava immediately felt underdressed—with a little girl behind her.

"Louise, this looks amazing," Ava gushed and she was not lying. Louise had clearly gone full out with the party; bunting, balloons, a large paddling pool, champagne, salads, and everything else you could think of.

"Thank you! I was so stressed this morning. Zoe got so cross with me," Louise was clearly flattered by Ava's compliment, and so Ava made a note of what Louise liked.

"Zoe? Is that your daughter?" Ava questioned, but Louise hastily shook her head.

"Zoe is my closest friend, you have got to meet her," Louise said loudly, and Ava noticed that she was ever so slightly drunk. Ava nodded.

"This is my daughter, Issie," Louise pushed her daughter forward in a polite fashion. Issie stuck her hand out to Mia.

"I'm four. What's your name?" Issie grinned at Mia, and Mia tenderly took the child's hand. Mia wasn't so gregarious as other children, especially this one.

"I'm Mia," Mia spoke quietly, but this earned a grin from Issie anyway. Issie stuck her hand out and pulled Mia away from Ava and towards the other children.

*   *   *

Nancy: Did you speak to Louise and Zoe?

Kelly: I did. Louise thinks it was an accident.

Nancy: Oh please. She's ridiculous.

Kelly: I know.

Nancy: Ever since the barbeque, she despised me more than usual. It must have been because Ava liked me. She's very territorial over friends.

Kelly: I agree. It was like Louise had Ava on a leash.

Nancy: Do you think Louise could have done it? Friendship loyalties and all?

Kelly: Louise? A killer? Where did that come from?

Nancy: I don't know what to think anymore. Ava used to be lovely. I would have considered her my friend . . . until the incident.

FOUR

Zoe was tipsy, but in her defence, so was everyone else. She was giggling like a teenage girl with Kelly Peterson. Kelly was not supposed to be friends with Zoe, and Zoe was not supposed to be friends with Kelly. Kelly was Nancy's friend and Zoe was Louise's friend. They weren't supposed to mix.

"I'm so irresponsible." Zoe giggled, and yet took another sip of champagne. "My three children are more mature than me."

Kelly just agreed. "Oh I know. Sometimes I think Ottilie is smarter than me." She laughed. "She thought she was too cool for this barbeque. Being year six and all." This made Zoe choke on her champagne.

"Poor Wren. I dragged him along." Zoe lowered her voice and continued, "Although I think he secretly likes being older than everyone else. Gives him a sense of power. Gets that from his mum." She winked at Kelly and they both laughed. Out of the corner of her eye, Zoe spotted a blonde woman walk into the barbeque next to Louise.

Kelly realised it before she did. "Is that the new girl?" Girl was the right term for her. She had curly blonde hair—Zoe didn't think she could ever have grown her hair that long—which was braided around her head. She wore flared trousers—the ones teenagers wore these days—with a crop top. God forbid! *How on earth is her stomach that toned after birth?* Zoe idly wondered.

"Her name is Ava." Zoe couldn't take her eyes off her. She was so gorgeous and so different to the rest of the mothers in Tansbury. Immediately she noticed that Louise had taken her under her wing.

"She's gorgeous!" Kelly exclaimed. "Just looking at her makes me want to skip lunch. I must be three times her size!" Zoe silently agreed. She was a slim mother herself, but in comparison to Ava she felt like an elephant. And they were heading her way.

"Louise!" Zoe exclaimed as they approached, as if they hadn't been watching them. Ava had a shy smile on her face.

"Zoe, Kelly, this is Ava," Louise introduced her new friend. "I need to go mingle, but Zoe, you'll look after Ava?" Zoe merely nodded as Louise scampered off.

"Hi. Sorry to intrude, I know no one," Ava muttered. Zoe immediately took a liking to her. She seemed sweet.

"We're not scary." Zoe touched her arm affectionately. Ava looked relieved and smiled at both the women. Zoe idly wondered how old she was. She looked no older than twenty-five, but she must be older.

"It certainly is intimidating walking in here. You're all so glamorous," Ava said. Zoe herself was a glamorous mother. She knew that. She styled herself so that she was seen as a glam mum.

"Look at yourself!" Kelly exclaimed, gesturing to Ava's individual style. "You are much cooler than us." Zoe coughed. "Well, much cooler than me."

"Thank you," Ava laughed nervously, and Zoe thought it was sweet. Kelly quickly excused herself as Nancy walked in. Zoe glanced over to see Mrs Ice Queen herself and her gorgeous arm candy strutting over to Kelly.

"Who is that?" Ava breathed, her gaze meeting the glamorous couple. Zoe noticed Ava's eyes immediately dart to Jake, Nancy's husband. Ava was staring in awe, and Zoe didn't blame her. Jake was very attractive; it must be said. Plus, he looked about half Nancy's age. Like her little toy boy.

23

"Nancy and Jake Gilbert. Ugh." Zoe turned to face Ava. Zoe despised Nancy, nearly as much as Louise did.

"Not a fan?"

"I am a loyal friend. Nancy and Louise are not friends, and therefore I am not either." Zoe lowered her voice and continued, "try to not involve yourself in the mother's politics."

"I am not one for conflict, so I think I'll steer clear." But Ava's eyes stayed on Jake Gilbert.

Zoe noticed Ava's eyes glued to Jake. "You're not the only one," she whispered in her ear. Ava snapped out of her trance and blushed.

"Sorry?" She tucked a strand of that long blonde hair behind her ear.

"We've all got a soft spot for Jake. I don't know why he's married to that witch," Zoe chuckled, "don't repeat that."

*　　　*　　　*

As the barbeque went on, Ava found herself loosening up. Zoe seemed less uptight than Louise, and she hoped that she would become friends with her.

In no time, Ava's glass had become empty, and she found herself hoping that food was soon, because drinking on an empty stomach would never turn out well.

Zoe and Ava were chatting about Zoe's husband—he seemed like a miracle husband and Ava was very jealous—when Louise returned.

"I'm sorry for abandoning you." Louise placed her hand on Ava's shoulder. "I've been doing the rounds." She glanced around before lowering her voice to a whisper and added, "I've been trying to avoid Nancy."

Ava stifled a giggle. She found Louise and Zoe's hatred for Nancy quite funny. She wasn't a malicious person, but it just

24

reminded her of school. All the bitchiness. She secretly loved watching the drama unfold.

"Ava fancies Jake." Zoe nodded at Louise. "You can fangirl over him together." Zoe winked at Ava, and Ava blushed like a teenage girl.

"I do not!" Ava fanned her face to stop the blushing. She lightly smacked Zoe's arm, but Zoe simply chuckled to herself.

"Ava, it would be weird if you didn't fancy him," Louise said soothingly. Her face suddenly dropped. "They're coming over here."

Ava glanced over to see Nancy and Jake wandering over. Ava grabbed another glass of champagne from the side.

"Louise!" Nancy exclaimed, and Ava noticed the display of affection was very fake. They embraced. "I am so sorry that I didn't come and say hello before. I was catching up with everyone!"

Nancy was clearly lying. Louise had a fake smile plastered on her face as she shook her head. "Oh, don't worry. I was doing the same." They chuckled together.

"Louise, this is a great set up." Jake stepped forward and gave Louise a kiss on the cheek. Ava felt as if she was watching a television programme, silently observing. And as she observed Jake, she couldn't help but notice something familiar in him. She almost recognised him, and she wondered if they'd ever met before. Or maybe she just had a type.

"Oh my goodness, I feel so rude!" Nancy turned her bright blue eyes to Ava, and Ava immediately felt nervous.

"You must be Ava!" she exclaimed and shot her hand out. "I'm Nancy, and this is my husband Jake." Ava shook Nancy's hand, and then Jake's.

"Lovely to meet you." Ava smiled at them, whilst being slightly anxious that Louise would hate her if she became friends with her arch enemy.

"If you don't mind me asking, how old are you?" Nancy asked lightly. "You look no older than twenty-five!"

25

Everyone chuckled, as if in agreement. Ava joined in; flattered by the compliment.

"Twenty-nine. I had Mia when I was quite young," she explained to them. Nancy put her hand to her forehead in mock horror.

"I feel like an old woman. Forty! Gosh. You're a little spring chicken." Nancy took a sip of her champagne. Everyone laughed with Nancy, but the tension that was building could not be ignored.

*   *   *

Zoe: Do you think Nancy could have been involved?

Louise: I've said it one hundred times and I've said it again; it was an accident.

Zoe: Ava's been arrested, Lou. You'd know, you were the one who bailed her out.

Louise: Under false pretences. It was an accident and the police just want someone to blame.

Zoe: So, you think it has nothing to do with Nancy? Even after . . .

Louise: She does hate Ava. But that's mad, even for Nancy.

Zoe: It's a possibility. Because if it wasn't Ava, who could it be?

FIVE

Louise watched as Nancy interacted with Ava. Nancy was laughing at something Ava had said, and Ava was blushing as if she was confused at Nancy's reaction. Nancy was trying to steal Louise's new friend.

Louise had always been territorial over friends. She was well aware of this. Nancy had once tried to be friends with Zoe, but Zoe knew Louise wasn't a fan. And so, she shut her down. Ava, on the other hand, didn't seem to be as fiery as Zoe.

"You are honestly so gorgeous," Nancy said loudly before putting her hand on her husband's arm. "Honey, isn't she gorgeous?"

This was a test. Louise noticed this because it was something she would do. Jake sipped at his champagne and nodded.

"Can't be ignored." Whoosh. Jake passed with flying colours. Louise noticed the slight flicker of Jake's eyes and idly wondered if Zoe was right. If, in fact, Nancy had been abusing him. The thought quickly passed from her head.

"My husband," Nancy whispered to Ava as if sharing some inside joke they'd had for years. "Such the gentleman!" And then she threw her head back in laughter. Ava looked utterly confused and merely laughed with her.

"So, Ava, what do you do for a living?" Jake asked, speaking to Ava for the first time. Louise felt a pang of jealousy.

"I work in marketing. I work from home, actually. So that I can still look after Mia," Ava explained to Jake, and Louise noticed a slight glimmer of something—she couldn't quite put her finger on it, hope, maybe?—in her eye.

"What type of marketing? Nancy's big in the industry." Jake placed a hand on his wife's shoulder, and Louise couldn't help but notice that it seemed fake.

"I'm the web producer for Xanos. The clothes line?" Ava clarified, but everyone in the conversation knew the brand. It was booming at the moment. Louise often treated herself one every couple of months by buying herself an item of clothing from there. After the purchase, her balance would dip hugely.

"Wow." Nancy seemed impressed; Louise rarely saw her impressed. "That's incredible. Xanos is my favourite shop. I'm actually dressed head to toe in it now!" Nancy spun around as if she was a model. *Oh, of course she could afford to spend all her money on Xanos clothing,* thought Louise enviously.

"So am I." Ava giggled, and gestured to her outfit. Louise made a note to ask Ava for a discount code later. She certainly wasn't going to ask in front of Nancy. Nancy would simply laugh and exclaim that she didn't need a discount code—she could afford everything!

Louise felt like a gooseberry, intruding on their conversation. She felt the need to leave them alone and join Zoe at the buffet. Zoe had disappeared after about five minutes; she hated Nancy even more than Louise did.

"I am going to grab some food," Louise said as nonchalantly as she could. She needed another glass of champagne.

"Oh, thank goodness, I'm starved," Ava agreed and so did the Gilbert couple. And so, they made their way to the barbeque.

*   *   *

Nancy: Ever since that barbeque, I knew things were not

right.

Kelly: I agree. We should have seen it coming.

Nancy: I even told her that she was gorgeous. It was like she took it as permission.

Kelly: I don't think she's that attractive. All hair and eyes, no personality.

Nancy: I actually got along with her really well.
It's a shame, really.

SIX

Ava's mind kept wandering to sex. It was like a plague. She hadn't thought this much about sex for a long while. Of course, when her marriage broke down, the sex soon followed.

Maybe it was the alcohol. She hadn't drank this much in a long time. She made a vague note of taking a taxi home later. She was well over the limit.

She knew that Jake had a lot to do with it. He was so attractive she could hardly believe it. She felt like a teenage girl again. But he was married. To a beautiful, successful woman. And as much as Ava tried to hate her, she seemed to be getting along well with Nancy—she was not going to tell Louise this.

But yet, as she ate her hot dog—reminding herself that the diet was going to start tomorrow—she found her eyes drawn to him. He was in conversation with the woman she met earlier. Not Zoe, the other one. Kelly, maybe? Yes, Kelly.

Kelly had one hand on his arm and her head was thrown back with laughter. She watched as her husband cut in the friendly banter and cracked a joke. It all seemed friendly. Louise and Zoe were chatting about some rumour, and Ava listened intently. She didn't want to be out of the loop.

"Rumour has it." Zoe leaned in and lowered her voice. "Miles is having an affair with one of the teachers." She raised her eyebrows.

"I don't believe it," Louise said in that sensible voice of hers. "Miles would never." Ava didn't feel she could comment.

"I heard it from Shira." Zoe turned her focus to Ava. "She's a year six mum, by the way."

"Well, how does Shira know?" Louise folded her arms. Ava noticed that this was a sore topic for her. Unfaithful men. Ava wondered if Patrick had ever been unfaithful.

"She allegedly saw it." Zoe shrugged her shoulders. "And she hasn't told Kelly."

"She's close with Kelly, though. Why wouldn't she say?" Louise asked. Ava was trying to put the pieces of the school together. She had only been around these mothers for an afternoon, but the secrets and mystery were already clouding her mind.

"Beats me." Zoe shrugged once more. "I need more champagne." (She didn't).

"I'll join you. Ava?" Louise asked, but Ava shook her head.

"I'm going to check on Mia. Catch up with you later," she told them. She was lying. Well, sort of. She was going to check on Mia, but she also wanted some alone time. Louise was smothering her, and the politics were already going over her head. She wandered over to where the children were playing and beckoned Mia over.

"Moma, we're playing a game!" she whined as she approached her mother. Ava crouched down and chuckled.

"Are the other children being nice? Are you having fun?" Ava asked. Mia looked very impatient.

"Yes, but can you go now?" Mia stomped her feet up and down. "I don't want to miss out!" Ava folded her arms.

"Fine." She placed a kiss on the top of her daughter's head, before she ran off. Ava sighed, before standing up and watching Mia join in with the current game.

"It seems we're not cool enough for them anymore." Ava heard a deep voice behind her and turned to see Jake. He had a

31

small smile on his face, and his eyes were on Ava. She still couldn't put her finger on why he seemed so familiar. He *did* look similar to Patrick, and so Ava concluded that it must be that she had a type.

"Not at all. I think she'd rather I just go home now," Ava laughed. Jake held out a glass to her.

"I saw you were empty handed. Awful etiquette. At these events, one must always have a full glass of champagne. It's rude, otherwise." He winked at the end.

"I'm awfully sorry," Ava said as she took the glass from his hand. "I did wonder how Louise could afford this much champagne. We must have got through ten bottles already."

"I'd say twenty," Jake corrected, "My wife must have had about five bottles to herself." Ava couldn't tell if he was joking.

"At least she can handle her drink. A couple more of these and my body will be hating me tomorrow." Ava looked at her glass with weary eyes.

"I agree." Jake threw the contents of his glass onto the grass. "I'm not one for the etiquette associated with these events."

"What a waste!" Ava exclaimed, but she then joined him by tipping her champagne away.

"Don't tell the mothers." Jake looked side to side as if someone could hear them. "They'd kill me."

"There's no point crying over spilt champagne." Ava laughed. "But I agree. The mothers are certainly very . . ."

"Territorial. Territorial over their children, their friends, and their husbands." Jake gestured with his champagne glass.

"I guess I will see with time." Ava didn't want to bitch about the mothers. But from what she could see so far, he was right.

"One piece of advice I will give you . . ." Jake leaned in as if he was telling her a secret. "Try to distance yourself from the politics."

32

"I've already been warned," Ava said, and she couldn't help grinning. This was the best part of the day so far. She wouldn't tell anyone that though. It was her dirty little secret.

"More specifically . . ." Jake looked around again, before adding, "Stay away from my wife and Louise."

Ava was shocked. "Your wife?"

"Indeed. She likes confrontation. And drama. That's why I rarely come to these events." He shrugged.

"Then why are you here today?" Ava raised her eyebrows at him. He smirked.

"If I'm being honest, the continuous stream of texts I received from Louise were persistent. I couldn't *not* come."

"I see." Ava wasn't surprised that Louise had been texting Jake non-stop. She seemed to be in love with him. Although, Ava couldn't blame her.

"We should get Mia and Kai together sometime before school starts. Kai loves making new friends," Jake suggested, and Ava felt a pang of wanting in her stomach. She quickly pushed it away.

"Sure, that sounds great."

"Unfortunately, it will be me doing the organising. I'm basically a stay at home dad." He looked disappointed with himself.

"Put your details in then." Ava was struggling to keep a smile off her face. A play date meant that she would be able to spend more time with Jake.

Purely plutonic. Keep it that way, Ava thought to herself. It was almost as if she was setting herself up for failure.

*　　　*　　　*

Kelly: You know, Jake and Ava were looking pretty cosy at the barbeque.
Zoe: Rubbish.
Kelly: Penelope Watkins said she saw then walking into the

woods together.

Zoe: Bull. Penelope is stirring the pot; that is all.

*Kelly: I'm not sure. I definitely saw Jake put his number in
on Ava's phone.*

*Zoe: That tells us nothing. I have Jake's number!
And I am a faithful wife!*

*Kelly: It tells us something. It was a foreshadowing of some
sort.*

SEVEN

Two weeks had gone by since the barbeque. School was starting soon and Ava was panicking. She didn't want to be alone all day. She knew she would miss Mia's company.

But today was the day. She had been counting down to it like a teenager—Today was Mia and Kai's play date.

Play date equalled Jake. She told Zoe about the play date—they were becoming fast friends, a weekly coffee was their thing—but not Louise. This was Zoe's advice. Ava felt bad keeping secrets but Louise was busy with the mother's council anyway.

It was exactly fifteen minutes before Jake was due to arrive. Ava had dressed herself well—a skirt from Xanos and a sweater. The other mothers loved to make fun of her hippie fashion sense.

Mia happily played with her train set whilst Ava cleaned the kitchen. She knew she was putting in too much effort, but she couldn't help it; she fancied Jake. Yes, he had a wife. She wasn't going to try anything. He was just nice to look at.

And like clockwork, the clock hit five and the doorbell rang. Ava sprung from her seat and walked as slowly as she could to the door. She opened it to find the gorgeous face of Jake. And his child, of course.

"Hello!" Jake exclaimed and leaned forward to give her a kiss on each cheek.

"Hello Kai." Ava crouched down so she was on eye level with the little boy. "Mia just got her train sets out. Do you like trains?" She had her baby voice on and she knew it. She was guilty of the baby voice most of the time. She hoped she would grow out of it.

The dark-haired little boy nodded and scampered past Ava to where Mia sat with her trains. Mia was shy and silently handed him a blue train. Ava stood up and gave Jake a smile. *God, he is good looking,* she thought.

"How are we?" Jake said with a cheeky grin. Ava lead him into the kitchen and sat down on a stool. He sat opposite her.

"Good thank you, panicking about school starting, but other than that, I'm great." Ava chuckled at how naïve she felt. A new mum. *The* new mum.

"You're panicking? Why is that?" Jake seemed genuinely concerned. Ava shrugged.

"Hold on, do you want coffee? Tea?" She glanced at her fridge. "Alcohol?"

"It is five o'clock." Jake gave a wink. "Maybe after supper."

Ava nodded and sat back down. "I'm panicking because I'll miss Mia," she confessed. "It'll be so strange being alone in the house."

Jake nodded slowly. "I'm only down the road if you need some company."

Ava's stomach flip flopped. *Friends. Just friends.* She reminded herself.

"Thank you," Ava said shyly, trying to not act as transparent as she felt.

"It's no problem. Nancy is never in. I never see her. Work work work." He looked angry about this, but Ava couldn't tell if she was reading him wrong.

"That must be exhausting for her."

"She loves it, but she never sees us. Kai misses his mum," Jake explained, and Ava realised it really was anger. Was he angry that he never saw her?

"My ex-husband was a doctor. So I understand," Ava told him in attempt to comfort him. Jake snapped his head up.

"Ex?" he asked; Ava realised she hadn't actually told Jake that she was a single mum.

"Sorry. I forget that people don't know. I am a single mum." Ava pulled a face. "Does that put me into a different category?"

Something flickered in Jake's eyes. "In a way."

Ava's stomach plummeted. His words cut deeper than she thought. She wanted to tell him that she was—or at least hoped—that she was the perfect wife. Patrick was the one who changed his mind. Clearly her feelings were shown because Jake spoke again.

"Not a bad way. Just different," he said quickly, as if he was scared he offended her. She felt a weight lift off her chest.

"Thank god. I get so worried of what people will think of me. I'm not a nightmare!" Ava tried to say it in a jokey way, but she meant every word of it.

"Why did you separate? If you don't mind me asking." Jake added the last bit in speedily. Ava was used to this question.

"Lost the spark. We grew apart. His long hours at the hospital was always a sore topic for us," Ava explained. Jake nodded as if he related to it; he probably did.

"Sounds similar to Nancy and I." Jake paused before leaning closer to Ava. "We have been arguing a lot recently. I don't know how much longer we can go on."

Ava felt hope flutter in her stomach. Was he insinuating what she thought?

"What?" Ava didn't know what else to say. She didn't want to assume.

"To put it plainly, Nancy and I have been thinking about separating," Jake said without hesitation. Ava almost fell off her stool. Why was he telling her this?

"Gosh, Jake." Ava was short of words. "I am so sorry. I would know, it's awful." She placed her hand on his arm. He flinched.

"It's been a problem for a while. We have just been putting it off," he said, but he didn't look sad. He looked *relieved.* Ava knew because she felt exactly the same way. He chuckled awkwardly. "I don't know why I am telling you this. We barely know each other."

Ava laughed too. "I won't say anything to anyone, if that's what you're worried about." Jake looked up at her and was silent for a couple of seconds.

"You're different to the other mothers," he said quietly, and Ava felt her heart race. She swallowed, but her mouth was so dry that it pained her.

"Just younger," Ava said as bluntly as she could. Before he could say anything else, she stepped off her stool. "I need to cook the supper. Is Kai okay with chicken pie?"

They had agreed beforehand to have supper together so that the children could get to know each other. As Ava pulled the pie out of the fridge, she wondered if it was a bad idea.

"'Course. He's not a fussy child," Jake answered slowly. Ava nodded but didn't turn around. She didn't know how to act. Jake had told her he was going to leave Nancy. She glanced at the clock to see it was 6 PM . Time was flying by. She hoped that it wouldn't move too fast, as she glanced over to see Mia laughing happily at something Kai had just said.

*   *   *

There was no more talk of Nancy over supper. Of course, there wouldn't be, since Kai was sat at the table. Ava couldn't help but notice the looks Jake was giving her. Or was she reading into things? She couldn't tell.

38

"That was delicious. Kai, say thank you to Ava for the lovely meal," Jake spoke to his child in a loving way. Kai blushed and said a small thank you, not meeting Ava's eyes.

"We better head off," Jake said as Kai and Mia scampered back over to the train set.

"Good luck trying to separate Kai from the train set," Ava laughed; she secretly didn't want him to leave yet.

"I'll put on my grumpy dad voice, he listens to that," Jake said before wandering over to the two children. "Kai, bud, time to go."

As predicted, Kai began to whine, but Jake managed to tear him away from playtime. The four of them walked to the door and Mia politely gave Kai a hug and thanked him for playing with her.

"Thank you for having me," Kai said in a slow, rehearsed, babyish voice. Ava chuckled and gave him a grin.

"It was lovely having you." And then it was Jake's turn to say goodbye. Jake puts his arms out.

"Thank you for supper. It was delicious." He put his arms around her and kissed her cheek. Ava felt her whole body tense. "And I know you feel it too," he whispered into her ear, sending shivers down her spine. Ava blinked slowly before releasing him. *What?* She felt it too?

Ava was speechless as Jake winked at her before turning around and heading out of the house. What had just happened?

*   *   *

Louise: I personally didn't see it coming.
Zoe: Get off your high horse, Lou. We all did.
Louise: It seemed friendly to me.
Zoe: There was nothing friendly about it. Jake saw what he
*   wanted and took it.*
Louise: You are acting like she is an innocent bystander in
*   all of this.*

39

Zoe: Oh, I know. She isn't.

EIGHT

"Mummy, I want the Spiderman one!" Callum whined as he solemnly placed his sandwich into the batman lunch box. Zoe sighed and looked over to Sam, who happily held his Spiderman lunch box in Callum's face. Wren was pretending to not care about lunch boxes, in fact, he thought he was too cool for them altogether.

"Well, how about you switch every week? Sam has it this week, then next week you can have it." Zoe thought the compromise was good enough, but it seemed enough to reduce Callum into floods of tears.

"What's all this fuss about?" Dave came into the kitchen and Zoe felt relieved. He would know what to do. He's a miracle worker.

"Daddy," Callum wept and ran over to his dad. Dave looked at Zoe and mouthed, 'what's this all about?'. Zoe shrugged. She hated the first day of school.

Whilst Dave sorted out the lunch box fiasco, Zoe idly wondered how Ava and Jake's play date went. She knew that Ava found Jake attractive, and she also knew that Jake and Nancy were separating. Zoe was close with Kelly; it was some rebellious friendship. At the barbeque Kelly—she was quite the gossip—informed Zoe of the separation.

Zoe wasn't shocked. Nancy and Jake were so different. They never spent time together. Jake was carefree, friendly, and gorgeous, not that Nancy wasn't attractive. And Zoe saw how Jake looked at Ava. She couldn't quite put her finger on it exactly. Maybe it was a look of longing? He almost looked angry when he looked at her, or maybe he was just angry that he couldn't have her. Ava seemed oblivious but Zoe certainly wasn't. She saw a spark. *You heard it here first,* she thought coyly.

"Sorted." Dave placed a long kiss on Zoe's lips, causing a series of protests from the boys. Dave loved to gross them out. Zoe loved his nature.

"What would I do without you?" She let herself lean onto his chest and he chuckled.

"The question is *who* you would do," he joked, making Zoe laugh. It was moments like these where she really felt sorry for Louise. She didn't mean that in a condescending way, but she couldn't imagine having no one to joke around with.

But she didn't feel sorry for Ava. This wasn't meant in a mean way, because she liked Ava a lot. Ava seemed to be the sort of person that could look after herself. Even though Louise was more than capable, Zoe really believed that she would benefit from a partner.

*   *   *

Ava parked her Polo as close to the school entrance as she could. She could tell that Mia was nervous; she kept opening and closing her lunch box.

"Are you feeling okay, honey?" Ava stroked her daughter's face. Mia nodded hastily and opened her door, before hopping out.

"Come on, Momma, I can see Kai!" And before Ava could get a word in edgeways, Mia scampered over to Kai. Her stomach dropped when she saw Nancy and Jake. They looked fine; each holding a child's hand and laughing. They looked like the picture of happiness.

Ava felt jealousy pool in her stomach. Ever since a couple of days ago, when Jake told her he thought she *felt it too*, Ava had been trying to figure out what he meant. He *had* been flirty, but Ava refused to let herself read into things.

Ava stepped out of the car and walked as casually as she could to where Mia was chatting to Kai. Maybe the play date had been a bad idea.

"Ava!" Nancy exclaimed as if they were best friends. "It's so good to see you, darling." She wrapped her arms around Ava, placing a kiss on her cheek.

"And you," Ava said, smiling as much as she could. She then turned to Jake and he was looking at her intensely. They gave each other a polite kiss on each cheek, but tension was in the air. Or was Ava hallucinating?

"I hear Mia and Kai's play date went well," Nancy said as if she was pleased that Jake and Ava had gotten to know each other.

"Yes." Ava snapped out of her trance. "They got along really well. And it's so nice for Mia to have a friend before starting school."

Nancy nodded in agreement. "I wish I could have come too. Jake says you're quite the chef!"

Ava realised that Nancy must not have known what Jake told her. Maybe they called the divorce off. But somehow, Ava thought that is unlikely. She knew how easy it was to pretend to be happy. She and Patrick did it all the time.

"I wouldn't go that far," Ava joked and Nancy just laughed. She wondered if Nancy was putting on a friendly facade to spite Louise. A small part of her hoped that was the case.

"Looks like Miss Junis is calling for line up," Nancy said, her gaze towards the school entrance. Ava took Mia's hand and briskly walked towards the entrance. She saw Louise near the front of the crowd and felt a surge of guilt course through her. Subconsciously or not, Ava managed to widen the gap between her and Nancy. She was scared of what it might look like to Louise.

43

"Hello to everyone!" the teacher, Miss Junis, said loudly to the small crowd of parents and children. Ava recognised most of the mothers—only a couple of men, Jake included—from the barbeque. She was suddenly glad that she had decided to make an appearance.

"I am so excited for you all to embark on your road of education," she said in a high-pitched voice. Ava noticed that her lines seemed very rehearsed. "And I am sure that, here at Tansbury View, you will all make friends for life," she spoke to the children. Ava withheld a laugh because she was talking to five-year-olds, who probably didn't know what she was talking about.

"So, children, if you could say goodbye to your parents, and come into the classroom!" Miss Junis finished her mini speech before letting the children say goodbye to their parents. Out of the corner of her eye, she could see Nancy giving Kai a brief hug before excusing herself.

"I am so sorry. I have to go to an emergency meeting." Ava heard her say in a small voice. She quickly tuned out of the conversation, crossed with herself for being nosy, and gave Mia a hug goodbye.

"Ava!" Louise rushed over to give Ava a hug, as if they hadn't seen each other in years. "Zoe and myself were about to go for coffee, would you like to join?"

"Thank God you asked." Ava put her hand on her heart. "Saying goodbye, even for a day, is heart breaking. I definitely need some company." She laughed and realised that she could be herself around Louise and Zoe. Nancy was a different case altogether.

"I feel you on that one," Zoe piped up, before embracing Ava as a way of greeting. "I'm on my third and I still can't say goodbye to him."

*　　*　　*

Zoe was observing Ava like she was watching an animal documentary. She had never seen someone so beautiful. Louise was obviously in awe of her as well because she couldn't stop chatting to her.

"You know," Zoe said after taking a sip of coffee. "Kelly's husband might not be the only piece of drama circulating this town." She loved to gossip. She often gossiped with Kelly since that's how she found about the divorce. She wanted to see Ava's reaction to the divorce.

"You are *such* a gossip," Louise said, rolling her eyes. Zoe laughed.

"I've been here a month and the drama is already going over my head," Ava said, taking a sip of her latte.

"You'll never guess who are getting divorced," Zoe said with wide eyes. She saw Ava frown and take a sharp intake of breath.

"Who?" Louise asked. Zoe knew Louise loved the drama really. She'd love this even more because it involved her arch enemy.

"Nancy and Jake." Zoe flitted her eyes between her two friends to observe their reactions. Louise's' mouth dropped open, and much to Zoe's surprise, Ava's face remained unmoving. She didn't seem surprised in the slightest.

"Why? How do you know?" Louise asked, clearly flabbergasted. Ava remained silent, her eyes darting back and forth as if she was trying to think of something to say.

"Kelly told me at the barbeque. Apparently, they argue all the time," Zoe said.

"Wow. I know we don't get along, but poor Nancy," Louise said. Ava was still silent. She took a sip of her coffee.

"I know. Poor Jake too. It will be so tricky for them," Zoe said. "But ever since I first met Jake, I thought he could do better."

"Thank God," Ava suddenly blurted out. Zoe was shocked at her outburst.

45

"What?" Louise and Zoe both said.

"The other day, Jake told me about the divorce," Ava said quickly as if it were a secret. Zoe started putting the puzzle together. Had Jake told Ava because he liked her?

"Really?" Louise sounded surprised but Zoe wasn't.

"Yeah. And I almost felt guilty that I knew. I don't know." She blushed. "I'm new here and I had this secret about someone. I felt guilty."

Zoe could tell Ava was telling the truth. But part of her noticed that Ava also looked like she was withholding something. And Zoe knew that it must have something to do with Jake. Something not good.

*   *   *

Zoe: All this talk of the incident is ridiculous. It has nothing to do with the murder.

Kelly: It all seems to be linked. I wouldn't jump to conclusions.

Zoe: No. I don't agree.

Kelly: You can't deny that the incident started everything.

Zoe: It was a coincidence.

Kelly: Maybe, maybe not.

NINE

Ava wasn't sure whether it was a good idea that she told Louise and Zoe that she already knew about the divorce. Louise looked surprised, and Ava wondered if she had been cross that Ava hadn't told her about the play date.

It was nothing, she reminded herself. *Just a play date.* Yet something in Ava's mind made her think differently.

"I can't wait for next week." Zoe quickly changed the conversation away from Jake. Ava was grateful.

"Oh, me either. It's my favourite time of the year." Louise laughed and Zoe just rolled her eyes.

"Of course. That's because you always win."

"By default, that means you win too," Louise pointed out and Ava felt baffled. She felt awkward interrupting their chat.

"What is next week?" she asked and immediately regretted her words. Maybe it was a party that she hadn't been invited to. She hoped she wasn't going to come across as needy.

"Oh, of course you wouldn't know!" Louise exclaimed. "Sorry, it's the annual Tansbury View ball. The headmistress, Mrs Lancar, is American, and I think she wishes she was teaching at an American high school. But because she's not, she basically puts on this 'homecoming' prom but for the parents. It's a lot of fun. It's a good way for the new parents to get to know each other. There are some games too."

Ava did like the sound of that. She loved dressing up, and she wanted to do anything she could to try to fit in more.

"Sounds great." She smiled, and she was glad that the Jake thing was leaving her mind.

"It's a black tie even, so get a dress," Zoe said with a wink. Ava loved how straight forward Zoe was. She wondered if she'd ever be like that.

"Oh, and everyone going gets put on a team," Louise added. "Normally, there are about six teams, with each member of the mother's council as a captain. So." Louise put her hand to her chest. "I am indeed a captain."

"Louise normally rigs it so Dave and I end up on her team," Zoe says. "I'm sure you'll end up with us." This was reassuring for Ava. She hated the idea of turning up alone to the ball, and then being stuck alone on a team with parents she didn't know.

"Everyone gets pretty drunk. It's quite the fiasco," Louise says in that self-righteous voice of hers. Ava stifled a laugh, because Louise was so uptight. She did like her, a lot, and she was grateful for her taking Ava under her wing. But they were very different.

"Being drunk is hardly a fiasco, Lou," Zoe said. "Get off your high horse." This comment made both Ava and Louise laugh.

"Where do I go about getting a dress in this town?" Ava asked, suddenly feeling excited about the upcoming ball.

"I'm actually going shopping tomorrow for mine, if you would like to join?" Zoe said. Ava felt the happiest she'd been since arriving in Tansbury.

"Sounds perfect."

*   *   *

The next day, Zoe picked Ava up from hers in the morning to take her to the shopping centre.

"If you don't mind me asking," Zoe started as she circled the car park, looking for a space. They had arrived in the Tansbury shopping centre, ready to buy their dresses. Ava was prepared to spend a lot of money on a dress.

"Go ahead."

"How was that play date? You know, the one with Jake?" Zoe asked, and there was a tone in her voice that Ava couldn't put her finger on. Ava felt her stomach sink.

"It was fine." Ava kept her voice cool, but guilt was surging through her. Why did she feel so guilty?

"What did he say about—oh shoot! I just missed that space," Zoe suddenly exclaimed as she put the car into reverse and manoeuvred the car into the small space.

"What did he say about the divorce?" Zoe said as they walked towards the shopping centre. Ava swallowed; her throat felt like it was closing up.

"He didn't actually say they were divorcing. He just said they were thinking about separating," Ava said, and she was pleased with her answer.

"Oh. Trust Jake to be so nice about it," Zoe said. "I wonder why he told you."

"I was telling him about Patrick and I.I think maybe he felt bad. I don't know." She bit her nails as his words from that day returned to her.

"Nice of him," Zoe said. All of a sudden, Ava felt the urge to confide in Zoe. Even though she was a self-proclaimed gossip, Ava believed she would keep her mouth shut about this.

"He said some weird things to me though," Ava said quietly, which caught Zoe's attention. She turned her attention away from the gorgeous shoes in the shop window and looked at Ava intently.

"What do you mean? About Nancy?" Zoe looked almost excited at the idea of new gossip.

"No, actually. About me. He told me that I was 'different to other mothers.'" She used her fingers as quotation marks.

"In what context?" Zoe was frowning now.

"No context. He just said it in the middle of our conversation." She paused, analysing Zoe's face. "I was confused too. But then later, when we said our goodbyes, he whispered in my ear: 'I know you feel it too.'"

"Shut up," Zoe said, and she looked genuinely shocked. "He said that? Are you sure?"

"Positive."

"Hand on heart, Ava, he sounds like he's coming on to you," Zoe said. "And he's normally so reserved."

"It's been eating away at me. I feel guilty because of Nancy, but maybe I'm reading into it." Ava kept her voice quiet as if there were other mothers around to overhear them.

"No, you shouldn't feel guilty. Jake should." Zoe hesitated. "You're not reading into it, hun. I would tell you if I thought you were."

Ava felt as if a weight has been lifted off her chest. "Phew. I just needed to tell someone. But please, don't tell anyone. Especially Kelly," Ava pleaded. Zoe nodded and promised her.

"Anyway, no more Jake talk. Let's get some dresses."

After two exhausting hours of shopping, both Zoe and Ava had chosen their dresses. Zoe had settled on a black fishtail dress, whilst Ava stuck to what she knew she liked and opted for a strapless white bohemian style dress.

"I better head off. I need to prepare a meal for three hungry boys." Zoe put her hand to her forehead. "I'm dreading the day they all become teenagers."

"See you soon," Ava said before heading to the supermarket. She pottered around, picking up as many healthy options as she could since her diet had officially started. As she approached the coffee aisle, she saw an all too familiar man at the end.

"Crap," slipped out of her mouth.

"Ava?" Jake walked down the aisle to greet her. She remained sturdily behind her shopping trolley.

"Oh, hey Jake!" She mocked surprise. "I didn't see you there." She felt herself reddening, because they both knew that she had been staring at him for about thirty seconds.

"You've been shopping?" He gestured to the bag in her hand.

"Oh, yeah. Just bought a dress for the ball next week." She nodded and felt so awkward. She felt like a teenager who had never spoken to a boy in her life. She felt like a complete idiot.

"You're going, then?" he asked. Ava nodded hastily. "Good. I'll make an appearance, then." Ava wondered what he meant by that, but she stopped herself from reading into it. She didn't want to step on anyone's toes. More specifically, Nancy's.

"I better go pay for this," Ava said awkwardly.

"Would you like to have lunch?" he asked quickly. "With me, I mean."

"Would that be appropriate?" Ava let the words slip out of her mouth before she could stop them. She immediately regretted them, as she saw a grin make its way onto Jake's mouth.

"A lunch between two friends. What would be wrong with that?"

*   *   *

The waiter took their order with a grin and a promise that their food would be with them as soon as possible. They had settled on a Japanese restaurant, and Ava still felt as if she shouldn't be there.

"You look nice today," Jake said to her, leaning over the table. Ava frowned because she did not look nice today. The compliment made her blush all the same though.

"Thank you. Back atcha," she said, and they burst out laughing at her lame comment. Ava felt her heart racing and the butterflies in her stomach fluttered nervously.

"How is Mia settling in?" Jake asked.

"She enjoyed yesterday. She told me Kai looked after her, so thank you for that," Ava said gratefully. This made Jake smile.

"My son. Such the gentleman." He laughed. Ava laughed with him and she couldn't help but notice how easy they got along. The conversation flowed from children to the ball, back to children and before they knew it, their food had arrived.

"How is Nancy?" Ava asked, because the question had been on the tip of her tongue all lunch. Ever since Jake told her about him and Nancy, the romantic feelings she felt for him were becoming stronger and stronger.

"Honestly? Not good. We keep arguing about the divorce. It's all so difficult." Jake ran his hand through his hair. "And the children. They're going to be so confused." He looked angry at himself, and Ava could understand that. She remembered oh so vividly when the topic had been addressed. Properly.

They had been sitting watching some talent show. Ava vaguely remembered it being a singing one. The X Factor, maybe? She liked trashy shows like that. Mia was in bed. Ava and Patrick sat on separate sofas.

"Can we change the channel?" Patrick had said. It was almost laughable that their divorce had started over something as trivial as a television show.

"Twenty more minutes," Ava murmured without thought.

"I'm going to bed then; I don't want to watch a minute more of this crap." Patrick stood up and marched across the room. Ava remembered this moment vividly because she was angry at his reaction. So angry that the worst part of herself had come out.

"That's ridiculous, Pat." Ava stood up also as if to square up to him. A flash of anger crossed his face. Ava knew that they were both being unreasonable. But that was how it was. As if they were looking for a reason to fight.

"A man can't go to bed without his wife getting angry. What a life to have, huh," Pat said in that know it all voice he had. This angered Ava further. She knew that their marriage wasn't good. She knew the way it was heading.

"What do you mean, a life to have?" Ava spat, her anger spouting from every extremity. She was furious that he had the balls to bring up their issues, when Mia was only a staircase away.

"Ava, we hate each other!" Patrick raged. "And we are kidding ourselves if we think it's going to get better!"

"It will be fine," Ava said through gritted teeth. "We can make this work. Anne knows this great marriage councillor-"

"Screw Anne! Screw this marriage!" Patrick had never been like this with her. In hindsight, Ava often wondered if his behaviour was purely so that she would agree to the divorce.

"What?" Ava remembered tears coming to her eyes. She didn't want to look weak.

"I want a divorce," her husband said with such conviction and hatred that Ava felt she had been slapped in the face. And the only thought that circulated Ava's head was Mia.

So, Ava understood that Jake had reservations about the divorce. She did. She often wondered if it would have happened if it weren't for that argument. But deep down, she knew it was always going to happen. It was just a matter of time.

"It will be okay." Ava found herself short of words, because even though she had been through it herself, it was one's personal experience. And Ava didn't want to dig her nose into someone else's business.

"Eventually, I hope." Jake stared intensely into Ava's eyes.

"It will. I promise. If I can get through it, so can you," Ava tried to make a joke, but Jake didn't laugh. He just kept on staring at her.

*   *   *

*Nancy: If it hadn't been for that ball, maybe things would
        have turned out differently.*
Kelly: Don't speak nonsense, Nancy.
Nancy: Hand on heart, I think we could have been friends.
*Kelly: You really think you could be friends with someone
        capable of murder?*
Nancy: I may hate her, but I don't think she did it.
Kelly: Maybe Jake did.
Nancy: What did I tell you about mentioning his name?

TEN

Ava felt like she was a teenage girl again. She sat by her mirror, anxiously watching the clock. 5 PM. She had two hours until she needed to leave for the ball.

All she had been thinking about for the most part of the day was the ball. She was excited to get dressed up. More importantly, she was excited to see Jake. She knew that it was a mistake to be fantasising about him, but she couldn't help it.

As soon as the clock hit half five, Ava began to get ready. She couldn't remember the last time she got this dressed up. She never really cared what Patrick thought of her outfit choices.

She curled her hair, applied makeup, and dressed herself in the space of an hour. She admired herself in the mirror and allowed herself to become the teeniest bit excited. She hoped that nothing would go wrong.

Heels were never Ava's forte, but Zoe had insisted she bought *at least* some wedges so that she would fit in with everyone else. And so she did.

Ava had agreed with Louise that they would turn up together, since they were both dateless. Ava liked the idea of turning up with Louise, since she had the mothers under some form of control. Ava was aware she sounded a bit like a social climber, but she wasn't. She had never been one for that.

They had agreed to get a taxi. Neither Louise nor Ava wanted to be the sober one, especially if they were going to be surrounded by happy couples. They knew they were being bitter, and they secretly enjoyed it.

The doorbell went off, and Ava was downstairs in a shot. The butterflies that filled her stomach were making her nervous and excited at the same time. Ava opened the door to see Louise dressed in an elegant grey dress that was made of satin. *She looked gorgeous*, Ava thought.

"Ava, you look stunning." Louise put her arms around her, and Ava felt her nerves lessen. Making friends with Louise was one of her best decisions since being here.

*   *   *

For a school event, the headmistress had certainly put a lot of effort in. The school hall had been transformed from a plain assembly hall to a hall covered head to toe with balloons, flowers, and bunting. It looked gorgeous.

Louise and Ava arrived there at the right time. It was filling up, and so their plan to be 'fashionably late' had worked. A crowd of parents had formed around a large board, where Ava assumed the teams were written down. Louise had told her that she was *sure* Ava was on her team but attempting to rig things could only go so far.

Ava wandered over to the board to see that she was not on Louise's team, and her heart sank. The team she had been put on was Kelly's, and her spirits lifted again when she saw that Nancy was on that team too.

Nancy equalled Jake.

Ava did not see herself as a homewrecker, and she certainly did not want to get involved with a married man. But part of her was drawn towards the danger of being with someone who was married. That part of her was dirty, and she shooed that thought away every time it entered her mind.

56

Ava found herself walking towards the bar. Louise was off organising something (probably flustered) and Ava didn't want to get in her way.

"Vodka martini, please," were the words that left her mouth. Mia was with the sitter and Ava was allowed to have a good time!

It was then when Nancy and Jake arrived. Nancy looked extraordinary—like an ice queen. A white dress with light blue makeup. Ava thought it looked a little over the top. That could just be jealousy though.

Jake met Ava's eyes quickly. He gave her a small smile before turning his eyes away. Ava felt a pang of jealousy as she saw him sneak an arm around Nancy. She reminded herself that it might just be for show.

Or it might not.

Ava tried to remove the toxic thoughts from her head by drinking more.

"Ava, darling!" said the high-pitched voice of Kelly Peterson. Ava turned around to see Kelly and her husband colour coordinated in maroon.

"Kelly, so good to see you," Ava said more enthusiastically than she felt. She knew from Zoe that Kelly was nice, but part of Ava didn't trust her.

"This is my husband, Miles," Kelly introduced, and the older man gave her a strange look. They shook hands and Ava distinctly remembered him as being the one who was having an affair. Poor Kelly.

"Nice to meet you."

"It's our lovely teammates!" came the loud voice of Nancy. Ava's stomach dropped and she immediately felt on edge.

"Yes!" Kelly clapped her hands together. "Ava, Nancy and I wanted to have a chance to get to know you a bit better."

Ava faked a smile. "I know! I've been here for a month and I still feel like I know no one."

57

"That's because Louise has got you cooped away!" Nancy slung her arm around Ava's shoulders as if telling a joke. However, Ava wasn't entirely sure Nancy was joking.

"Oh, no, it's not that." Ava laughed awkwardly. "I'm a bit of a recluse." Ava wasn't sure Nancy would believe that. Ava found her eyes darting over to Jake, whose eyes were on her. He gave her a half smile.

"Ladies and gentlemen!" the headmistress' voice boomed through the room. "Please take a seat at your allocated table! And don't forget to get a drink from our fabulous bar."

"Oh yes," Nancy said. "I need my second drink already. Ava, I'll get you one too!"

"Oh, really, it's fine—"

"Nonsense!" Nancy seemed as if she was already drunk. Ava wondered if Nancy's gregarious behaviour was to show that she was the alpha female. And so, Nancy left to go to the bar, ordering Ava a drink that she knew she didn't need.

"She's already had a lot to drink," Jake said into Ava's ear. "We had a big argument before we left."

"Oh." Ava didn't know what to say. "I'm so sorry."

"Don't be. One week's time and it'll be over," Jake said as Ava felt his hand touch hers. "Shall we go to the table?"

*　　　*　　　*

Jake was right about how much Nancy had had to drink. She was laughing loudly—well, louder than usual—and her behaviour was sloppy. Ava made sure she was drinking slowly; otherwise, she feared she would be acting in a similar fashion soon.

The quiz had been going on for half an hour and Kelly's team was losing. Obviously, Louise's team was winning. Ava felt a pang of jealousy as she saw then win yet another point. Ava had lost track of the quiz. She remembered that Geography was not her strong suit as the headmistress asked what the smallest country in the world was.

"I'm going to the loo," Ava excused herself. She didn't need to go; she just wanted some air. She felt as if Nancy was constricting her with her constant jibes at Louise and her incessant cackling. And, despite Ava's best efforts, the drink was most definitely going to her head.

Ava walked as quickly as she could out of the doors, and onto the flat lawn. She welcomed the cold air into her lungs and sat down on the bench.

Now that she was outside and away from the noise, Ava realised just how drunk she was. She must have only had three drinks, yet she felt herself swaying slightly. Oh gosh, she was *drunk*.

"I figured I'd find you here," came a voice. Ava looked up to see none other than Jake. She wanted to tell him to leave her alone, because she was not in a good state. Yet somehow, her mouth wouldn't form the words.

"I think I'm drunk," Ava said as Jake sat down next to her. He chuckled and held out a glass of water.

"I figured as much." Ava took the water and sipped at it tentatively.

"Why did you come out here?" Ava asked, the alcohol taking control.

"I needed some air. And I wanted to talk to you, away from my very drunk wife." He chuckled at the end, but it was forced.

"You're just swapping one drunk woman for another." Ava hesitated. "Talk away."

"I, er," he started. "I am not one to flirt when I am married. I have been very loyal to my wife," he said, his words staccato and rigid. Almost rehearsed.

"Do you want a medal?" Ava joked, finding herself extremely amusing. Jake laughed and suddenly took Ava's hand in his. She was shocked at this gesture, but she didn't stop him.

"But you. You're the opposite of her." He seemed to be struggling to get his words out. "It's no wonder I'm so attracted to you."

Ava felt her breath hitch in her throat. She feared that was where he was headed.

"Oh," was the only word that came out of her mouth.

"And I keep telling myself to behave. I am a married man. I know that in theory, I will not be a married man in no less than a week, but still. I am married nonetheless."

"Yes, you are," Ava said, nodding as she sipped at her water. Jake's hand moved from Ava's hand to her leg, and Ava felt herself tense.

"So, I should probably stay away from you."

"That would be the right thing to do," Ava said, flabbergasted that her drunk self had such amazing self-restraint.

"Screw the right thing to do." And before Ava knew it, Jake's mouth was on hers and they were kissing.

*   *   *

Nancy: I think her behaviour was disgusting. Having an affair with my husband whilst we were still married. Trashy behaviour, trashy girl.

ELEVEN

"What the hell?" were the words that filled Ava's stomach with dread. She pulled away from Jake, breathless and embarrassed, and saw Nancy standing in front of them. She thought she was going to be sick.

"What the hell is this?" Nancy shrieked. Ava was shaking so much that she couldn't form words. Jake stood up hastily, cursing.

"Nancy." He ran his hand through his hair. "I'm so sorry." He walked up to her and tried to put his hand on her shoulder, but she slapped it away. She then pulled her hand back and slapped him across the face.

"Sorry?" Nancy raged, before turning her attention to Ava. "What about you? Are you sorry?"

"Nancy, oh my God." Ava felt the words tumble out of her mouth. "I didn't even know what was happening—"

"You were sticking your tongue down my husband's throat, that's what was happening!" Nancy yelled. The commotion was clearly heard, because that was when Louise rushed out of the door.

"Is everything okay out here? I heard yelling." Louise looked worried and rushed to Ava's side. Ava felt a sense of relief and felt tears gather in her eyes.

"Ava, do you want to tell her?" Nancy snapped, folding her arms across her chest. Ava didn't know what to say. She felt so awful.

"It wasn't Ava's fault," Jake stepped in. "I kissed her. She hasn't done anything wrong. I have," Jake said to his wife. Louise gasped and quickly put her arm around Ava.

"Oh really! Because from where I'm standing, it looked pretty mutual!" Nancy snarled, and Ava felt the tears drip down her cheeks. She felt humiliated.

"You heard your husband," Louise stepped in, protecting Ava. "Don't put this on Ava."

"Oh, step out of this, Louise, you weren't even here," Nancy snapped.

"I heard what your husband said. I believe him, and so should you. Don't take this out on Ava, because she isn't the one in the wrong." Louise pulled Ava closer and Ava leaned into her friend. She felt like a child being comforted by her mother.

"Kissing a married man is wrong," Nancy shouted.

"Nancy, we are getting divorced!" Jake's voice began to rise, and Ava just wanted to go home.

"But we are still married right now!" Nancy shrieked, but Louise wasn't having any of it. She turned away from the squabbling couple.

"Ava, I'll take you home," she said, and Ava merely nodded.

"Don't you walk away from me," came the angry voice of Nancy, but the two friends ignored it. This was not their battle to fight, and so they left the married couple alone to bicker.

*   *   *

When Ava woke up the next day she felt as if her heart had been broken into two pieces. Last night, she had kissed a married man. And his wife caught them red-handed.

She didn't want to get out of bed. Thank goodness it was the weekend, giving her two days to recover before returning to school. Her phone bleeped.

> Louise: Hope you're okay, hun. I'm with my cousin today, but if you need anything, just send me a text and I'll come over.

Ava sent Louise a text of thanks before slowly getting out of bed and wandering downstairs. She felt like a zombie with a hangover. She had *kissed* a married man. And even though it wasn't her fault, she hadn't tried to stop it. She even enjoyed it.

There was a text from Jake on her phone, but she didn't want to open it. She had archived it as if trying to rid her phone of any evidence of an affair.

But it wasn't an affair, was it? Ava was certainly not an expert, but she did not think one kiss with a man who was about to become divorced counted as an affair.

She attempted to rid these thoughts from her head as she made her coffee. She was aware that Patrick was coming to collect Mia today. It was a bank holiday on Monday, and so he was going to have the entire weekend with her.

Ava hated the timing. She was going to be alone in the house when she needed company the most. Mia hopped into the room in her pink pyjamas.

"Morning," she squeaked as she rushed over to her mother. Ava picked her up and hugged her tight. If only she could go back in time and stop herself from kissing Jake.

"Would you like some breakfast?" Ava put on her best mummy voice. Mia nodded and sat at the table, excited for her upcoming trip to see daddy.

After breakfast, Ava packed Mia's clothes into a suitcase and showered before Patrick would arrive. She wanted him to think that she was over it. *She was.* She wanted him to think that she had her life together. *She didn't.*

The doorbell rang and Mia sprinted to the door. Ava felt nervous at the prospect of seeing her ex-husband.

"Daddy!" Mia shrieked and soon, she was up in the air and in Patrick's arms. He had sunglasses low on his nose, and Ava noticed he had had a haircut. She folded her arms and gave him a smile.

"Good morning," Ava said from across the hall. She was unsure of how to greet him.

"How are you?" Patrick walked into the hall; Mia sat on his hip. "Honey, why don't you be a big girl and get your suitcase?" Mia nodded, excited at the idea of being a *big girl*.

"I'm okay. Just settling in." Ava nodded and gestured for Patrick to sit down at the table. "And yourself? How are things in Grennly?"

"I'm okay. They're good. Missing my lovely Mia, though," he said. Ava observed her ex-husband in fascination. He looked the same, but different. She found it hard to explain. He looked the same physically—that brown floppy hair, dark eyebrows, and wide eyes. But he looked tired; his frown lines were much more pronounced and the bags under his eyes were a shade of purple. Ava wondered if work was finally wearing him down.

"She is just as lovely as ever." Ava laughed. Patrick nodded and remained silent. *What was wrong?*

"Right. Well we'd better be off, pumpkin," Patrick said as Mia emerged from upstairs. He took her suitcase in his hand. "I'll see you on Monday."

The door slammed and they were gone.

*   *   *

After saying goodbye to her cousin, El, Louise wandered into the bar, and she was, of course, early. She took it upon herself to order her and Zoe an exotic sounding cocktail that was most definitely going to give her a hangover. As she took her first sip, her thoughts fled to Ava. Poor, naïve Ava. She didn't know what to think of the whole situation. It was a bit of a mess, really. Of course, she felt for Nancy. Louise was cheated on, and so if she put herself in Nancy's shoes, she felt very sorry for her indeed.

But Ava didn't seem like a bad person, and definitely not the type to get it on with a married man. She had just come out of a divorce herself, and for all Louise knew Patrick could have cheated too. *Men*, Louise concluded, *are exhausting*. It is simpler to be alone. Well, that's what she tried to tell herself, anyway.

"So sorry I'm late!" Zoe exclaimed as she entered the bar. Louise smiled at her friend and gave her a kiss on the cheek.

"Not a problem. I got us some drinks." Louise pushed the drink over to Zoe, and she grinned.

"Yum. Plus, Dave is coming to get me. I can drink as much as I like!" She took a sip of the drink, the extravagant flower in the centre poking her eye. Louise laughed.

"Me too. Although, I don't have a doting husband. Just a lovely taxi driver." She shrugged and sipped her drink, reminding herself that she does not need a man.

"Speaking of husbands . . ." Zoe looked around as if to check if anyone from school was here. "Jake has gone down in my estimation."

Louise nodded. "Yes. Even I feel bad for Nancy." Zoe looked shocked and pulled the flower out of her drink.

"Surely not!" Zoe said a little too loudly. Louise shushed her.

"Being cheated on is not nice, even if you are getting divorced." Louise felt the drink was going to her head already. She made a note to take smaller sips from now onwards.

"Yes. Poor Nancy. And Christ, what was Jake thinking? And Ava, for that matter?" Zoe tutted slightly, and Louise immediately felt the need to protect her newest friend. Ava was by no means in the right to kiss a married man, but Louise believed that the fault laid with Jake, not Ava.

65

"Jake was in the wrong. Yes, Ava shouldn't have kissed him, but for all we know he could have come onto her," Louise pointed out, and Zoe chuckled.

"You really like her, don't you?" Zoe looked at Louise thoughtfully, and then shrugged. "She is very sweet. I can't imagine her preying on Jake. You're right, it was probably him." Louise smiled and took another sip of her drink.

"I think we should make a pact to protect her. Nancy will probably rally up a team to make Ava's life a living hell." Louise explained sternly. She didn't want Ava getting hurt; she'd only just gotten here.

"I agree." Zoe lifted her glass. "To protecting Ava." And they clinked their glasses together.

*   *   *

It wasn't until the evening when the loneliness set in. Ava had been busying herself; cleaning, washing, unloading, decorating. But now, as she sat in front of the TV watching the X Factor—how ironic!—she felt incredibly lonely.

It had come when Ava was in the kitchen. She was making herself a cup of tea—decaffeinated, of course— in hopes that it would help her sleep.

The phone ring was loud and shrill, making Ava jump. She covered her chest with her hand, before wandering over to the phone and picking it up.

"Hello?"

But there was no response. There was only silence.

"Hello?" she tried again. But there was, again, silence. She was about to hang up until she heard something that made her blood run cold.

She could hear slow breathing. It was faint, but Ava could hear it nonetheless. The breaths were slow and absolutely terrifying.

She hung up the phone in terror. Placing the phone down on the counter, she held onto the sides and took slow breaths.

It's nothing, she told herself. Just someone with the wrong number. She convinced herself of this until she was certain, then she took herself upstairs and got into bed.

*   *   *

Louise: Did she ever tell you about the calls?
Zoe: Calls?
Louise: I never thought much about them, but now . . .
Zoe: You're going to have to explain.
Louise: She received these calls.
Zoe: So?
Louise: No one spoke. Just breathing.
Zoe: Creepy.
Louise: Do you think it is just a coincidence?
Zoe: I don't know what to think anymore.

TWELVE

When Ava woke up the next morning, she had precisely two missed calls and three text messages from Jake. She hated the part of her that got excited about it.

She managed to ignore the texts until lunchtime. She found herself doing anything to distract herself from her phone. She planned a new layout for her company. She gave herself a manicure. Spoke to her boss. Took off the nail varnish and repainted it another colour. Spoke to her boss again Changed the layout. Repainted her nails again.

But by lunch time, she couldn't help herself. Including the one from yesterday, she had three in total.

> Jake: *I just want to apologise about last night. It wasn't fair on you. I'd love to see you so that I can apologise in person.*
>
> Jake: *Ava, I know this is an awful situation to be in, and I'm the last person you want to see, but I really need to talk to you.*
>
> Jake: *Nancy and I have just signed the papers.*

Ava felt her stomach drop. He was now divorced, and she was *happy* about it. What kind of person did that make her? *A bad one*, she concluded. But still, she composed a simple text, telling him to come around for coffee whenever. She was free all day.

Ava did not expect Jake to come over as quickly as he did. Half an hour after she sent the message, the doorbell rang.

Immediately, Ava's stomach filled with butterflies. When she opened the door, Jake stood there in blue jeans and a black t-shirt. He looked tired, but gorgeous nevertheless.

Ava gave him a small smile and let him in.

"Hey," was the only word that she could say. He muttered a small hello back again, before Ava led him through into the kitchen.

"Would you like a drink?" Ava's voice was quiet, so she cleared her throat. "Coffee, tea?"

"Tea would be great." Jake sat down on one of the bar stools. Ava gave him a quick glance before turning to her kettle. How was this going to go? She hoped she wouldn't start crying, although that was highly likely.

Ava brought the pot of tea to the island and passed Jake a mug and a milk jug. She sat opposite him and poured herself a mug. There was silence. Ava felt extremely awkward. What was she supposed to say?

"I, er," Jake started. He took a sip from his mug. "I need to apologise. My behaviour at the ball was totally inappropriate, and I shouldn't have pulled you into my marriage. I can't put into words how sorry I am."

Ava nodded slowly. She wasn't cross with him—how could she? She was just as guilty as he was. "I think the best thing to do is put it behind us."

"That's probably a good idea." Jake chuckled. "But I am sorry. Just one more time."

"There's really no need to apologise, Jake. I am just as guilty as you," Ava told him, upset by how angry he was at himself.

"Not quite. I came onto you, I recall," he said with a half-smile, and Ava couldn't disagree. But she knew that her feelings for Jake were bad too. She shouldn't have felt that way about a married man.

"Let's forget about it, okay?"

"Ava, if I'm being honest, I really don't think I can forget about it." Jake suddenly looked up, staring deeply into her eyes. Ava felt her stomach turn over.

"Oh."

"Yeah."

"Nancy's bed isn't even cold . . ." Ava started, but Jake cut her off.

"Nancy's bed has been cold for the past couple of months. And I really don't think I can pretend I don't have feelings for you. Not anymore."

The butterflies in Ava's stomach were going so crazy that she felt a little sick. "But the divorce . . ." She knew she was making excuses.

"Nancy has been so controlling. I think it's time I put myself first," Jake said, before reaching over to take Ava's hand. "I like you, a lot."

"Obviously this is hard for me." She swallowed. "Because I've got very conflicting emotions."

"Which are?" Jake asked curiously.

"Well, obviously I feel extremely guilty." She paused. "But on the other hand, I've got quite strong feelings for you that I don't think I can ignore."

Jake's mouth burst into a grin and he squeezed her hand tight. "Then it's settled. Next week I will take you on a date."

*   *   *

Jake left shortly after they discussed the whereabouts for their date. Ava felt guilty but after having heard how Nancy behaved towards Jake, she felt almost glad Nancy had caught them kissing.

Though it was extremely lonely without Mia, it meant she had some peace and quiet, and time to do some work for the company. As she checked her emails, she noticed that she had an

70

email from her boss telling her to refurbish the website and add a few discount codes onto the page.

Coding was difficult, and despite having been the Web Producer for Xanos for a while now, she still worried that she would slip up. During her summers whilst still doing her psychology degree, she took several computer coding courses as she knew she would always end up with a career along the media line.

She refreshed her emails, and a new one popped up. The subject read: *Homewrecker.* Her stomach dropped. Her thoughts immediately went to Nancy. Had Nancy emailed her? Ava shakily opened the email and read the content.

You better watch your back.

Ava slammed her laptop down as if had electrocuted her. It must be Nancy. Who else could it be? Her heart raced as she slowly opened her laptop up again. The sender was blocked. Ava wondered if she could track an email, but the email quickly disappeared from her inbox. Confusion rushed through her as she refreshed the page.

The email had vanished. She immediately went to her recently deleted folder, but it wasn't there either. It had completely disappeared.

Had she imagined it?

Had her paranoia about Nancy caused her to hallucinate an email? Ava rubbed her temples in distress and refreshed the page one more time. No email.

She sighed heavily and shut her laptop, deciding that her paranoia had gotten the best of her and she must have imagined the email.

But somewhere in her subconscious, there was a pit of unease telling her that she hadn't imagined anything at all.

*   *   *

71

Zoe: These calls . . . they might not have been related to the murder.

Louise: Yes, we can't assume anything.

Zoe: Could they have been from Nancy?

Louise: That's what Ava thought.

Zoe: Maybe she was trying to scare Ava; get some revenge.

Louise: How far might she have gone though?

To get revenge?

Zoe: Are you insinuating that she could have done it?

Louise: Maybe.

THIRTEEN

The email remained in the back of Ava's mind for the rest of the day. She coded, cooked, cleaned, showered, and yet it remained. She checked her emails several times in order to see if the email had miraculously returned, but she was unlucky.

She should be happy that she imagined it. She knew that. The fact that there was no email meant that Nancy wasn't telling her to *watch her back*. But at the same time, how could she have imagined something so vividly?

Ava shook her head as if to shake off the thoughts plaguing her before settling down on the sofa to watch TV. It was 9 PM and she was already tired. She considered taking one of her sleeping pills and going to bed now, but she knew that was a bad idea. She'd wake up in the middle of the night, completely wide awake.

She aimlessly flicked through the programmes, until one caught her attention. A game of baseball was on. She loved baseball. She remembered joining the society in her first year of university to be sociable, but she ended up loving the sport.

She must have been watching the game for about half an hour before her eyes slowly began to close.

Ring ring!

Ava was woken up suddenly by the phone ringing. She stood up quickly and went to the phone. "Hello?" she said groggily.

But there was no reply. There was complete silence on the other side of the phone. Ava's blood ran cold as she remembered the call from the other day. With slightly shaking hands, she turned the volume up on the phone.

And there it was. Slow breathing. It was so slow that it seemed deliberate, so it could only just be heard. Ava's heart was pounding as terror ran through her veins.

"Who is there?" Ava brought herself to say. And then the breathing stopped. "Hello?"

Suddenly, a long sigh came from the other end. Ava's blood ran cold and she hung up the phone. She raced to where her mobile lay and dialled Louise's number as quickly as she could.

"Hello?" Louise sounded upbeat.

"Sorry to spring this on you, but is there any chance I can stay with you tonight?" Ava asked, her heart thumping. She placed her hand on her chest in attempt to calm herself down.

"Sure, my cousin is out tonight so the spare room is free. Are you okay?" Louise asked, sounding concerned.

"I'm fine. I'll explain when I get to you." Then, Ava hung up the phone. She was aware it was probably rude, but she needed to get out of the house. She needed to get away from the phone. She sprinted upstairs and filled a bag with essentials before rushing out of the house and locking it behind her.

The sky was dark. Ava moved as quickly as she could to her car. She reversed speedily out of her driveway and to Louise's house, away from her mysterious caller.

*   *   *

Louise didn't know what to expect when Ava came rushing through her door. She thought that maybe Ava was regretting her divorce and needed comforting, or maybe that she missed Mia. She certainly did not expect what Ava told her.

"I've received two calls from unknown numbers. One yesterday and one today," Ava said slowly. Louise nodded. She received blocked number calls all the time. They always tried to sell her something. She found them extremely annoying.

"What did they say?" Louise asked.

"Nothing." Ava gulped. "There was complete silence, and then I could hear breathing." Ava was twisting her hands around nervously. Louise could tell that she was scared by these calls.

"Breathing?" Louise asked. It definitely sounded creepy, but Louise didn't think it was anything to panic about.

"Slow breathing. And then when I spoke, I heard a long sigh. It was so scary." Ava let out a long breath and Louise could tell that Ava was really shaken up.

"I can imagine. But Ava, I'm sure it was nothing. They sound creepy, but it could be something else."

"What if its Nancy? What if she's trying to scare me?" Ava was curled up on Louise's sofa like a child. Louise immediately felt sorry for her. She reached out and placed her hand on top of Ava's.

"Nancy may be a little bit psycho, but I don't think she would do that," Louise said, but she wasn't sure she even believed herself. How far *would* Nancy go? Louise had seen Nancy's rage after she caught Ava and Jake kissing. But how mad could she be if they were getting divorced? Clearly, they weren't in love anymore, so what was it? Louise wondered if Nancy's pride had been knocked. She had been replaced by the younger, skinnier version.

"I don't know." Ava covered her face with her hands and Louise saw a tear run down her cheek. "I'm just so lonely without Mia, and I got freaked out."

"Anyone would." Louise paused. "You can stay here for as long as you want. You are always welcome."

*   *   *

Ava didn't sleep well at Louise's house. And so, the evening after she was exhausted as she sat on her sofa. She had decided that she was going to be brave today, and sleep on her own bed. The weekend was going to be over soon, and her little Mia would be back. It was all going to be fine.

Ava was attempting to tire herself out. Earlier she had gone on a run, and now, she was sat in her bed reading her book. Her eyes were drooping slowly when she heard a sound downstairs.

Her heart leapt into her mouth as she froze in bed. There it was again. *Footsteps.*

Someone was in the house.

Ava's heart was beating so loudly that she could swear it could be heard. She daren't move—although she knew she should ring the police.

How had someone got in? The door was locked, and she had shut every window. A brief thought crossed her mind: Nancy. Could it be? Could she be going to these lengths to scare her?

Even so, breaking and entering was illegal. Ava's phone was on her bed side table. Ever so slowly, she pulled the covers down and reached for her phone. She dialled 999 as quickly as she could.

"Which service do you require?" the operator asked, but Ava barely heard the question.

"There's someone in my house," she stammered, and then she hung up the phone. She couldn't bear the thought of her intruder hearing her on the phone, and so she silently prayed that they could track her location. She was in panic mode, and she felt as if every muscle in her body was frozen until she heard the sounds of the police sirens.

*   *   *

The police had searched the house through and through, and nothing had been found. Ava felt like a fool.

"I heard footsteps, I swear," she said, hugging her large jumper around her. The policeman eyed her sympathetically.

76

"I believe you heard a noise, Miss Milberry. However, you must understand our struggle. There is no sign of break in. There are no fingerprints on the door handle, and no damage to any of the windows. So again, I ask; are you positive it was footsteps you heard?"

"Yes!" Ava was frustrated; her ears did not deceive her. She did hear footsteps. There *had* been someone in her house.

"Have you noticed anything missing? Any valuable belongings?" he asked again, impatient. Ava cursed herself immediately for not doing this earlier. If something was missing, then it was proof of the break in. Proof she wasn't going mad. She searched the house immediately. However, everything seemed to be in place. Nothing was missing.

Had her ears deceived her? Had she maybe, just maybe, imagined the footsteps as she had the email?

She felt frustrated with herself. Was there something wrong with her? How was she imagining things so vivid? And so, she apologised to the policeman for any inconvenience and watched as they disappeared from her house.

Her sleep that night was disrupted, to say the least. Every time she woke, she was convinced it was because she heard footsteps downstairs. Her dreams were filled with pictures of Nancy, Jake, and even Louise and Zoe, conspiring against her, trying to scare her. She felt as if she was going mad.

It was a relief when morning came; the clock struck six AM and Ava was out of bed and making breakfast. She gifted herself with a breakfast of avocado on toast with poached eggs and bacon in an attempt to distract herself.

But despite her best efforts, the sequence of last night's events were on a continuous loop in her head. She was certain that she had locked the door. And the windows, for that matter. So how had the intruder got in? Or was there an intruder? She didn't know now.

The phone rang, disrupting her thoughts. In a cloud of confusion, she didn't think twice to answer it.

"Hello?"

And then ice-cold fear ran through her veins as silence answered her. Could the break in and these calls be connected? And the email? She forced herself to be calm and stay on the phone.

"Whoever this is, please leave me alone. The police know about the break in. If you don't stop, they will soon know about these calls."

She didn't know what she expected to hear in reply. She hoped that her caller would hang up in fear of the police. But she was answered with silence, and that slow breathing that made Ava's hairs stand.

And then she heard it. She turned her phone volume up to be sure. She could hear the tapping of a computer. The person on the other end was typing. Her fears were answered when she heard the tell-tale sound of a new email on her laptop.

Staying on the phone, her heart in her mouth, she rushed to her laptop to see.

Subject: Let's play.

Tell anyone and you'll get what's coming for you.

"What is coming for me?" Ava now knew she wasn't going mad. She hadn't imagined the email, and she hadn't imagined the break in. Someone was after her. Could it be Nancy?

Her question was answered with silence once more, and Ava hung up the phone. She glanced at her laptop to see the email gone, again. But she wasn't fooled this time. She went to her recently deleted, and the email was there. She felt some victory then, which quickly diminished when she saw the email disappear once more.

Her stomach lurched as realisation coursed through her. Her caller, her *stalker,* had hacked into her emails.

If he, she, whoever they may be had managed that, what else could they be capable of?

*   *   *

Louise: The only thing I am unclear about is why. Why would someone kill him?

Zoe: So, you finally agree that it is murder?

Louise: Yes. The evidence points to it.

Zoe: The police think it was Ava, they really do.

Louise: The evidence also points towards that. But even so, it couldn't have been her.

Zoe: Do you think she was framed?

Louise: I don't know. The only thing I know is this: she is being too quiet. She has barely said a word since it happened. It's like . . . she's just accepting she's going to be incarcerated. So maybe we shouldn't be asking who killed him; we should be asking why Ava is being blackmailed.

FOURTEEN

Ava hadn't moved from her laptop for half an hour. She was too frightened to move. She had a stalker. Someone was out there, hacking into her emails, watching her every move. Someone had gotten into her house.

But why?

Ava knew she had to find what they had taken. They must have taken something. Something that they could use against her.

But what?

Money?

Something of sentimental value?

Mia leapt to her mind. Would her stalker dare threaten Mia? Ava's heart was pounding. She grabbed the edges of the sink as she keeled over it, retching.

She grabbed her phone as quickly as she could and dialled Patrick's number. He answered quickly.

"Ava? Is everything ok?" he asked as soon as he picked up.

"Is Mia there? Have you got Mia?" Ava said breathlessly.

"Yeah, she's sitting right next to me . . . is everything okay?" Patrick sounded genuinely concerned.

"Can I talk to her?" she demanded, ignoring Patrick's concern.

"Mummy?" came her sweet daughters voice. Ava let out a sigh of relief. The panic slowly drained out of her. "Mummy? Are you there?"

"Yes, sweetheart." Ava eventually managed. "I just wanted to hear your voice. I'm really excited to see you tomorrow." *One more day*, she thought to herself. One more day and she can monitor Mia's every move.

The phone hung up after they exchanged their goodbyes. Ava idly wondered if this is all some sick prank from Nancy, trying to get back at her. The thought has crossed her mind more than once. But the email sounded menacing enough—she didn't care if it was Nancy, Patrick, or anyone she knew. She wasn't going to tell anyone if it put her little girl at risk.

*   *   *

That afternoon, Ava scoured the house for any sign of a break in. So far, she could find nothing. Everything was as it seemed. She had nearly given up hope when she opened a storage cupboard and saw a piece of wood leaning against the wall. Curious, she reached in to pick it up.

It was a baseball bat.

Ava examined it up slowly. She was sure she hadn't brought any of her university stuff with her. But right in front of her eyes, plain and simple, was her university baseball bat.

She examined it slowly. The base of the bat still had her initials carved into it, albeit faded and dusty, but they were still there. Confusion filled her head and she tried to remember packing it. She concluded that she must have had. Then, she placed it back to where she found it and shut the door.

The afternoon slowly ticked by, and Ava found herself wanting her stalker to call, or email, or even break in again. They must be connected; they must. A small part of her wanted to confront Nancy. *Yes, I kissed your husband. Yes, I'm sorry. But please, stop stalking me. It has scared me; there is your revenge.*

But what if it wasn't Nancy?

Ava didn't want to consider that possibility. Because who has it out for her? Who wants to scare her? Ava knew that nine times out of ten, the person who is stalking you is someone you know. So, who could it be?

Her mind flashed back to her university days, terror running up her spine.

But she couldn't let herself think of those days.

To take her mind off the toxic thoughts swirling through her mind, Ava messaged Zoe asking to go for a coffee.

> *Zoe: Perfect! I need to get out of the house. The kids are driving me mad . . . God save me! See you in a few.*

She checked the door was locked once, twice, and thrice before she eventually tore herself away from the house. Her paranoia was driving her insane, and a small part of her remembered the safety of having Patrick.

And like that, without any thought, Jake crossed her mind. Jake. Jake! Her date was later this week and she wasn't sure if she was going to go.

She did not want to be *that* girl. The girl who is *so* desperate to find love that she leaps into the bed of the first man who shows her attention. Of course, Ava was not looking for love. To clarify. Half of her was tempted to sack the whole thing off, and then if in half a year or so Jake was still available, she could try something then.

But then the other half of her . . . that more dominant, thrill-seeking, childish part of her. That side was winning. She wanted to remember what it was like to be loved. To be touched. She wanted to know what it felt like to be alive again.

Ava decided to leave the battle between her naughty and nice sides as she pulled into the parking spot outside the coffee shop. Zoe was prompt as ever, already sitting in the window seat. She gave Ava a brief wave.

"Good afternoon, *mon cherie*," Zoe said in the worst French accent Ava had ever heard. Ava chuckled.

82

"How are you?" Ava sat down to see Zoe had ordered her a cappuccino. She sipped it slowly, careful to not burn her tongue.

"I think the better question is, how are you?" Zoe asked. "I haven't seen you since . . ."

"Don't remind me." Ava's heart thumped. Amongst the stalker calls, break in and emails Ava hadn't had the time to see anyone. She dreaded to think what Zoe thought of her.

"Seriously, though. How are you?" Zoe repeated. Her warm eyes were so trusting, Ava was half tempted to tell her everything. But then she remembered the menacing email.

"I'm good. Obviously totally ashamed at my behaviour." Ava nodded.

"You shouldn't be. I mean, it wasn't the best thing to do, but you know that. But that doesn't mean you should be ashamed," Zoe said. Ava touched her arm affectionately.

"Thanks. I feel awful. For Nancy, I mean. I don't know if I can bear to show my face on Tuesday."

"Louise and I will protect you," Zoe joked and Ava felt her heart swell. Because honestly, what would she have done without Zoe and Louise?

"Has Kelly said anything?" Ava asked, feeling like a little girl in trouble with the headmistress. Zoe nodded bashfully.

"You can tell me," Ava said quietly. "I won't get upset."

"It's nothing specific . . . Kelly just told me that Nancy thinks you're just a younger version of her. And that Jake will get bored. And then you'll 'get what's coming for you.'"

Ava sensed that Zoe was sugar coating it slightly. She thanked her and moved the conversation on. Even though she was trying to deny it, every it seemed clearer and clearer every day. Nancy was behind the emails, phone calls, and maybe even the break in.

*   *   *

Louise tottered around the kitchen, preparing breakfast for her children. She'd silently hoped that because it was a bank holiday, they'd have a lie in, meaning she'd have one too. However, when her little munchkins leapt on top of her at seven AM, she realised she'd never be so lucky.

"Are you making pancakes, Mum?" Luca asked as he swirled on the bar stool. He'd got into the habit of calling her 'Mum' rather than 'Mummy'. She thought he was growing up way too fast.

"I am. Why don't you do Mummy a favour and put some toppings on the table? There's some Nutella in the cupboard," she told her son as she stirred the batter. He nodded and obediently wandered over to the cupboard, dragging his feet as he did. She wanted to tell him off, because she hated that habit, but she remembered it was a bank holiday. A rest for everyone.

"Good morning!" came her cousin's voice from the bottom of the stairs. Louise looked over to El and beamed. El used to live with Louise, but a few months ago she decided to start her own life elsewhere. But from what Louise knew, her attempt wasn't successful, so she'd asked to move back in. They'd always been close, ever since they were little. El had always been a fiery character, just like Zoe. They balanced each other out well.

"I'm making pancakes!" Louise said enthusiastically. She always felt this inherent need to please her cousin. She was a people pleaser, she guessed. El pushed her silky hair behind her ears and looked at Issie, whom she held on her hip.

"Did you hear that, Issie Wizz? Mummy's making pancakes!" El exclaimed, before spinning Issie around, who yelped in delight. El didn't have her own children and was single like Louise. Louise liked that about her—El was the ideal vision of a single woman thriving in life. Sure, she'd had her ups and downs, but who hadn't?

"So, what's the plan for today then?" El asked as she took a seat at the breakfast bar. "Any fun bank holiday surprises for the munchkins?"

Louise poured some batter into the pan before turning back to her cousin. "I thought we could go to the park. It's a nice day," Louise said, taking a spatula and scraping underneath the cooking pancake. "What do you think of that, kids?"

"Sounds good!" Luca exclaimed, who was still laying the table with toppings. Louise's heart swelled as she looked around her kitchen; her two lovely children and her beautiful cousin. What more did she need?

Certainly not a husband.

*   *   *

Ava's bank holiday creeped by slowly. Ava was counting down the hours until Mia's return. Patrick had sent her a couple of pictures from their trip, with Mia grinning in every single picture. She was scrolling through the photos, when the phone went off.

Ava was so distracted by Mia's return that she barely had time to process the call. "Hello?" she said down the phone.

When she was answered by silence, her blood ran cold. *Her stalker.*

"Nancy, if this is you . . ." she began, unsure of what to say. She could barely hear herself over her thumping heart. "I am so sorry. Genuinely. You did not deserve what I did to you. I am so sorry."

Ava didn't know what she expected. She didn't expect Nancy to suddenly jump out and tell it her was a prank, or even her to say anything. But what she was replied with covered her body with goose bumps. The voice was so low and quiet, Ava could barely hear it. But it was there.

"And now, you'll get what you deserve."

Ava slammed the phone down as quickly as she could. Her entire body was shaking as she stared at the phone in shock. *And now, you'll get what you deserve.*

*   *   *

Nancy: It wasn't me. I was not the one who killed him. I know that's what you're thinking. But between you and me, that little bitch deserved it.

FIFTEEN

Ava was still shaking fifteen minutes after the phone call. The words from her stalker were ringing through her ears. It must be Nancy. Who else would want her to get what she deserved?

She glanced at the clock. 4:30 PM. Half an hour until Mia would be back. She thought about confiding in Patrick. If it was Nancy, there would be no way she'd find out about Ava telling him. But what would he say? He'd probably say she was crazy. Unhinged. Mentally unstable.

Ava remembered the argument they had when she realised it had all gone wrong. Not the X Factor argument—that one was ridiculous—but the first one.

"I was talking to Kiera Mol-shit today and she was telling me that her daughter has already been registered for a gifted and talented program."

"Kiera who?" Patrick looked up from the table wearily. Mia was barely walking and already competition was setting in.

"Molship. But I call her Mol-shit because I don't like her," Ava reminded him as she stirred the bolognaise.

"Ah yes." Patrick nodded. "What gifted and talented program? Aren't they a little young?"

"Pat!" Ava put a hand on her hip. "This is important. I want Mia to have the best education she can. I want her to have as many possibilities as she can."

"You sound like Kiera Mol-crap."

"It's Mol-shit!" Ava groaned, feeling frustrated. Patrick rolled his eyes.

"You're being pushy, Ava." He took his reading glasses off and looked away from the TV.

"I'm not being pushy, Pat." Ava walked over to him. "I just want our little girl to be successful!"

"And she will be. But you have to admit, this is a little ridiculous. She's two," Pat said. Ava's anger boiled under the surface.

"I just want her to have the best education she can, Pat," Ava said, pushing her anger away. Pat rolled his eyes once more.

"It's not like you had the best education, Ava, and look at you now. You're doing perfectly fine," Pat snapped, malice in his voice. Where was this coming from?

"My parents did everything they could for me, Pat. Not all of us come from such wealthy backgrounds," Ava seethed, not able to believe her ears.

"And you don't let me forget it." Pat sighed. Ava frowned at her husband, sensing that this anger was coming from somewhere else. This couldn't just be about Mia.

"Where is this coming from, Pat?" Ava felt tears rush to her eyes. "Have I done something to upset you?"

"I don't know, Ava. Recently, I just . . . I don't know how I feel about us anymore." Pat looked at his wife with sad eyes. "Sometimes, I just think you take things too far. You can be a little crazy, sometimes. Bat shit crazy."

Bat shit crazy. Ava could remember that argument as if it was yesterday. And so, she decided that she would not tell Patrick about her calls. Or Nancy.

The sound of a car pulling into a driveway snapped her out of her daze. She looked to the front window to see Mia climbing out of the car, Patrick following her closely.

Ava ran to the door and embraced her daughter lovingly. "Mummy!" she screamed into her ear.

"Are you trying to deafen me?" Ava giggled as she tickled Mia's tummy. "How was your weekend?"

"It was 'mazing, Mummy! We went to the beach and I saw baby seals! They were so cute!" Mia squealed. Ava tickled her again, making Mia squirm.

"Good afternoon." Patrick sauntered through the door. "How long did it take for her to tell you about the seals?"

"Precisely two seconds." Ava chuckled and stood up. "Was she good?"

"An angel. Honestly. That new school is good for her, evidently." He looked down at his daughter. "You're doing a great job."

Ava smiled. "Thanks Pat. That means a lot."

"Momma, can I go play with my Barbie?" Mia asked. Ava nodded before letting Mia scamper off. All of a sudden, she felt Patrick's hand on her arm. She looked over to see him looking at her with concerned eyes.

"Ava, I really need to tell you something," he said. Dread filled her. Had he met someone new?

"Yeah?" Ava said, trying to keep her voice steady. She did not feel steady at all. But then Patrick shook his head.

"It's nothing. I just miss you, that's all," he said. "I'll see you around." And just like that, he disappeared from the house.

In hindsight, Ava should have stopped him. She wondered how things would have ended up differently. She wondered if he would have told her.

*   *   *

The night was cold. Very cold. Ava even put the fire on. Some form of pathetic fallacy, if anything. Mia was in bed. Ava was watching some rubbish reality TV program. She was even contemplating ringing up to vote.

The time was 10:22 PM. Ava knew this because she had just checked her phone. The doorbell rang.

Ava sat up immediately. Who would be coming to her house so late in the evening?

She opened the door, her eyes widening as she saw the last thing she had expected to find on the other side. *What were police officers doing at her front door?*

"Are you Ava Jules?" asked the female police officer. Ava nodded.

"Milberry. But yes. Is everything okay?" Ava crossed her arms over her chest. The police officers looked very serious.

"Is it okay if we come in, Miss Milberry?" the female officer spoke again. Ava shook her head, her heart in her chest. Police officers at your door was never a good sign.

"First, tell me what this is about," she said, her words shaking as they left her lips.

"Miss Milberry, I am extremely sorry to inform you that your ex-husband, Patrick Jules, has been found dead on the outskirts of Tansbury."

SIXTEEN

18th September 2009

"Are you sure you have everything sweetie?" Mum and Dad hovered in the doorway of my university bedroom. We had just finished unpacking what felt like my entire life into a tiny box.

"Yes," I told them for the one hundred millionth time. I saw so many people out in the corridor socialising already—I needed to be too! This was university for Christ's sake

"Okay," Mum said. "Oh, I told myself I wouldn't cry." Oh god, she was so embarrassing. I pulled her into a quick hug.

"I'm so proud of you sweetie," Dad told me. I hugged him too before shooing them both out of the door. It was a relief that they were gone; I was anxious to start meeting new people. I had been told great things about the Bristol nightlife, and I just couldn't wait to go out tonight.

I heard a knock on my door. I opened it tentatively and found a girl with long strawberry blonde hair behind it. She was very petite and looked about fourteen. Half of me wondered if she was someone's sister.

"I'm Annabelle." She stuck her hand out in an official kind of way.

"Ava," I replied as I shook her hand. She walked into my room and glanced around.

"Cool room. Very boho," she commented. "What are you studying?" she asked, casually sitting down on my bed.

"Psychology," I answered shyly.

"Oh my god. That is so cool," she said energetically. "I'm studying medicine. Yawn." I thanked her and watched as the babbled on.

"You've got to meet everyone else on our corridor. They are super fun," Annabelle informed me as she stood up. I wasn't quite sure about this girl. She seemed a little... over the top to me.

"Oh okay. I haven't had a chance yet." I unwillingly followed her out of the door. Part of me just wanted to have some time to myself. But the other part of me was grateful to her; I had said I wanted to meet people as soon as possible, so I needed to be brave.

When we arrived at room 4B, I heard voices inside. It sounded like there were already a lot of people in there, which put me on edge. Annabelle walked into the room with an air of confidence I wished I had.

"Guys, this is Ava!" she announced. I looked around to see three girls and four guys. They all smiled and waved at me.

"Take a seat," uttered the guy with dark hair, patting on the bed. "I'm Matt."

"Thanks. Ava. Although Annabelle did just tell you that so . . ." I mumbled awkwardly. Matt smiled. He had one of those contagious smiles, where you couldn't help but smile with him. I felt my nerves lessen already.

"Hey." A red-haired girl turned to join Matt and I's conversation. "I'm Lucy, by the way. Sorry for Annabelle, she's a little over the top." She grinned and shook my hand.

"She's sugar coating it. Annabelle is ridiculously annoying," Matt said with a slight chuckle. Lucy hit him on the arm playfully and laughed.

"It is true," Lucy said. "A couple of us are having drinks in my room tonight before going out. Elite only. You're totally invited."

"Just don't tell Annabelle." Matt put his finger to his lips. A small part of me felt bad for Annabelle, but my eagerness to be friends with these apparently very 'cool' people took over me.

"I'm in." I grinned and Lucy smiled at me with a glint in her eyes. "So, what do you guys study?" I asked and I caught Matt's eye. He laughed, and I wondered what he's laughing at.

"Well, Ava, it depends what year you're asking." He laughed again, and everyone else joined it. I frown, confused. "I've changed my course three times. I'm technically in fourth year. But I just can't make my mind up."

"So, you're . . ." I asked, only now noticing that he looked a lot older than us.

"Twenty-two. Four years older than you guys. Jeez, I feel like a granddad." Another chuckle escaped his mouth as he put his arm around my shoulder. I giggled, feeling settled in already.

SEVENTEEN

"You might want to take a seat, Miss Milberry," the male officer told Ava as they both walked past her into her home. Her whole body was frozen, her mouth open in an 'o' shape. The blood pounding in her ears was deafening—like waves crashing through her brain, muting all other sounds.

"Is this a prank?" were the only words she could form. That could be the only answer. There was no way that Pat . . .

"Of course not. I am very sorry," the woman told Ava. Ava looked at her in horror and her eyes immediately filled with tears. She covered her mouth with her hand.

"How?" she stuttered as she made her way to the sofa. She collapsed and curled into a ball. The officers followed and sat opposite her.

"I understand this is an extremely traumatic time for you, Miss. We can give you some time—" the male officer began, but Ava cut him off.

"Tell me what happened to him!" she said loudly, tears streaming down her face. The officers looked at each other wearily.

"We cannot say anything conclusively at the moment. However, it was not a suicide or a car accident. Whilst the car was off the road, there is sign of struggle," the female officer told Ava slowly.

"So, he was . . ." Ava's voice broke. "H-he was killed?" She began to sob heavily.

"That is what it's looking like. The forensics team are currently collecting the evidence, so more information should be available soon," the female officer continued. She looked at her partner unsurely. The male officer nodded.

"We do need a formal identification of the body, Miss Milberry," the female officer said, turning Ava's stomach to coils of snakes. "You can do that when it suits you. If you need some time to process this . . ."

Ava cut the woman off. "I'll do it tonight. It might not be him, right?" A glimmer of hope found itself in Ava's heart. The officers looked at each other, before nodding and standing up.

"I'll need to drop my daughter off at a friend's house, first," she said, making her way to the stairs. As she made her way up to her daughter's room, she looked up, and said a silent prayer.

Patrick couldn't be dead.

He just couldn't.

*   *   *

As Ava made her way into the room, she felt sickness rising within her, making all previous nerves go to dust. Nothing in her life could ever measure up to how she felt in that moment.

The coroner stood by the table, a white sheet covering the body. Ava's eyes filled with tears as she turned to the police officers.

"I'm not sure I can do this," she said, a tear trickling down her cheek. The female officer looked at her sympathetically and put an arm on her shoulder.

"Is there anyone we can call?" she asked, and Ava's mind went to Patrick's family. Oh God, his lovely family. But she needed to identify him, first. She had to do this.

"I'm ready," she told the coroner, who nodded and pulled the white sheet back from the body. Ava's legs collapsed from underneath her, throat constricting as an ugly cry escaped her.

It *was* him.

*   *   *

Ava wasn't sure when she fell asleep that night, and when she awoke at 6 o'clock she felt as if she hadn't slept at all. The first few moments were bliss, having forgotten the disastrous string of events from the past evening. But as she arose from the sofa, she remembered.

Patrick was dead. A sob caught in her throat and she felt bile rise. She just made it to the sink before throwing up. How had it happened? Why? Why had someone murdered her ex-husband? And Mia wouldn't have a father . . .

Mia.

Ava needed to get herself together for Mia. She turned the tap on and cleaned her mess from the sink. She needed to get Mia out of the house in time for the detectives arriving. She took a deep breath and took herself upstairs.

Shower. Clean teeth. Put fresh clothes on. Brush hair. Look presentable. Look like a normal mum. A mum that did *not* kill their ex-husband.

She was ashamed at her outburst at the officers; she was worried that it made her look guilty. But she wasn't guilty. She did not kill Patrick.

Ava reached for her phone and dialled the number she knew all too well.

Ring ring. Ring ring.

"Hello?" came her mother's voice from the phone. Tears filled her eyes and suddenly Ava felt like a ten-year-old again.

"Mum?" she croaked.

"Ava, darling. Is everything okay?" Carol Milberry's voice was suddenly alarmed. Ava let out a sob, tears falling down her cheeks.

"Patrick's dead, Mum. He's dead." She sobbed, and she was met with a gasp. There was commotion over the phone.

"Darling, oh my goodness, I am so sorry." More commotion. "Oliver, pack your stuff, we're leaving."

"It's okay, Mum, you don't have to—" Ava started, but her mother cut her off.

"We're in Scotland at the moment, on a spa retreat. We'll be with you as soon as we can darling." Ava could hear her mother shouting at her father over the phone, who clearly wasn't moving fast enough to fit Carol's timetable. Ava thanked her mother, barely keeping herself together. After saying goodbye, she took a breath, and then made her next phone call.

"Hello?" Louise sounded extremely upbeat.

"Hi, Louise." Ava didn't know what to say. "Um, I need you to take Mia to school today. I'll explain when you arrive."

"Is everything okay?" Louise asked. Ava tried to keep herself together, she really did. The tears reformed and she let out a sob.

"No," was the only word she could say through her tears.

"Oh honey." The sound of keys jingling could be heard over the phone. "I'll be at yours as soon as possible." The phone hung up.

Louise was there within five minutes. Ava fell into her arms as soon as she opened the door and cried on her shoulder like a little girl.

"What's happened?" Louise said soothingly.

"Patrick." Ava choked. Louise looked at her unsurely.

"Your ex-husband?" she asked, seeming unsure of what tone to take. Ava nodded and slowly pulled away from her.

"He was killed last night," she stammered. Her jaw was clamped shut, as if she was trying to stop a sob from exploding from within her. Louise's mouth dropped open. Ava didn't expect Louise to know what to say. Because, really, what could you say to that? Even if you were the most composed, sympathetic person on

97

the planet, there was really nothing you could say to 'someone I love was killed'. Nothing.

"Oh, Ava . . ." Louise put her hand on Ava's shoulder. Ava waved her hand quickly as if to tell her to not comfort her.

"I've just managed to stop crying. I need to compose myself." She sniffed. "What if the police think I did it?" Ava said. Louise did know how to answer this one.

"They won't, Ava. You loved him; anyone can see that. But if they do, you know that Zoe and I, and probably even Jake can be character witnesses." Ava's eyes widened in shock, so Louise quickly added, "But I'm sure it won't get that far."

"I just don't get it. Who would want to kill Pat? He knows no one here." A single tear traced down Ava's golden cheek, shining as it took its path.

"That makes it the perfect plan for whoever did it," Louise said slowly, and just like that, a flicker of doubt crossed her face. Ava tried not to let herself imagine the worst, but could it be possible that Louise suspected her as a killer?

*　　　*　　　*

Ava got Louise out of the house with Mia as soon as she could. She could barely keep herself together with that patronising tone. Ava knew Louise was only trying to help. However, it took all her will power to tell her to shut up because she had never been loved like Patrick loved Ava. But that thought was toxic.

The detectives arrived five minutes past eleven, giving Ava the perfect amount of time to compose herself. They were both men—unfortunately—and looked very stern. Ava felt nerves bubble in her stomach as they asked to come in.

"Miss Milberry, I am Detective Martin Brown, and this is my colleague, Steven Piper. We are the detectives assigned to this case." They reached out to shake her hand. Ava nodded slowly.

"Can we take a seat?" Detective Brown asked (evidently the man in charge), and before Ava gave him an answer, they both made their way to the sofa.

"Have there been any more developments in my husband's case?" Ava asked in a small voice.

"Ex-husband. Correct?" Detective Piper asked. Ava shook her head in confusion.

"Yes, sorry. Um." She was unsure of what to say. "It's an easy mistake to make," she told them, trying to be as convincing as possible. But she had nothing to lie about. Didn't she?

"I'm sure it is." Piper looked at his colleague with a look that Ava most certainly could not read. Did they think she did it?

"Miss Milberry, does this picture look at all familiar to you?" Brown pulled a photo out and gave it to Ava. It was the baseball bat she found in her cupboard not too long ago.

"Yes. It's my baseball bat from university. Why is that relevant?" she asked. Immediately, she felt as if she should have lied. *'No, I do not recognise that, Detective. I'm innocent I swear!'*

"That is what we believe to be the murder weapon, Miss Milberry. Which, as I'm sure you can imagine, puts you in quite the predicament."

EIGHTEEN

25th September 2009

I'm telling you. Freshers' week was awesome. Seriously! Who knew life could be like this? I couldn't remember most of what happened in the whole week—apart from hooking up with my flat neighbour. Whoops. And maybe a couple of others . . . but who could blame me? I was drunk!

I managed to land myself an awesome group of friends. We managed to ditch Annabelle on day three—when she finally got the hint that she just wasn't our type of person.

And although I loved everyone in my clique, Lucy stood out. I felt like I had known her forever. She was the best friend you could ever ask for. She was the sort of girl everyone couldn't help but be jealous of. The sort of girl *everyone* wanted to be friends with. But she picked me.

"Knock knock!" Lucy announced as she entered my room. She was all glammed up for tonight and—as usual—looked beautiful.

"You look HOT!" I told her as she made her way over to me and placed a wet kiss on both of my cheeks. She shrugged her shoulders and winked at me.

"Never as good as you though." She collapsed onto my bed. I swivelled around on my desk chair to face her.

"Guess what I found out today," I told her.

100

"Ooh gossip." She eagerly sat up. "Tell me, tell me."

"You know that hot guy from the block across?" I told her. Of course, she knew who I meant; we've only been stalking him since day two.

"Of course."

"I found out that he studies medicine," I explained. Her eyes widened and her mouth dropped.

"That's so hot! How'd you find out?"

"Okay, don't call me a stalker . . . but I saw his medical school lanyard at dinner tonight." I giggled and watched as she burst into a fit of laughter.

"You are such a stalker. But kudos to you." She clapped her hands and I tossed my hair behind my shoulder.

"Thank you, thank you very much." I took a bow, making Lucy laugh even more. And then her mouth dropped open again.

"And we know who studies medicine . . ." Lucy trailed off before raising an eyebrow. At first, I was confused, and then I realised.

"Annabelle. I bet she knows him." I slapped my leg. "Damn, we shouldn't have dropped her last week! She could have been useful."

"That is where you are wrong, dear friend," Lucy said slyly. "She still can be useful."

"Is that so, oh wicked one?" I laughed before realising what she meant. She meant to make friends with Annabelle again so we could use her to get to the fit medic. And although a small voice in the back of my head was telling me it was so, very wrong to use a person like that, I was too lost in the middle of being Lucy's minion to even spare it a minute of my time.

*　　　*　　　*

101

After informing the rest of the group of our plan, we decided to go with it. There was a bit of resistance from Matt, but Lucy swore that it was just because he fancied me.

Annabelle had always preferred me—even Lucy could admit that—so it made sense for me to be the one to go and see her.

I knocked on her door slowly. She opened it and was definitely shocked to see me standing here. She narrowed her eyes and looked me up and down.

"What do you want?" She didn't even try to be nice. And I totally got why; we were horrible to her. The way I acted was something my previous self never would have done . . . but with Lucy, you couldn't help but go along with her ploys.

"I feel like I haven't seen you in ages!" I exclaimed, walking past her into her room without an invite. She continued to look at me with that look on her face.

"That's because you and little miss bitch dropped me on day three." She folded her arms and looked at me sternly. I bit my lip awkwardly. She was not wrong.

"How do you mean? And I get that Lucy can be harsh and all, but she isn't a bitch." I tried to feign innocence, but Annabelle wasn't stupid—she was studying medicine after all.

"Come on, Ava. I sat on the same table as you and your little entourage and you all got up and moved. Pretty harsh, if you ask me."

Okay, that was a nasty thing for us to do. But I couldn't help it, I wanted in with their group, so I followed what they did.

"Yeah. I'm so sorry about that. But really, that wasn't Lucy and I." A lie, it was Lucy's idea. "The boys were just unsure of you, that's all. I don't think they're used to such a big character." Another lie. Annabelle never spoke to the boys, and they never spoke to her.

"Really?" Annabelle looked hopeful, and I knew that it was my time to pounce.

"So, we were thinking . . . it would be really cool if you came out with us tonight. I'd really like you to." I told her, and I saw her eyes light up. Immediately, I feel guilty.

"I'm not really ready to go out . . ." she said timidly. I shook my head.

"That doesn't matter! I can do your makeup for you," I said. "But only if you'd like."

"I would really love that. Thanks Ava," she answered. And that little voice in my head was just yelling, 'you are such a bad person. This will definitely have consequences.' But yet again, I ignored it.

NINETEEN

"I'm sorry?" were the only words that came out of my Ava's mouth. The detectives looked at each other with unease.

"To reiterate, Miss Milberry. Mr. Jules received a few blows to the skull with a long hard object. A couple of metres from the crime scene, this bat was found. Covered in Mr. Jules' blood," Brown slowly explained to Ava as if explaining a math problem to a kid. But she could do the math. Her bat, plus her fingerprints, and Patrick's blood? The answer was screaming at her in the face. They suspected her to be the killer.

"I didn't kill Patrick," Ava told them as convincingly as she could. "I . . . I don't know how that bat got there. It was in my cupboard a few days ago . . ."

"Until you used it to kill your ex-husband?" Piper snapped, causing Ava to bolt upright. Brown turned to his colleague and told him to be quiet. Yes, he was definitely in charge.

"Of course not!" Ava said a little too loudly. "I thought I didn't even own it anymore."

"Then, please explain to me how it was in your possession a few days ago, as you have just stated, and how it found its way to the outskirts of Tansbury yesterday evening," Brown said sharply. "Sounds unlikely, no?"

Ava agreed with him. That did sound unlikely. "Maybe it is a replica?" Ava regretted the words as soon as they came out of her mouth. The detectives looked at her like she was crazy.

"Can I just check that my bat isn't still there? Please?" Ava asked, but the niggling voice in the back of her head knew it wouldn't be.

As she made her way to the cupboard, her suspicions were confirmed. Her university baseball bat was no longer there. And like that, her blood ran cold. Because she knew she did not kill Patrick. And someone did, with her baseball bat. And that person must have been in her house.

Ava's legs collapsed from underneath her, and she fell to the ground with a crash. She felt her heart rate leap and her breathing quicken. She felt faint, and she idly wondered if she was having a panic attack. She barely felt Brown's hand around her arm to help her up.

"It's not there." Ava said in a small voice and Brown just nodded slowly. He knew it wasn't going to be there, and let's be honest, so did Ava.

"Let's go back downstairs, Miss Milberry," he told her softly as he helped her back down to the sofa where Piper was waiting obediently.

"Are you going to arrest me?" Ava asked weakly. She wasn't sure how murder investigations worked, but she knew that they thought she was guilty.

"Not yet," Brown said. His eyebrows crumpled as if realizing the implication of his words. "No," he quickly corrected himself. "When we have enough evidence to suspect you to be guilty, we will bring you down to the station. For now, we are still in the process of collecting evidence."

"I think I'm being framed, detective," Ava burst out without being able to stop herself. The detectives almost looked amused. Ava was sure people said that to them all the time.

"And why is that, Miss Milberry?" Piper was the one to speak this time. Ava wanted to tell them about the emails and the calls. The suspected break in. *They must all be linked*, she thought. It was logical.

But then she remembered the threats that were made by her stalker. "Because I didn't do it. And someone is trying to make it look like I have."

*   *   *

Zoe heard about Patrick's death before it even came out on the news. Zoe was supposed to be taking Louise's kids to school, so that Louise and her cousin, El, could go out for breakfast. However, it turned out that Louise had to take Mia to school anyway. "Why are you looking after Mia?" Zoe had asked. Louise had to inform her that something very, very bad had happened to P A T R I C K. She spelt it out, not wanting her children to know what she was talking about.

And she certainly didn't want poor little Mia to find out that her father was dead.

Zoe felt as if she was in some sort of television show. It was the most surreal thing—a murderer in Tansbury. Of course, it was terrifying as well. She was scared for her children, her family, and her friends.

She could not deny it. Part of her wondered if it was Ava who did it. Because, in this small town, who on earth would want to kill Patrick? The only person with a motive was Ava. And thinking about it, they really didn't know Ava at all.

In the time she had been in Tansbury, she had barely spoken to anyone other than Louise and Zoe. She had an affair with a married man—not really an affair, but Zoe was dramatic. For all they knew, Ava could be capable of murder.

"Everything okay, sweetie?" Dave sat down at the table and placed a latte in front of Zoe. The coffees he made her almost made her feel justified for spending such a large amount on a coffee machine.

"Yeah. I'm just worried," Zoe told him as she took a sip of coffee. He looked at her with concerned eyes, and Zoe realised that she hadn't told him about Patrick.

"Oh. There is no easy way to say this . . ." She looked at her husband in order to gauge his reaction. He'd say the right thing; she knew he would. "Someone has been killed on the outskirts of Tansbury."

Dave coughed slightly in surprise, but quickly regained composure. "Someone we know?"

"Vaguely. You know the new mum, Ava?" Zoe asked, and when Dave nodded, she continued, "Her ex-husband."

Dave's eyes widened. "Poor Ava. How was he murdered? Shit. That's the wrong thing to ask." He rubbed his head.

"I don't know. They haven't even released it on the news. But as soon as its out . . . Gossip gossip gossip." Zoe sighed and warmed her hands on her coffee.

"How awful. Have they caught who did it?" Dave asked. But Zoe knew he was thinking the same as her. *Could it have been Ava?*

"I don't know. I don't think so." And the next words came out of Zoe's mouth before she could stop them. "I just really hope Ava has an alibi."

*   *   *

Ava wondered if she should get a lawyer. She didn't know much about how all of this work, but she'd read enough crime novels to know that lawyers tended to get involved when things got bad. She also knew that it would make her look guilty. But she wasn't.

She knew that the only person on her side was Louise. Kind, caring Louise. Louise, who seemed to be willing to take a bullet for Ava despite having only known her for over a month. She idly wondered if she had Zoe in her corner. Her corner? What was she thinking? This was not some sort of battle—her against the police. It should be her and the police against whoever did this.

And without warning, her brain quickly flickered to Nancy. Nancy, whom she suspected was pranking her with those calls and emails. Could Nancy be capable of murder? She dismissed the thought as soon as it entered her brain. Nancy would have to be crazy to kill someone over a small kiss.

Jake!

Ava had completely forgotten about the date. With everything that had been going on, the prospect of seeing Jake again had completely slipped her mind. She was due to see him tomorrow if she remembered correctly.

But she just couldn't. How would it look? She daren't even think it. Her ex-husband had just been killed, and two days after she would be seen frolicking around with a *still married* man.

Ava: Hey, Jake. I'm so sorry, but I'm going to have to cancel on tomorrow.

She wasn't sure whether she should explain the situation or not. She knew he'd find out soon enough, so she decided to let him find out in his own time. Her phone bleeped soon after her message was sent.

Jake: I heard about Patrick. I am so sorry Ava. If you need anything, please just let me know. J x

Butterflies erupted in Ava's stomach, but not because of Jake. But because if he already knew about Patrick's death, who else knew?

TWENTY

25th September 2009

We managed to get Annabelle out—much to the boys' sadness. Success.

"I feel like I haven't been out in forever!" Annabelle said, her voice a little higher pitched than usual.

"I know!" I replied, slinging my arm around her. We were in the queue for the club. My job was to keep Annabelle happy, and Lucy's job was to look out for the hot medic. Of course, she got the better job. We came up with a code—when Lucy spots the hot medic, she would ask Annabelle how her course was going. Hopefully that will lead onto her friends . . . and boom. Hot medic.

Part of me was worried about what will happen if we did meet him. Lucy and I could hardly share him, and let's be honest, she was definitely the more outgoing one out of the two of us. Oh well, I guess I would be happy for her if she was the one to get him.

Once at the front of the queue, we paid the entrance fee and went into the club. Of course, Matt offered to buy me a drink—I had been noticing more and more that Lucy was right; he did like me. Once we all had drinks in our hands, we headed over to a booth to have a seat.

"Looking good tonight, Ava," Matt whispered into my ear, and I felt myself recoil. I murmured a small thanks before turning the conversation back to Annabelle.

"Hey, so what drink did you get?" I asked her. I'm hoping it was something strong, so that she would let her hair down a bit more.

"Vodka cranberry." She giggled. "I haven't drunk this much all year!" she whooped. Out of the corner of my eye, I saw Lucy roll her eyes. I gave her a quick wink before pretending to listen to Annabelle.

Suddenly, Lucy hit my leg. I frowned at her before realising that the hot medic had just walked into the club.

"So, Annabelle, how's your course going? It's medicine, right?" Lucy put on her best 'I'm so interested in your life' voice.

"Yeah, it's good. Pretty hard already." She looked a little confused that Lucy was talking to her. I smiled and nodded.

"But you're really clever, I'm sure you'll be fine," I reassured her. "But I hear it's a lot of hours. Do you fit in any time to have fun?" I made a joke out of it, and thankfully, Annabelle laughed with me.

"Yeah, the hours are long. But I guess I get to spend so much time with the other students that we make our own fun. We're kind of like a family." She shrugged. *Bingo.* But before I could get another word out, Lucy jumped in.

"That's super cute. Do you go out with them then?" I knew where she was heading.

"Yeah, I guess. We normally go out together on Fridays, so we don't have lectures the following day. I actually think some of them are out tonight," she said nonchalantly. She had no idea that she was saying all the right things.

"That's so cool. If you want to go hang out with them instead of us, go ahead." Lucy suggested.

Annabelle frowned. "Do you want to get rid of me?" she asked slowly. Lucy shook her head quickly.

"No, of course not. I've just heard that medics are super fun on nights out. I didn't want to bore you," she said smoothly.

Nice save, I wanted to say that to her. I simply flicked her leg to tell her she did a good job.

"Yeah, they are fun. Actually, it would be nice to see them," she said, taking a small sip of her drink. "There's enough space here, isn't there? I could introduce you?" she asked timidly. Lucy and I looked at each other as if we were thinking about it, but we already knew the answer.

"That would be nice!" I exclaimed, and just like that, Annabelle wandered over to the bar. Lucy and I turned to each other in glee.

"That couldn't have worked better. Nice work," I told her, and she flicked her hair backwards.

"I know." Her eyes darted over to the bar. "They're coming over. Act natural." I nodded and took a sip of a drink before pretending to laugh at a joke that Lucy just told.

"Hey guys!" Annabelle cooed and we turned around mid-laugh. And there he stood, looking absolutely phenomenal. "These are my friends from medicine: Luca, Patrick, Missy, and Julia." She pointed at them as she said their names.

Patrick.

"Hey, I'm Lucy." My best friend suddenly dived in before patting the seats next to her for them to sit down. I could barely get my name in before she started chatting with Patrick.

You snooze, you lose.

TWENTY-ONE

Two days had passed since Ava last saw the police. She was still completely lost on what to do with herself. Her parents were trying to get back from Edinburgh but weren't having any luck on getting a flight. All she wanted was her mum. She hadn't dared look up potential lawyers, in fear her internet history would be examined. She was at a loss. Of course, Louise was being brilliant—taking Mia to school most days, and constantly asking if she was okay. Ava couldn't face dropping Mia off at school anymore, not after what happened at the ball.

Ava planned to tell Mia today after she got back from school. She had been going through all the possible ways she could tell her four-year-old daughter that she no longer had a father.

It was 4 PM. She had put it off for as long as she could. Ava made her way up to her daughter's room, where she found Mia playing with her Barbie.

"Hey, sweetie." Ava felt her voice break. *Be strong,* she told herself.

"Mama, will you be Ken for me? I can't do the low voice as good as you." She held the Ken doll to Ava.

"Honey, we need to have a little chat about daddy." Ava felt her eyes glistening with tears. *Breath in, breath out.*

"Is he coming to play too?" Mia smiled and placed the Ken doll down. Patrick was always the best at playing Barbie with Mia. A single tear fell down Ava's cheek.

"No, baby. Daddy has gone . . ." She couldn't bring herself to say it. How do you tell your child that their parent is gone? In what world is that ok?

"Where daddy gone?" Mia began to look concerned. Ava pulled her daughter into a tight hug.

"Daddy has gone to heaven, sweetie."

*   *   *

Mia had reacted like any child would. She refused to believe that Patrick wasn't coming back. She cried and kicked and screamed at Ava until she wore herself out. She was now asleep.

Ava wasn't sure how long she had been crying on the sofa. Maybe hours? It must be at least 8 PM. She managed to stay strong whilst Mia was crying, but as soon as her little girl fell asleep, she collapsed.

She was so angry at whoever did this. She felt sick to her stomach that someone had deliberately torn her family apart. She was angry at herself for ruining her marriage. The pillow she was crying into was soaked now, but she didn't care. Her eyes felt as if they were on fire, but she didn't care. The only thing she cared about was finding out who did this.

Ding dong.

"Crap," Ava muttered to herself. There was no way she was going to pull herself together in time, but yet again, she didn't care. She shuffled over to the door and opened it.

"Jake?" she said with a sniff. Standing before her was beautiful Jake, holding a brown bag in his hands. He looked at her for a couple of seconds before pulling her into a hug.

"I'm so sorry," he said. Once he pulled away, he held the bag out for her. "I brought curry. I figured you might need a little food. Food would definitely be the last thing on my mind."

Ava nodded. He was right. Ava couldn't actually remember the last time she ate. She gratefully took the bag from his hands and ushered him in.

"Oh, I only came over to drop the curry off. I don't want to intrude," Jake told Ava softly. She felt her eyes glistening with tears again.

"Please come in. I need some company." She felt the tears slide down her face. Ava knew how bad it would look if she was caught seeing Jake, but right now she didn't care. She needed someone.

Jake shut the door behind him before embracing her once more.

"I am so sorry, Ava. I know there is nothing I can say or do," he whispered into her hair. But at that moment in time, Ava didn't care what the detectives would think, or what anyone else would think. Because her ex-husband had just died, and all she wanted was someone to look after her.

"Shall we watch a film or something?" Jake suggested as he guided Ava over to the sofa. She nodded, finding words difficult. She just wanted to lie down and cry forever.

"Okay, lets watch some Netflix," Jake said as cheerfully as he could before picking a comedy film Ava had seen a thousand times before.

"Good choice," Ava mumbled as she curled her legs underneath her. Jake looked at her thoughtfully.

"Are you going to eat the curry?" he asked carefully as if walking on eggshells. Ava nodded, suddenly realising how hungry she was. Slowly, she took the first mouthful. *Of course, he's a good cook*, she thought. Practically perfect in every way.

"How are you doing? All things considered," Jake asked slowly. Ava looked up from her curry with blurry eyes and looked him in the eye.

"I have never been more terrified in my life," Ava whimpered as a tear dropped down her cheek. "The police think it's

114

me. Everyone seems to think it's me. I don't understand how they think I could to that. To my family. To Mia." She clenched her hand into a fist.

"I believe you," Jake told her. "If that helps in any way." He chuckled and looked at her. "It's easy for the police to blame you. It makes their lives easier."

"They have evidence. The murder weapon has my fingerprints all over it. I just don't know how it could have happened."

"The murder weapon?" Jake asked slowly.

"Yes." Ava felt nerves wrack her body. "A baseball bat— my baseball bat. It was there one day, and then when the detectives were here, it was gone. I thought I got rid of it after university."

"It's the same one? Are you sure?" Jake asked. Ava nodded. She was sure it was hers; it had her initials engraved into the bottom.

"Yeah." Ava fiddled with her fingers, unsure of what to say. She knew what it looked like. Everything was pointing to her. But it wasn't her.

She wondered whether she should mention the calls and the emails to Jake. It terrified her because if her hacker was in her emails, where else could they be? She knew they were linked to the murder; she *knew it*.

"Jake?" she asked, the word stalker on her tongue. And then the phone rang. "I'll get that." She rushed over to the phone.

"Hello?"

"Miss Milberry? It's Detective Brown." Her blood ran cold.

"What is it?"

"We need you to come down to the station."

TWENTY-TWO

25th September 2009

"Are you having a good night?" Annabelle asked over the music that pounded in my ears. I wanted to tell her to leave me alone. To make herself useful. Get the fit medic to notice me, not Lucy. Tonight was the first time that I resented my best friend. I sat in the corner of the booth—alone, may I add—while she was almost on Patrick's lap, making me resent her very much indeed.

She looked over at me, a sly glint in her eye. I knew that look. It was her 'I'm going to get lucky tonight' look. I plastered a large smile on my face. It was fake, of course. I had never been one to be fake, but ever since landing myself into Lucy's friendship group, I had noticed another face appear from nowhere. I was becoming as two faced as Lucy herself.

I love my best friend, I reassured myself. But as I saw Lucy lean over and stroke Patrick's leg, I felt a fire in my blood that I had never felt before. Jealousy was an ugly face to add to my collection, but it had been added nonetheless.

"Would you like a drink?" Matt snapped my attention away from Lucy by placing his hand on my leg. My instant reaction was no, because I knew what Matt wanted, and I couldn't give that to him. I pondered his question for a moment, leaving his words hanging in the air with hope.

"Sure." I stood up, pushing his hand off my leg. I glanced back to him. "But you're buying." Glee lit up his face, and Annabelle stood up next to him. I suspected she liked Matt quite a bit.

"I'll join!" she slurred as she looked over to Matt adoringly. I did not dislike Annabelle, but sometimes she could be a real nuisance. If I wanted to make Patrick jealous, I needed to be alone with Matt. I gave Annabelle a pointed look before casting my eyes up and down her body.

"I think you've had quite enough; don't you think?" I said in a sickly-sweet tone, and I almost hated myself for it. Annabelle had done nothing to warrant the unpleasantness she kept receiving from Lucy and I.

Her face fell as she heard my words and sat back onto the seat submissively. Guilt trickled through my veins, and I wanted to take back the action immediately. Instead, I took Matt's hand in mine and pulled him over to the bar.

"That was a little savage, don't you think?" Matt asked me with a raised eyebrow when we reached the bar. I ran my tongue over my teeth slowly, already bored of his company. I rolled my eyes and turned my attention to the bar man.

"I'm just being responsible," I told him before catching the bar man's attention. He casted his eyes up and down me approvingly. Matt snaked his arm around my waist, and for once, I didn't recoil because any attention he gave me might get Patrick's attention.

"Two tequila shots, please," he ordered. I butted in and held four fingers out; I needed to be drunk if I wanted to flirt with Matt all night. I felt him squeeze my waist before letting him pay the bar man.

"Cheers to uni!" Matt said as he held his tequila to clink mine. I poured the liquid back down my throat, the sickening taste almost causing me to gag. I took the second shot almost immediately, and before the taste hit the back of my throat, I bite into the sour lemon.

"God, I don't even know why I buy tequila," Matt said as he stuck his tongue out in disgust. I hummed at him before turning my attention to see where Lucy and Patrick were. Dread filled me when I noticed that they were no longer at the booth.

"Fancy seeing you two together." Lucy's voice crawled into my ear as her hand snaked onto my arm affectionately. I turned around to see my best friend and Patrick leaning against the bar. I planted another fake smile onto my face.

"Just getting some shots. I'm not drunk enough," I told her, trying to keep my eyes off Patrick. It was hard because the fit medic really did live up to his name.

"Us too." She leaned into him and gave me a devilish smile. I wanted to punch her. Instead, I politely held my hand out.

"I'm Ava." He took my hand and gave me a smile.

"Patrick." His hand didn't leave mine, and neither did his eyes. Bingo. *Sorry Lucy, but you might have to sit this one out.* I felt my best friend's eyes on me, willing me to let go of his hand, but I ignored her. Just as she had been ignoring me the entire night.

"Fancy another shot? Lucy and I are buying sambuca," Patrick asked me, and we finally released our hands. I gave him a small smile.

"It would be rude to say no," I told him before leaning against the bar next to Lucy. Her eyes were still on me, and so were Matt's.

"It would indeed." Patrick's eyes glinted as he raked his eyes over me, and I licked my lips. Maybe Lucy wouldn't be getting lucky tonight after all.

TWENTY-THREE

Ava sat behind a large table, her knees jittering with nerves. Why had detective Brown called her down to the station? Were they going to arrest her? Questions buzzed around her head so quickly that she thought it might fall off. *That would make this easier,* she supposed. Her phone buzzed, and she glanced at it to see a text from Louise.

> *Louise: Mia is okay, eating all her veggies at supper. Plus, her and El get on so well! I hope everything is ok.*

Ava let out a sigh of relief. When she received the call from the detective, Ava had to ask Jake to leave and to take Mia to Louise's. She could hardly bear to leave her baby without her after having received such sad news, but she had to.

The door slammed open and detective Brown walked in, head held high. *He means business,* Ava thought.

"Evening." His voice was stern, not warm as it usually was. Something bad had happened. Ava's mouth was so dry that she could barely muster a word, so she remained speechless. "I suppose you're wondering why we called you down."

Ava nodded. Detective Brown nodded before he pressed a button on the table, which Ava highly suspected was there to record her. She gulped.

"Ava, whilst your fingerprints on the murder weapon was suspicious, it did not place you at the scene of the crime. It was understandable that your own prints would be on the bat, and it's not too far-fetched to believe that someone could have taken it from your home," he said. Ava didn't reply. He was leading up to something.

"Your alibi was iffy as you had no one to validate it, but of course, there also wasn't anyone to disprove it." He cleared his throat and rubbed his face. "Until now. We received a phone call earlier this evening telling us that you were seen walking around the woods at the time of Patrick's murder." Detective Brown looked at her with sad eyes and Ava's stomach dropped.

"That's not true." Her voice came out as a gasp, her words shaking as they left her lips. "I was at home, I told you that."

"The caller informed us that you appeared disorderly. Drunk, even." Detective Brown looked deep into Ava's eyes. "Holding a long item, that the caller believed to be a bat of some sort."

"Convenient." The sarcasm dripped off Ava's words as anger rushed through her. Someone had done an extremely good job of framing her. And she couldn't tell the detective about the calls, for she feared the threats on Mia would become real. She didn't doubt Patrick's killer for one moment.

"You see, Ava, this puts me into a predicament." Brown clasped his hands together, his fingers intertwined. "I have physical evidence. I also have evidence that places you at the time of the murder."

"It's not true." Ava was at a loss for words. "The caller could be making it up. Or maybe, just maybe, did you consider that the real killer may have called you?" She tilted her head to one side, eyeing the detective.

"I am a detective, Miss Milberry. It is my job to explore every possible route, so watch your manner." His voice was stern. "The issue I have here is that the evidence I have is sufficient to establish probable cause." Confusion clouded Ava's mind. *Probable cause?*

"It means that we have enough evidence to conclude that you committed the crime, Miss Milberry." Brown looked saddened by that news, but the rocket of emotion that surged through Ava outweighed any emotion the detective was feeling.

"The bat and the phone call." Ava struggled for words. "That doesn't seem enough to me."

"That's for the court to decide." Brown looked down, and Ava realised that he believed her. She couldn't put her finger on it, but Brown seemed reluctant to be telling her this information. But it was his job, so he had to do it. And she understood that.

"Ava Milberry, I am arresting you for the murder of Patrick Jules. You have the right to remain silent. If you do say anything, what you say can be used against you in a court of law. You have the right to consult with a lawyer and have that lawyer present during any questioning. If you cannot afford a lawyer, one will be appointed for you if you so desire."

The words echoed in Ava's ears, and the world around her seemed to stop moving. She was under arrest for a crime she did not commit. The words replayed in her brain over and over, trying to make sense of them. Her stalker—the one who had called her and emailed her and *broke into her house*— had done this. As her world moved in slow motion, the only thought that spun in her brain, like a spider spinning its web, was that she was going to find the son of a bitch who'd done this.

*   *   *

When Louise received the phone call from Ava, she could barely believe her ears. Ava had been arrested for the murder of Patrick? The thought had crossed her mind, but she had decided that there was no way that Ava was a killer.

Of course, Louise immediately agreed to bail her out, and drove straight to the station, grateful that El was there to look after the kids and Mia.

When Ava stepped out of the police station, Louise didn't have to say anything to make Ava crumble. The moment Ava reached Louise she melted into her arms.

"It's okay." Louise stroked her hair, like a mother does for a child. The hot, angry tears streamed down Ava's face and onto Louise's jumper. Louise almost wanted to cry for her.

"I have a trial," Ava managed when Louise released her. "To decide if I did it or not." Ava looked at Louise with wet eyes. "I didn't do it, Louise. I didn't."

"I believe you. Only a mad man wouldn't." Louise took Ava's hands in her own. "Are you okay to drive?" Louise asked, her tone motherly and calm. Ava shook her head.

"Okay, we'll leave your car here overnight, alright? We'll go get Mia from mine, and then I'll drop you both off. That sound okay?" Louise asked, wanting to do as much as she could for her friend. Ava nodded.

The car ride back to was silent. Even after collecting Mia, Ava seemed lost for words. Louise made as much conversation with the little girl as she could, but even Mia seemed to know that something was up with her mum.

When they pulled up into Ava's driveway, Ava didn't seem sure what to say to Louise. Louise wanted to tell her that it was no problem, that she would do anything for her. It seemed extreme, but nothing was too much when someone you love has died.

"I'm only a phone call away, Ava. Please call me if you need me." Louise looked deeply into Ava's eyes, and Ava nodded briskly. She gave her a small smile before retreating into her house. Louise let out a sigh of exhaustion.

*   *   *

After Ava put Mia to bed, assuring her that everything was okay, Ava felt consumed by loneliness and fear. She knew her husband's murderer had been in her house, but for some reason they hadn't killed Ava herself. Whilst that provided some comfort, it also caused confusion. Why would the killer murder Patrick? Had he been involved in some business that Ava didn't know about?

But if so, why would they frame Ava?

Ava tried to stop the thoughts whirling around her mind, and amongst those thoughts, she almost missed the knocking on her door. She glanced at her watch, which read 9:33 PM. Dread pooled in her stomach. Who would be coming to see her this late? Could it be the police again? Or worse, had the murderer come to kill her?

She certainly wasn't expecting to see Patrick's family standing behind the door, arms wide open.

"Ava." Lily, Patrick's sister, engulfed Ava in a hug before she could process what was happening. Ava returned the hug, seeking comfort in a girl she used to be so close with. Patrick's mother, Agatha, took Ava's hand with tear brimmed eyes. Ava was surprised at the welcome she received from her ex-husband's family. They were always close, especially Ava and Lily, but once the divorce had gone through, Ava received no word from any of them. Not that she expected it.

"I know it's a bit late, but please come in," Ava said to them, her voice slightly strangled. "I'm sorry I didn't call; it's been a bit of . . ." she began, but Ian, Patrick's very stern father, cut her off.

"We didn't expect you to call, dear." He looked at her with kind eyes. Ava didn't think he'd ever said anything so nice to her before. Her eyes filled with tears and the words came from her mouth before she could stop them.

"I've been c-charged with his murder." Her words were so rushed and tear filled that she wondered if they had understood her. Agatha's mouth was a hard line.

"We expected no less." And that was all that was said about the matter. Ava guided the family over to her seating area before regaining her hostess instincts.

123

"Can I get you drinks? Tea, coffee?" she asked, and Lily surprised them all by letting out a sharp laugh. She looked over at Ava with expecting eyes.

"I think we all need something a little harder than that, don't you?" Lily gave Ava a sad smile and Ava let out a small laugh before looking at Patrick's parents, who were smiling in agreement. Ava decided to make four vodka martinis, Patrick's favourite drink. She brought them over on a tray with a bowl of crisps, still trying to impress the parents.

"Thank you, dear," Ian said. Dear again. He clearly felt sorry for Ava, which was something. At least they didn't think that she did it. She rose her glass to the Jules family, tears brimming in her eyes.

"To Patrick. He was an incredible doctor, husband, son, brother, and person. We will miss him dearly," Ava said, struggling to get her words out. Agatha nodded at Ava and a single tear fell down her face.

"And to that arsehole who took my brother from me," Lily spoke with venom in her voice, surprising them all. "When I find you, I will kill you." And then she smiled a sickly-sweet smile. Ava clinked her glass with Lily's. They would *find* the bastard together.

TWENTY-FOUR

26th September 2009

I woke up in a room that seemed familiar but wasn't mine. The familiar pristine walls of the hall of residence that I lived in. But this wasn't my room. I rolled over in the dark blue sheets and saw dark hair and a bare torso. All of a sudden, the memories from last night started to piece itself together in my head.

I hooked up with Patrick Jules. The fit medic.

Oh god, Lucy would be fuming. I swung my legs off the bed and looked for my bag with a face full of hair. My clothes scattered the floor, but thankfully, I had a large t shirt on, which I suspect was Patrick's. When I found my bag, I noticed that my phone was dead. *Great.* I looked over at Patrick, who was gently snoring away.

Christ, he was attractive.

I looked around his room, in hope to get to know him better. Posters covered the walls, varying from the human anatomy to pictures of bands I had never heard of. I glanced back to Patrick, who still slumbered away. I picked up my outfit from the night before and regretfully redress myself. Walking through the halls in my thigh high boots was not going to be a highlight of my year, I could tell you that for free.

"Going so soon?" Patrick's voice alarmed me so much that I fell backwards onto his desk chair. He propped himself up on his forearms and gave me a devilish look. "I'd much rather you got back into bed."

I felt myself blush. "I have lectures today. I really should head back," I said as I zip my boot up. He cocked his head to one side.

"Don't be a bore, take those boots off and get back here. Skip the lectures. I'm taking you out for breakfast," he commanded, and his charm got to me. I rolled my mouth inward and gave him a small smile.

"In this?" I gestured to my outfit. He chuckled before leaning forward and grabbing my arm, pulling me back onto the bed. I made a small yelp in surprise before turning my face to his with a grin. He was really quite something. He put his finger underneath my chin, beckoning me closer to him.

"I think you look sexy as hell." And then he pressed his lips to mine. "Who cares what everyone else thinks?"

*   *   *

As we walked into the pub, I received a multitude of disapproving looks. I couldn't blame them; I was wearing thigh high boots, a leather mini skirt, a red crop top, and a large jacket of Patrick's. It was quite the combo.

"A table for two?" The waiter looked me up and down as he spoke, his eyes resting on the gap of skin between my boots and my skirt. I coughed and looked up at Patrick, whose eyes narrowed with anger. I felt triumphant.

"Yes," Patrick said to the waiter, whose eyes were still on my legs. *Pervert.* "She has eyes too, mate." The waiter blushed red and looked over to Patrick for the first time. He kept his eyes off me as he gestured to a table in the corner. I took the seat by the window before lifting the menu to my eyes to hide my embarrassment.

"What an arse," Patrick said after the waiter was out of earshot. "He couldn't get enough of your legs." I peeped at the gorgeous medic opposite me. He cocked his head to one side and shrugged. "Not that I blame him." I felt myself blush once again, giggling and returning my focus on the menu.

"I think I'll feed my hangover with a fry up." I snapped the menu shut. "What are you getting?" Patrick's eyes were still on me and he gave me a small smile.

"The same." He looked over to our waiter and called him over before telling him our orders. He nodded, a bead of sweat trickling down his face. He didn't look in my direction even once.

"You've embarrassed him." I tutted, but I silently felt glorious. It felt great to have a man stand up for you, and Patrick was a real man.

"Rightly so. I don't think I want anyone else looking at your legs." He took a sip of water, and my mouth dropped open in surprise. The confidence of him!

"You've only just met me." I pointed out as I fiddled with my boots, but I quite liked his cockiness. Patrick shrugged.

"And look how well we're getting on. I think I'll marry you." He grinned and I almost choked on my water.

"You want to marry a one-night stand? Who even are you?" I tried to fight the grin that was making its way to my face, but I was enjoying Patrick's company too much.

"I don't know how you remember it, Ava, but we certainly did not shag." He raised one eyebrow. "Not that I'd say no." I felt embarrassment surge through me. How silly of me to just assume that we had sex. I felt blood rush to my face once more, humiliated at my assumption.

"Sorry, I just . . ." I began, but Patrick hastily cut me off.

"Don't apologise. You were pretty hammered. The most action I got last night was changing you into one of my t-shirts. That was pretty challenging." He laughed at the memory, and his explanation jolted a memory in me that made me want to crawl under the table and never resurface. I remembered wiggling around on his bed, refusing to get dressed.

"Christ." I put my head in my hands. "Any other embarrassing stories you want to reveal? We may as well get it out in the open." Patrick looked at me with a half-smile.

"Only one more thing." He rolled his lips inwards as if trying to suppress a smile. "You kept calling me fit medic. Not Patrick. Just fit medic."

I groaned.

TWENTY-FIVE

Ava and the Jules family spent their evening drinking vodka martinis and reminiscing about Patrick and their fondest memories of him. Ava couldn't think of a better way to reflect on his brilliant life.

"Oh wow, it's late," Ava stated as she saw the time on the clock. Almost midnight. She wanted to offer them a lift home, but she knew she was over the limit. Lily stood up with her phone in her hand.

"I'm going to book a taxi to take us to our hotel," she said. They had explained to Ava that they were going to stay in town to help Ava work out the funeral arrangements and Ava was glad. Her own family were due to be coming to stay tomorrow, and she finally felt like she had people on her side.

"It was lovely to see you," Ava told them as she took each member of Patrick's family in a warm embrace. They all said their goodbyes and left Ava.

Suddenly, she was alone again. Slowly and drunkenly, Ava made her way up to bed, collapsing in a heap.

*   *   *

The tell-tale ping of a new email awoke Ava from her slumbers. As she groggily made her way to her laptop, her stomach plummeted.

129

Subject: Murderer
You killed him as much as I did.

Ava slammed her laptop closed and her world came to a halt. She felt as if her throat was being constricted, her breathing ragged and raw, the blood pounding repeatedly in her ears. She took her shaking hands and slowly reopened the laptop, but the email was already gone. She slammed her hands on the table, sending fireworks of pain up her forearms.

"Dammit!" she shouted before hitting her hands on the table again. "Dammit!" Hot tears pooled in her eyes. She wiped them immediately, refusing to let her stalker get to her. She rubbed her face and looked to the ceiling, willing her tears to stop. And then, the doorbell rang.

Ava looked at her watch and saw that she had severely overslept. She swore loudly before running into Mia's room to wake her up.

"Knock knock!" Louise's voice echoed from downstairs. Ava ran down to greet her. The pounding in her ears began to slow as she took deep breaths. "Sorry, I'm a little early. Are you alright?" Louise asked, noticing Ava's pyjamas.

"Yeah. Sorry. Overslept," Ava said monotonously. "Sorry, I need to help Mia get ready, but please help yourself to coffee." Before Louise could say anything, Ava rushed up the stairs to the aid of her daughter. But as she reached Mia's room, Mia was practically ready.

"Hey, mama!" She looked up with her big eyes and round cheeks. "I got ready alllll by myself. See?" she exclaimed, lisping every s. Ava's eyes filled with tears, impressed with her daughter, especially after the news she received last night. She remained in hope that her daughter didn't quite understand the true meaning of her fathers disappearance.

As they made their way down the stairs, Mia asked if she could have a sleepover with Issie.

"They were planning it all of yesterday, apparently." Louise laughed as Ava made her way into the kitchen. Mia clasped Ava's legs, giving her those puppy dog eyes that she always did when she wanted something. Ava wasn't sure whether to say yes or not.

"It's a school night, pumpkin," she said slowly. "Don't you want to be in your own bed?" But after that email, she felt as if Mia would be safer in Louise's house than her own, so she agreed to her daughter's pleas.

When Mia ran up the stairs to pack her suitcase—which Ava suspected she'd have to repack instantly—Louise placed her hand on Ava's arm.

"Are you okay? You look a little shaken up." Louise's kind eyes bore into Ava's, and she almost felt like she could tell Louise. But then she spied her laptop on the counter, a reminder of the threats her stalker had taunted her with.

"Yeah." Ava took a deep breath. "I'm fine."

*   *   *

Ava was filled with a terrifying loneliness as Louise drove her daughter to school. She needed to get over her fear of Nancy and her posse. Whilst she was afraid to be alone, she was glad that Mia was in the safety of school, where the stalker can't get to her.

She checked her phone and saw a couple of missed messages from Jake.

> *Jake: Hey, sorry for not checking in after you got called*
> *to the station yesterday. Nancy called me with*
> *an emergency. I hope everything is okay.*

Ava smiled despite her current level of fear and sent a quick reply.

> *Ava: I wouldn't say things are okay, but I'm managing.*
> *Thanks for checking in.*

After clicking send, Ava decided to make herself some food. She couldn't remember the last time she had a home cooked meal. As she gathered the ingredients for breakfast, she tried to remember the last thing Patrick ever said to her. It was when he dropped Mia off. Did he say he missed her? She thought so, and she hadn't said it back. She wished she had, now. But there was something niggling at her, at the back of her brain, trying to reach the surface. *Ava, there is something I really need to tell you.* His words suddenly rung in her ears like foghorns. She didn't want to leap to assumptions, but could he have possibly been trying to tell her about the stalker? Had he been a victim before he was killed?

And if that was the case, did that mean that Ava was next?

Ava took a deep breath and ran her fingers through her knotted hair, panic seeping through every bone in her body. She couldn't let her stalker get to her like this, she needed to stay strong.

The day crawled by. Ava tried to get back into work, even though Xanos had given her leave following Patrick's death. As the clock spun, the outside light began to dim, and Ava began to feel a panic for her daughter. She pulled her phone out and composed a message to Louise.

Ava: How's Mia? Was school okay?

The reply was instant.

Louise: She's fine, don't stress. They're having a great time.

Ava let out a sigh of relief and made her way into the kitchen, before taking a bottle of Merlot from her shelf and pouring herself a large glass.

"To you, you bastard. If you hurt my daughter, I will kill you." She held her glass up in a toast before taking a large sip and returning to her food.

Ava was three glasses of Merlot down when she heard her email ping again, and in her drunken state, she didn't think anything of it. She glanced at the clock as she walked over to the counter, which read 11:30 PM. Time was getting away from her. But as she opened her laptop, she felt the familiar sensation of panic as she saw the subject line of the email.

Subject: I'm no bastard, bastard

132

You're hurting my feelings, Ava. And when I'm upset,
I never know what I may do.

Ava's heart leapt into her mouth as the attachment in the email loaded, and the glass in her hand fell from her hand, smashing into a million little pieces on the floor, coating the white tiles in red.

The picture was of Mia, sound asleep, cuddling a teddy bear. Beside her was a note, which read:

Don't do anything stupid now, Ava.

Ava barely made it to the sink before she threw up the entirety of her supper.

133

TWENTY-SIX

Patrick and I had been dating for three weeks now, ever since that breakfast. To my surprise, Lucy was more than happy when I returned from our date—thrilled even.

"Less competition for me with the other boys." She had winked at me when I nervously told her. I was so lucky to have such a supportive best friend. Someone who was less thrilled was Matt. He kept sending me angry texts, telling me I led him on. He wasn't wrong, but it definitely didn't warrant cyber abuse.

And even less pleased was Annabelle. After Lucy and I used her to get to Patrick—I still felt guilty about that, by the way—Lucy forced me to drop her again. Annabelle reported to the residence life team that we were bullying her. All we received was a stern letter.

Lucy and I strutted through the dining room arm in arm, striding past the hot food—because God forbid that we ate anything other than a salad—and over to the salad bar. Of course, when I was not with Lucy, I would eat how I wanted. But when I was with her . . . well, let's just say that she had this power over people. This power that just made you do whatever she wanted you to do. We each placed a couple of lettuce leaves on our plates, carefully selected some vegetables and dressing, and took our seats at our table.

As I took my first mouthful, I saw Annabelle wander into the dining room with a sullen look on her face. Lucy immediately laughed at her outfit— long shorts and a black shirt. I wanted to point out that she was a medical student, so she needed to dress practically, but I kept my mouth closed. I didn't want to get on Lucy's bad side.

"If it isn't my beautiful girlfriend." I heard the familiar voice of Patrick from behind me. He kissed me then sat next to me. Lucy coughed and cocked her head to one side. Patrick chuckled.

"And her gorgeous sidekick." He rolled his eyes and Lucy gave him a big grin.

"Oh Patrick, you're too kind." She batted her eyelashes, making us both laugh. Our laughter stopped when Annabelle made her way over to our table. Lucy rolled her eyes at me, and I wanted to tell her to stop being nasty but, again, I stopped myself.

"Hey, Patrick. I was just wondering if you could send me your notes from today? I didn't manage—" Annabelle began, but Lucy cut her off, flashing her manicured nails in Annabelle's face.

"Sorry, did I say you could come over here?" She frowned as if Annabelle had just run over her dog. "You should really keep up, or you might get kicked out." Lucy looked at poor Annabelle up and down before giggling. "But then again, that wouldn't be a shame, would it?" Lucy looked at me for backup, and I didn't know what to say.

"Lucy, that was a bit harsh, don't you think?" Patrick said, his eyes darting between Lucy and I. Lucy's frown deepened and she ran her tongue over her teeth.

"Ava, don't you agree with what I said?" Lucy asked me, her eyes floated over to me as her red lips pulled into a smug smirk. I rolled my lips in, scared of what to say. I was not a nasty person, but I didn't want to disappoint Lucy. I looked at Annabelle, guilt coursing through me.

"She's right, you know. You should do everyone a favour and fail." I laughed. I felt Patrick's eyes judging me. I wanted to cry
135

for Annabelle, but I didn't. I saw her eyes gathering with tears, and my moral self punched me in the gut.

"One day, you will get what's coming for you. You can't treat people like this and get away with it," Annabelle said, directing all her anger at me. I kept my smile on my face before lifting my hand and shooing her away.

*   *   *

"Ava, that was really harsh, what you said to Annabelle," Patrick said as we entered my room. *Sure, now he tells me off after Lucy has gone.* I turned to him and shrugged.

"You know what Lucy is like. I have to agree with her," I said in an exasperated tone. He gave me a look and sighed.

"Babe, you can say and do whatever you want. Lucy doesn't own you, you know." He pointed out. But he didn't know what it was like to be friends with Lucy. And he didn't know what it was like *not* being friends with Lucy, but Annabelle did.

"You know what she's like, Pat. She'd hate me if I disagreed with her." I sat down on the bed and grabbed the control for the TV.

"That isn't a friendship though, is it?" he said in a patronising tone, and I frowned at him. He didn't understand. Lucy was my best friend; she was what made my university experience amazing. I couldn't lose her.

"It is, Pat." I turned the TV on and began to flick through the channels. "What shall we watch?" He reached over and took the controller from my hand. I sat back, shocked at his actions.

"Don't change the topic. Ava, you need to stand up for yourself. I hate watching her walk all over you. It's not right." He ran his hands through his hair. "You don't even agree with half the things she says. Plus, Annabelle is actually really nice."

I rolled my eyes. "If you think so, then why don't you date her then!"

"Ava! Don't be ridiculous." He threw his arms in the air and I felt anger rising in me. He didn't know what he was talking about.

"Why can't you just understand that she's my friend?" I argued, the volume of my voice rising. I really didn't want to fall out with Pat, but he needed to understand that sometimes, friends came first.

"Why can't you just understand that she's manipulating you?" Patrick looked so frustrated that his face was beginning to go red. I sighed.

"Fine. I'll stand up for myself next time. Happy?" I said, defeated. He did have a point. I knew what we were saying to Annabelle was wrong. He put his head in his hands in relief and sighed.

"I'll believe it when I see it."

*   *   *

It was breakfast when we next saw Annabelle, who piled a large portion of hash browns and baked beans onto her plate. With Pat next to me, and Lucy nowhere to be seen, I decided to ignore my diet for a day and copied her. She looked my way and gave me a sad look. Pat nudged me.

"Hey Annabelle," I called out as she began to walk away from me. She turned back with a nervous look on her face. "I just wanted to apologise for all my behaviour towards you. It's not right, and I'm really sorry." I tried to smile, but the look on her face was making it hard. She looked . . . scared of me.

"You think an apology can fix everything?" she said, her eyes filling with tears. "You're wrong." She turned away and walked towards a table by herself. I felt horrible. I turned to Pat and shrugged my shoulders, wanting to cry.

"I tried." My voice was weak, and Patrick gave me a sympathetic look.

"I know, babe. I'm sure she'll come around." He rubbed my shoulder before grabbing some food and heading over to our table. Lucy was a little late today, and I already saw her eyeing my portion as she grabbed a yoghurt. When she made her way to our table, she leaned over and kissed my cheek. She ignored Patrick.

"Eating for five today, Ava?" she joked with a smile. I didn't smile back, and I remembered what Patrick said about sticking up for myself.

"I'd say this is a portion for one, personally," I retorted, my words trickling out of my mouth like acid. I immediately wanted to take them back. Lucy looked shocked as she took a mouthful of yoghurt. I looked at Pat, who gave me a subtle thumbs up, reassuring me.

"It's just that I thought you were trying to lose some pounds." She looked me up and down. "And those types of food won't help. I'm just looking out for you." She raised her eyebrows. I felt a little angry at my best friend.

"I've already lost half a stone since being at uni. I think it would be unhealthy to lose any more," I told her, impressed with myself. Maybe it was easier to stand up for myself than I thought. Lucy frowned at me.

"It doesn't look like it," she said, her lips pulling into a smirk. I heard Patrick make a noise, but all I could hear was the blood pounding in my ears. How dare she comment on my weight.

"That's really nasty, Lucy," I said with a stern voice. "You should never comment on a friend's weight." And to make a point, I stuffed a large mouthful of hash browns into my mouth. Lucy laughed and narrowed her eyes.

"I'm not being nasty. And you shouldn't tell me what to do." She turned her attention to Patrick. "What have you been saying to her, huh?" Patrick looked at her as if she said she was the Queen.

"Are you serious?" He looked angry. "I just told her to stick up for herself, Lucy. You're a bully." I looked at Lucy, feeling nervous. She breathed in deeply before turning to look at me.

"Are you really going to let your boyfriend talk to me like that?" She pursed her lips and tilted her head one side, trying to manipulate me. I folded my arms and took a deep breath.

"Yes, Lucy. I am."

TWENTY-SEVEN

As Ava stared at the picture of her daughter, her heart felt as if it might escape her chest. She reached for her car keys, ignoring the four glasses of wine she'd had earlier and got into her car. Her mind was running wild. Somehow, Patrick's murderer had gotten into Louise's house. Somehow, Patrick's murderer could hear everything that Ava was saying. What else were they capable of?

Ava sped along the roads, her vision swaying. She knew it was a bad idea to be driving drunk, and she hated herself for it, but she had to get to her baby. The arrest and the conditions of her bail didn't even cross her mind. The only thing that mattered was Mia.

As she pulled onto Louise's road, she thought she'd made it safely despite being drunk. But when she spotted the tell-tale flashing lights of the police, she knew she'd messed up.

She pulled over, and the police car followed. She felt her eyes fill with tears. Of course, this would happen. The officer stepped out of his car and wandered over to Ava. She reluctantly rolled down her window, willing herself to act as sober as possible.

"Good evening." He peered into the car, looking at the contents. Ava plastered a smile on her face, but she knew the officer wasn't buying it.

"Pretty late to be driving about. Did you know you have been driving on the other side of the road?" He cocked his head to one side, and Ava felt dread pooling through her. Drunk driving; how could she be so stupid? Ava was stumped for words.

"Been to the US recently?" He was playing with her; Ava knew it. She knew she couldn't lie, so she shook her head.

"I'm not used to driving in the dark, and the road markings confused me." The words tumbled from Ava's mouth in a chaotic mumble, and she wished she'd thought them through a little more.

"Is that so?" He narrowed his eyes and nodded slowly. "I'm going to have to breathalyse you, ma'am," he said, and Ava's stomach flipped over. *No, no, no.* This could not be happening, not when Mia's life was at risk. The officer pulled the small device out and clicked the nozzle on. He raised his eyebrows at her.

"Are you sure you don't have anything you want to tell me?" He narrowed his eyes at her, that was when it struck her. Could it be possible that her stalker had set this all up? Could it be that they knew she was drunk, and knew that she'd drive in any state to save her child? Had she fallen into their trap like a fool? She knew she couldn't be arrested *again.* Drunk driving on top of a murder charge? She may as well not even bother going to court. Then, an idea popped into her head.

"I think I know why I was driving badly," she said as she spotted an old tub of Prozac pills in the cup holder. They were old; she hadn't used them in ages. But the officer hadn't recognised her yet, which could only mean he didn't realise she had recently been arrested. If he was to realise, then she'd be done for.

"And why is that, Miss?" the officer asked, looking sceptical. Ava took a deep breath and continued.

"I've recently started re-taking Prozac. It's an antidepressant," she explained, and the officer nodded. "I haven't taken it in a while so I forgot about the side effects it can have." Tears were streaming down her cheeks now, and she realised that they weren't an act. They were real.

The officer glanced around the car, and spotted the tub. He frowned before standing up a little straighter.

"I understand." The officer placed his hand on Ava's shoulder. "I'll give you the benefit of the doubt this time, but please be careful next time you take it." He winked at her before strolling away from the car.

Ava released a sigh of relief, and within seconds her phone bleeped. Terror ran through her as the anonymous sender came up again.

Subject: Congrats!
Well played, baby. Well played.

*　　　*　　　*

When Ava arrived home, she climbed into bed immediately. Her body was still shaking from the events earlier. She'd sent Louise a text asking her to check on Mia, and according to Louise, all was fine. So, Ava had to trust that.

Her mind went back to the email from earlier. Of course, it mysteriously deleted itself after Ava had read it. *Well played, baby.* It had read. The words shook her to her core. Who was taunting her like this? Calling her baby? It made her sick to her stomach.

But she couldn't carry on being scared. She needed to be strong for Mia and figure out how to expose her stalker. She needed to be clever about it. Play along with the stalker, figure out who they are.

Because as they say—your stalker is most likely to be someone you know.

*　　　*　　　*

Louise was shocked to see Ava turn up at the school gates next morning. She'd imagined that it would be months before Ava could have faced Nancy again. When Mia spotted her mother, she ran over and hugged Ava's legs. Ava's face crumpled. Louise could tell something was up; something more than just Patrick's murder.

"How was your sleepover, pumpkin?" Louise heard Ava ask as she made her way over. Mia gave her mother a gap-toothed grin.

"Soooo good. We had popcorn and watched Barbie." Ava looked up to Louise, mouthing a silent 'thank you'. Louise gave her a small smile, wanting to comfort her friend, wanting to ask what made her come to school today.

"You and Issie need to get to your classroom, or you'll be late," Ava said, and her tone seemed reluctant. Louise looked at Ava intently, and as the two girls skipped away, a single tear fell down Ava's cheek.

"Oh Ava." Louise put her hand on Ava's shoulder. "What happened?" Ava shook her head, as if willing the tears to disappear.

"Nothing. After everything I'm just finding it hard to see her walk away." She wiped the tears from her cheek and sighed. "I'm just being pathetic. I need to get back into a routine and sort myself before I have my court hearing." She put her hands to her head. "Christ, I need to get a lawyer."

"Ava, you're not being pathetic," Louise told her, running her hand up and down her arm in attempt to comfort her. "The court date is miles away. We have time." She nodded and gave Ava a small smile.

"Miss Milberry?" A voice came from behind the two friends, and they both swivelled around to see a blonde woman Louise didn't recognise. Maybe it was a mother she had not met before, although Louise did make it her mission to know every mother at the school. Ava shook the hand that was outstretched before her.

"My name is Audrey Winkle from the BBC," the women said with a large smile, and dread pooled in Louise's stomach. She knew this was going to happen; it was always going to. "Can I ask you some questions regarding your ex-husband's recent passing?"

"No, you can't." Louise put her arm around Ava and ushered her away from the woman. But clearly, Audrey Winkle was not the only journalist to have received the memo that Ava was going to be at the school today. The gates were swarmed with reporters shouting questions and cameras flashing as Louise attempted to pull Ava out of the crowd.

"Why did you kill Patrick, Ava?"

"Did your ex-husband abuse you?"

"What was the reason for the divorce?"

"What aren't you telling us, Ava?"

"Are you fit to be looking after Mia?"

The questions fired around, and Louise kept a tight grip on her friend, telling her to ignore them. But she knew there was nothing that she could say to comfort Ava. Absolutely nothing at all.

TWENTY-EIGHT

7th December 2009

"So." I sat down on Patrick's bed and looked at him with dopey eyes. "Are we doing Christmas presents?" Patrick leaned over and pecked my lips.

"Of course." He winked at me and pulled me onto his lap. "I've already got you yours." He nuzzled his head into my neck, and I squirmed away from him.

"What!" I groaned. "You're so hard to shop for. Can you give me a hint of what price range you went for?" I asked, and Patrick shook his head. I hit his chest playfully.

"I don't want anything. Having you in my life is enough." He wrapped his arms around my waist and placed his head on my shoulder. I pulled a face and turned to face him.

"Seriously, Pat. What do you want?" I wiggled my eyebrows. "I could dress up like a sexy elf?" He chuckled and rolled his eyes.

"Well . . . that is something I could get on board with." He ran his finger down my arm. "You know, there is something I do want."

"Yes, please tell me," I exclaimed, thankful that he was giving me an idea. He ran his hand through his hair slowly and exhaled. He looked nervous.

"I think you should make up with Lucy." He didn't meet my eyes as he spoke. I frowned at him and pulled away from his arms.

"What?" I folded my arms across my chest. "You do realise that it was you who caused us to fall out, right?"

He groaned. "I know, I know. And that's why I feel so bad. You didn't want to lose her, and I made you." He shrugged his shoulders and cocked his head to one side. "Please. Just think about it."

"I don't know, Pat. You were right. She was toxic and manipulative. And I love being friends with your friends. Annabelle is my new Lucy." I shrugged. Since falling out with Lucy, I had moved on to bigger and better things. Annabelle was now one of my best friends, and I loved hanging out with the medics. They were carefree and non-judgmental, everything that Lucy wasn't. But part of me did miss her. She was the best friend that all girls dreamed of having—glamorous, loyal, strong, and a feminist. Maybe I should talk to her.

"Okay, I'll go and see her," I said. Pat grinned. "But, if she shuts me down and eats me alive, it's all on you," I said, only half-joking. Pat laughed and pinned me down onto the bed before kissing my nose.

"Go get her."

*   *   *

When I reached Lucy's door, I felt compelled to turn around and leave. Since our face off at the cafeteria, we hadn't said two words to each other. Occasionally, I would see her at dinner, but she would barely eat. It did made me worry; she had had lost even more weight since we fell out.

Here goes nothing.

I knocked two times on the door and took a deep breath. When there was no reply, I was almost relieved. But that was when I heard her voice from behind me.

"Ava?" I spun around to see Lucy standing there with her arms over her chest. She had zero makeup on—I had never seen her without any makeup on—and the clothes she was wearing were falling off her body. She looked unwell. Very unwell.

"Luce." Tears sprung to my eyes. Before I could stop myself, I threw my arms around her small frame. It took her a while, but eventually she wrapped her spindly arms around me. I heard her release a sob, and I let go of her.

"I've missed you so much," she said, tears streaming down her cheeks. "I'm so sorry for everything." I reached up and brushed a finger over her cheek.

"I've missed you too," I told her. "Let's never argue again." She nodded and braved a smile at me.

"Never."

TWENTY-NINE

Ava felt like she was underwater. The noises downstairs were unclear, faded even. It was as if they were miles away and she was all alone. But she wasn't. She stood in front her mirror, smoothing the black material over her thighs. The material hung loosely on her hips, barely clinging to her waist. There was a time where she couldn't do the zipper up. There was also a time where she had a husband. A husband who was alive.

But things had changed.

"Ava?" The sound of her name paused her thoughts and disrupted her peace. She looked over at Lily, her dark hair framing her sweet face. She looked too much like him. Too much. Her eyes were red, just like Ava's.

"Is it time?" Ava's voice came out coarsely as if she hadn't spoken in days. Lily nodded and held her hand out. Ava took a deep breath and reached out to Lily's hand, taking it with every strength in her. *Time to be strong again.*

Stepping into her living room felt like a step into the past. Her parents had finally made it back from Edinburgh, promising to never leave the country again. It was weird seeing her parents and Patrick's parents together again. It could almost have been a family dinner, only they were missing Pat. But this was not a happy affair—it was a funeral.

"Are you ready, darling?" Carol Milberry asked as Ava approached her. Ava nodded slowly, looking over to her daughter, who was dressed head to toe in black. The sight broke her heart.

"Yeah, Mum. Let's go."

The drive to the church was a quiet affair; it was as if people were scared to speak. Ava wasn't scared to speak; she just didn't have anything to say. It wasn't the kind of day where one could just talk about the weather or ask how the family was. It was the type of day to mourn the loss of her ex-husband, and everything that came with that—her independence, her dignity, and her strength. Her stalker had taken almost everything from her. The most important thing that they hadn't taken was Mia, and the only way to ensure her daughter's safety was to keep her mouth shut. About everything.

When they arrived at the church, Ava felt a sudden peace come over her. If Pat had been going through something similar to her—if the stalker had been taunting him—then at least he was resting now. Part of her was almost jealous.

Ava, her parents, Mia, and Patrick's family wandered into the church slowly, taking in the site in all its beauty. Ava was glad that Patrick's family had organised the service with an incredible funeral director. She had too much on her mind to be organising a whole service.

"Are you okay?" Lily softly took Ava's arm, her eyes wet with tears. "All things considered."

Ava nodded. "To be honest, I just want this over with," she muttered, sighing heavily. "I can't believe how many university friends I'm going to see. I don't know what I'm going to say to them. It's been years."

Lily gave her a faint smile. "You don't have to say anything. They'll understand." Ava returned her best smile and turned to the door. She could hear cars arriving, meaning that people were beginning to arrive. She took Lily's hand and they both wandered into the garden to greet the guests.

The first to arrive were members of Patrick's family, some that Ava hadn't even met. She was polite and considerate, paying her regards to each of the guests. They returned the favour, but everyone seemed unsure of what to say to Ava. They almost seemed scared. It was as if they believed everything that they read in the papers—that she had done it. She couldn't blame them, she supposed. They had no reason to think anything else other than what they read.

When Louise and Zoe arrived, Ava almost cried with relief. She did her best not to run over to the two of them as their car pulled in.

"Ava," Louise greeted, taking her friend in her arms. Ava clung to her as if Louise were her life support. Ava then turned to Zoe, hugging her tightly too.

"Thank you so much for coming." The tears threatened to surface, but Ava pushed them away. "I'm going to really need you two today."

"Don't thank us. We're always here for you, Ava," Louise said, stroking Ava's arm. Ava nodded and let out a shaky sigh.

"I don't know how I'm going to make it through today without sobbing my eyes out," she said quietly, aware of other guests arriving. She looked between her two friends, wondering what they were thinking. Did they think that she had done it?

"Ava, don't hide your emotions. Of course you're going to cry today, it's your husband's funeral," Zoe said sternly, and Ava could read between the lines. She knew what Zoe meant—she needed to grieve; if she didn't, she would look even more guilty.

"Of course." Out of the corner of her eye, she spotted Jake get out of a car. Dread pooled through her. *What was he doing?* She excused herself from her friends and rushed over to Jake.

"What are you doing here?" she hissed at him. He looked startled at her outburst and put a hand on her shoulder slowly.

"What?" He frowned at her. "I was invited, wasn't I?" Ava narrowed her eyes and put her hand on her forehead. And then it

150

dawned on her. Could . . . her stalker have invited him? To make her look bad?

It made sense—get her new 'lover' in front of a huge crowd of people who were most likely suspecting her already. She took a deep breath and cleared her head.

"Sorry, I forgot." She rubbed her forehead in frustration. "It's been a manic day."

"Do you want me to go?" he asked, unsure of what to say. "I can go, if that would make you feel better." It would make her feel better; having him here put her on edge. It was inappropriate having him here; her stalker knew that.

"Yeah." Ava nodded slowly. "I'm sorry, but you need to go. It was a mistake sending you that invitation." Her words obviously upset Jake; she could tell by the way his face crumpled ever so slightly. But she couldn't have him here.

"Okay." He bit his lip. "I'll go." With that, he turned around and walked away. Ava wandered back to the main crowd, trying to say her greetings over the pounding of blood in her ears.

And just like clockwork, her phone buzzed to notify her of a new email. She almost rolled her eyes at the ridiculousness.

Subject: Heartbreaker
Oh Ava. That wasn't very nice, was it?

She wasn't even scared this time because she had almost guessed it. Somehow her stalker had bugged the church, or her phone, or *something*. But Ava couldn't do anything about it because if she were to tell anyone, her stalker would find out somehow. She couldn't put Mia's life at risk.

Her thoughts of the stalker were disrupted by a familiar voice calling her name. She looked up to see a petite blonde woman walking towards her. It took Ava a while to recognise her but when she did, it became blindingly obvious.

"Annabelle." She wandered over to her old university friend cautiously, unsure of how to approach her. Annabelle had changed a lot since she last saw her. She was no longer the geeky,

151

clingy girl who obsessed over Ava. She was glamorous and elegant, smelling strongly of an expensive perfume.

"How are you?" Annabelle asked, her head cocked to one side. Her tone was condescending. That annoyed Ava. A lot.

"Fine, all things considered," Ava said in a strained voice. "You look well."

"Yes, well, I'm the lead neurosurgeon at my hospital now," she boasted, a smirk on her face. "What do you do? Some sort of . . . marketing?"

"I'm the web producer for Xanos," Ava said as strongly as she could, and Annabelle scrunched her face a little.

"Oh, you were always into fashion, weren't you?" Annabelle didn't seem impressed. "Well. I guess things have changed since university, haven't they?" Ava wanted to leave the conversation immediately.

"They definitely have." She looked over to see some more guests arriving, giving her a perfect excuse to leave. "Sorry, I better go and greet the other guests." As she turned to leave, Annabelle uttered words that made her blood run cold.

"You killed him, didn't you?" Ava spun around in response to her words, rage boiling through her. Annabelle looked smug, happy that she received such a reaction from Ava. When Ava didn't reply, Annabelle continued, "It's all in the papers. I don't know why there aren't any journalists here, to be honest. They'd love to document you pretending to grieve his death. It's all bullshit. Everyone knows it." The urge to slap Annabelle was immense, but Ava couldn't. She took a deep breath and raised her eyes to the sky.

"It's great to see you Annabelle. Really, it is." Ava locked her eyes onto her old acquaintance and kept her voice steady. "It's impressive that you made the effort to come all this way. But then again, you did always have a thing for Patrick, didn't you?" Annabelle's mouth dropped open, and Ava didn't wait to see her reaction. She simply turned away and walked into the church, her blood boiling.

*　　*　　*

The ceremony moved slowly, but it was beautiful. The funeral director had done an incredible job. The prayers were tear jerking but necessary, and the choir was spectacular. Ava almost forgot the nerves for her speech.

"And now, Ava will say a few words about Patrick." The vicar nodded at Ava with a small smile. His kind eyes gave her the strength to stand and slowly make her way to the lectern.

"Hi," she said, her voice wavering. "Not all of you know me, but I am Patrick's ex-wife." This generated some murmurs, but Ava powered on. "I get what most of you are thinking; why is she giving a speech? Doesn't she hate the bastard?" The murmurs turned to chuckles, and Ava's confidence grew. "And that is partly true, I guess. I hate that we didn't work through our marriage. I hate that we didn't give our lovely Mia the upbringing she deserved. But most of all, I hate that he's gone.

"When I first met Patrick, my life was a mess. I was a wild university student with no direction or career aspects. He showed me that there was more to life than just partying. He showed me how to be me. He was the most amazing person that I have ever known—funny, smart, kind, and an amazing husband and father." A tear fell down Ava's cheek. "'I will love you for infinity.' We always used to say that to each other. And I still mean it, I will love you for infinity, Pat. I will—"Ava's words were suddenly cut short by someone shouting. It took her a while to see who it was at first, but as her vision cleared, she saw that Annabelle had stood up, tears pouring down her face.

"You are a killer!" she screamed. "Are you all seriously listening to this bullshit? She killed him, and we all know it. She never loved him; she just wanted his money! She's a murderous, gold-digging bitch!" Ava's mouth dropped open and her eyes filled with tears. Not here, anywhere but here.

153

"She's a murderer!" Annabelle screamed. "A murderer!"

THIRTY

"Hey, Ava." Annabelle called me as I walk out of the cafeteria. I bit my lip and turned to face her. "You okay?"

"Yeah." I nodded, unsure of what to say. "I have some stats work to do, so I need to rush off." Annabelle frowned and took my arm.

"You've been so weird with me recently. Have I done something to offend you?" she said. I felt guilt trickle though me. I had to tell her the truth.

"Lucy and I . . . we've made up," I said cautiously and Annabelle's face dropped. "She's not in a good mental state right now, so . . ."

"So what?" Annabelle crossed her arms angrily. "So, you can't be friends with me anymore?" I ran my hand through my hair frustratedly.

"It's not that, Annabelle. Admit it, you and Lucy have never got on. Ever. And she's been having a really tough time, so I need to be there for her. I'm sorry." I tried to turn away from her, but she grabbed my arm.

"You can be friends with more than one person, Ava. She's manipulating you; everyone knows it." Her eyes started to fill with tears. "Ava, you're my best friend. Please don't do this to me." I

155

rolled my lips into my mouth, the feeling of guilt growing stronger and stronger.

"I'm sorry, Annabelle. I truly am." I mentally prepared myself for my next words. I knew that once I said them, Annabelle would hate me forever. "But you need to leave me alone. You're obsessed with me! I was only ever friends with you because I pitied you. Plus, you're clearly in love with Patrick. And quite frankly, I feel uncomfortable being friends with someone who's in love with my boyfriend."

I couldn't have prepared myself for the pain from the slap that came from her. It knocked me senseless.

*   *   *

"Ow." I winced as Lucy placed an ice pack to my cheek. "That stings." Lucy chuckled and readjusted it.

"Sorry. I still can't believe she slapped you." Lucy shook her head. "I always knew what she was like. You were right to be honest with her. It's not okay that she is so obsessed with you, and Patrick for that matter. Quite frankly, it's just weird." She brushed a strand of hair behind my ear. "I don't blame her though. It devastating to lose you as a friend." She shrugged her shoulders before sitting back on the bed and passing the ice pack to me.

"Luce, you won't lose me again. I'd pick you over Annabelle any day." I placed my hand on her arm and smiled at her. She smiled back and took my hand in hers.

"You're my everything, do you know that?" she said. "I know that sounds weird, even Annabelle-esque. But it's true. I don't know what I'd do without you." I wrapped my arms around her and gave her a tight squeeze.

"It doesn't sound weird. It's sweet." My phone buzzed, but before I could reach for it, Lucy snatched it from my grasp. I frowned at her as she read my text message for me.

156

"Just a Dominoes ad!" she exclaimed before placing my phone next to her—out of my reach. "God, those pizzas are so unhealthy. Something like two thousand calories per pizza. It's disgusting." She shivered as if the text personally bothered her. I didn't comment on it. *I never do.* I had studied anorexia and I knew that Lucy had a bad case of it. I had been trying to conjure up the confidence to tell her to speak to someone, but I knew that she would react badly.

"I gotta pee." She leapt up from the bed and disappeared into the toilet. As the door shut behind her, I checked my phone. Confusion teared through me as I noticed that there was no Dominoes text. Instead, there was a text from Pat asking to hang out.

Why would she lie?

I place my phone down next to me and wait for her to come back in.

"So, the boys just texted me to ask if we want to go out tonight. You in?" Lucy announced as she re-entered the room. When she saw the look on my face, she frowned. "What's wrong?"

"Why did you lie to me?" I asked her calmly. "Why did you say that Dominoes texted me, when it was really Pat?" It could just be a mistake; maybe she opened the wrong text message. But when her face dropped, I knew that it wasn't a mistake.

"I'm sorry." Her eyes filled with tears. "It's just that you spend so much time with Patrick, I feel like I never see you anymore. I thought if you didn't see his text, then you'd spend more time with me." She sobbed and collapsed on my bed. I sighed and placed my arm around her.

"Don't cry, Luce. It's fine. If you want to spend more time with me, tell me, okay? Just don't lie to me," I said in the sweetest voice I could, but in all honesty, I was a little pissed off. I had barely seen Patrick since Lucy and I made up because she would demand almost every second of my time. I didn't say that though. I couldn't have her getting any more upset.

"Of course, Ava. But will you stay with me tonight? And not see him?" She looked up to me with tear-stained cheeks. And I had no choice but to say yes.

THIRTY-ONE

"She's a murderer! A murderer!" the petite blonde woman screamed, and Louise felt sick. Poor, poor Ava. She glanced back at her friend, who was staring at the woman in horror.

"Jesus Christ," Zoe said next to her. "This is next level." Louise didn't reply. Instead, she just stared at the woman. She had tears running down her cheeks, her face screwed, and makeup smudged. Louise recalled seeing her earlier, talking to Ava. The conversation did not seem like a pleasant one. A man from the front row stood up, rushing down the aisle to the woman.

"Calm down, Annabelle," he said slowly, and calmly for that matter. Louise could barely hear him over the sound of her heart thumping. Annabelle finally tore her eyes away from Ava and stared at the man in shock.

"Calm down? How can I calm down? He was your *son,* Ian. And she killed him! She's been arrested for his murder, don't you all know that?" the woman screamed at the man—Patrick's father.

"Annabelle, calm down before you're removed from this service," he said, his voice becoming louder now. Louise removed her eyes from the woman and looked back at Ava, who was still on the stage, her hand covering her mouth. Tears were trickling down her face. Louise swore under her breath and moved out of her pew as quietly as she could.

"What are you doing?" Zoe hissed, grabbing Louise's skirt. Louise smacked her friends hand away and pointed to Ava. Zoe breathed out heavily and closed her eyes. Louise quietly scampered up the aisle, hearing Patrick's father remove Annabelle from the church.

"Ava," Louise said as she approached her friend. Ava hadn't even noticed Louise was there. She looked over as she heard her name, her eyes glazed over with tears. She shook her head at Louise, tears streaming down her face.

"Let's go sit down." Louise reached her hand out to take Ava's, but as she did, she heard a small voice from beside her.

"Mummy?" Mia stood next to Louise, staring up at her mother with big eyes. "Don't be sad." And the little girl took her mother's hand, slowly leading her back down to the front pew, leaving Louise alone on the stage in shock.

*   *   *

The service ended shortly after Annabelle was removed from the church. Ava was grateful for Ian's actions; she didn't know what to do when Annabelle had stood up, guns blazing. Her first thought was that Mia was there, and she didn't want her daughter to think she was a killer. But Mia was mature; she'd shown that when she helped her mother off the stage.

But Annabelle's words weren't the reason that Ava was shocked. She knew that the news of her arrest would come out sooner or later.

She was shocked that she hadn't seen it sooner; could Annabelle be her stalker?

Her first thought was no; she was obsessed with Patrick at university, she would never lay a finger on him.

Her second thought was that her obsession with Patrick gave her a pretty big motive. He chose Ava over Annabelle, and maybe Annabelle never got over that. Plus, Ava knew how she treated Annabelle at university. She and Lucy bullied her relentlessly. Ava always knew that there would be consequences.

160

But would she have really gone that far?

Ava was lost in her thoughts as she slowly sipped her champagne. The reception was beautiful; it was if people had forgotten about Annabelle's outburst in the church. Or maybe they were choosing to ignore it. Ava suspected the latter.

"Ava." Zoe's voice came out from nowhere and disrupted her thoughts. She turned to see her two friends wandering over, champagne glasses in hand.

"Hey guys," she said weakly. She really hoped that they didn't believe Annabelle. Louise had been an angel, swearing to help Ava in every situation. But Zoe? Ava could tell that Zoe was sceptical.

"How are you doing?" Louise placed her hand on Ava's shoulder soothingly. "After . . . you know." Ava shrugged her shoulders.

"Fine, I guess. I don't really know what to say, to be honest." And that was the truth—Ava had nothing to say about Annabelle because she was scared that her theory was right. Maybe Annabelle was the killer.

"Where's Mia?" Zoe asked, her voice sharp. Ava frowned at her and pointed over to her parents, where Mia sat on her grandmother's lap.

"She's with my mum. I'm going to take her home soon. This day hasn't been fair on her." Ava nodded and the three of them fell into silence.

"Ava . . ." Louise begun; her voice uncertain. "Before I say this, you have to believe that I know you didn't kill him. Okay?" she asked and Ava nodded.

Then, "Where's your fight? Why aren't you trying to find the person who did this?"

Good point, Ava wanted to tell her. She also wanted to tell her that Patrick's killer could be nearer than they thought. And then an idea came to her as if her motivation had finally kicked in. It was risky, almost too risky. But she had to try.

161

"Sorry, I need to excuse myself." She told her friends before running to the bathroom. With her phone in her pocket, she took a deep breath, and then removed her phone and dialled Detective Brown's number. When the call went to voicemail, she left a message.

"Hey Detective, I have something to tell you. Can we meet at the park in 15 minutes?" she said, and then hung up the phone. Before she could waste any time, she ran out of the bathroom and over to her parents.

"Hello darling, how are you doing?" her mum said as she approached. Ava nodded, a little breathless.

"I'm okay, but I was just wondering if you could take Mia back to your hotel room this afternoon? I have something to take care of," she told her mum, her phone heavy in her pocket.

"Well, yes, that'll be fine. Are you sure you're okay? That woman was –" her mother began, but Ava cut her off.

"I'm really fine." And then, she slowly removed her phone from her pocket, placing it on the table. She then took her father to one side, away from her phone, and put her hand out.

"Dad, I need to use your phone. Quickly," she said, aware of the time. This needed to work. He frowned at her but placed his phone obediently in her hand. Ava didn't even say thank you as she rushed off to a quiet corner and dialled Detective Brown's number once again.

"Hey Detective, it's Ava again. I just wanted to tell you to scrap the last message, I'm no longer free to meet up. See you soon." And then she hung up.

*   *   *

Ava got to the park with a couple of minutes to spare, her phone safely restored in her pocket. If her theory was true, then she might be able to get ahead of the killer. Just maybe.

162

Her theory was that somehow the killer had bugged her phone. Therefore, they would believe that Ava was about to meet the Detective, not knowing that she had actually cancelled.

She sat down on a bench and waited. When fifteen minutes had passed, her phone pinged in her pocket; this was it.

Subject: Tattletale

Nice try, son of a snitch. Looks like you've been stood up. What a shame! I wonder what you were going to tell him.

She was right. Her phone was bugged. And that's how the stalker had been hearing everything Ava was saying.

Ava felt as if her world was being turned upside down. How on *earth* had her phone been bugged? It had been on her at all times.

And then, she remembered the break in. She always kept her phone downstairs. Could the break in have been the murderer? Could they have bugged it when they broke into the house? That would explain why nothing was stolen.

If that was the case, then Patrick's death was not an impulsive crime. Whoever did it had it planned for a while.

But why? Who would go to these lengths to frame her?

*　　*　　*

Ava didn't get rid of her phone. Because if she did, the stalker would know she knew about the bug. Having that advantage was the first sliver of hope Ava had experienced since Patrick's death.

On her way back to her house, she picked Mia up from her parents' hotel. Of course, they offered to have her for the night. But Ava had spent too much time away from her baby; it was time to be strong. She definitely wasn't going beat this psycho by being weak.

"Mummy, why did that lady say those things?" Mia asked in a small voice as they approached the house. Ava's stomach dropped. She had hoped that Mia was young enough to not understand what Annabelle was saying. But she was wrong. Aware of her phone in her pocket—and her new revelation that Annabelle could be behind it all—she lied.

"That woman was not right in the head. She needs to be taken care of," Ava told Mia, who looked shocked by her words.

"She's crazy?" Mia asked, and Ava nodded. Another lie to add to the ever growing pile. But when would they all catch up with her?

"Time for bed, pumpkin." She took her daughter's hand and ushered her up to her bedroom. After she shut the door, her phone pinged once more.

Subject: Bully
Well, that's not a very nice thing to say, is it?

THIRTY-TWO

14th December 2009

"Hey, so I was thinking that we should go out with the OGs tonight," Lucy told me as she slipped her arm around mine. I looked at her and shrugged my shoulders.

"Yeah, I guess since being with Patrick, I haven't seen them that much." I said and I immediately regretted my words. Something flickered in Lucy's eyes and she nodded her head in agreement.

"You know, you do spend so much time with him. I'm a little worried that you're becoming too reliant on him." She turned and faced her body towards me. "Boys don't like clingy girls, Ava." I stepped back on reflex and frowned at her.

"Are you saying that my own boyfriend doesn't like me because I'm 'clingy'?" I used my fingers for air quotations, and Lucy shrugged noncommittedly.

"It's just that he keeps asking me to spend time with you because he feels like you're being full on, that's all." She rolled her lips into her mouth and gave me a guilty smile, although I was sure she didn't feel guilty at all.

"He is my boyfriend, Lucy. I am allowed to see him."

"Oh, and don't we all know it. I think it's pathetic, really." Her voice was sharp and suddenly, I felt as if she was attacking me.

165

"Look, I know you've never been the biggest fan of Pat, but please don't take it out on me." I pleaded her with my eyes. I really didn't want to have another spat with Lucy.

"Don't take it out on me," Lucy mimicked me in a high-pitched voice. "I'm not. I just think you've become really desperate."

"Desperate? Lucy, he's my boyfriend." I felt my temper rising. I was not in the mood for this today.

"As you mentioned. But don't you think spending this much time with him is a bit desperate? He told me he thinks you're really clingy."

"Really, Lucy? Did he really say that?" I asked, but I knew it was one of her many fibs. She had always been envious of Patrick and I, especially recently. It was like she was obsessed with me.

"I swear. But it was probably out of context anyway." She turned around and slipped her arm back through mine as if nothing happened. "I gotta go. Got some work to do. See you later." She blew me a kiss and skipped into her room too quickly for me to tell her that I was seeing Pat tonight.

*   *   *

As I wandered to my room, Matt's door opened, and he stepped out. I gave him a small smile and he gave me a wave.

"How are you?" he asked, leaning against his door. I nodded.

"I'm alright," I said; I didn't have the energy to lie. He frowned, almost sympathetically.

"Wanna talk about it?" he opened his door and gestured to his room. Despite the fact I knew Matt had a crush on me, I found myself wandering in. I sat down on his desk chair and placed my head in my hands.

"What's up?" Matt asked, sitting on the bed opposite me. He looked at me with kind eyes.

166

"Lucy," I said. "I know you two are tight, so I don't want you to get in the middle of it. She's just being . . ."

"Lucy," he chuckled. "Ava, I'm not stupid. I know what Lucy's like. To be honest, I don't really like her."

I was surprised at his words. "But you worship Lucy."

Matt chuckled. "No, I don't, Ava. I only hang out with her because of you. You're a really cool girl, Ava. Mature, unlike Lucy."

And despite the fact I know Matt meant it in a different way, it was exactly what I needed to hear. I gave him a smile before wrapping my arms around him, blinking away my tears.

"Thanks, Matt."

*   *   *

I was quiet around Pat that night. Whilst I didn't believe Lucy's lies, they did strike a chord.

"Everything okay, babe?" he asked as he leaned over to reach into his mini fridge, grabbing a beer. He held one out to me and I shook my head.

"Yeah." I nodded and hugged my knees. "Lucy is just being weird again." Pat frowned at me and sat down on the bed, taking a long sip of beer. I refrained from telling him that it was only four o'clock in the afternoon.

"Oh God, really?" He rolled his eyes. "Look, I know I said to make up with her, but I genuinely think that there's something wrong with her." He took another sip and I rolled my lips into my mouth. He was not wrong.

"She said that you told her that I'm clingy." I cringed at my words as they left my mouth, cursing myself that Lucy had got to me. Pat looked at me and chuckled.

"And you believe her? I barely speak to her." He shook his head and reached over to take my hand. I sighed and shrugged.

"I don't know, Pat. Lucy has a way with words. She can be very believable." I looked at the ceiling. "She's just . . . manipulative."

"Babe, I don't think you're clingy. If anything, I'm clingy. I'm obsessed with you." Pat grinned at me, and I cracked a smile for the first time today. "Maybe that's the problem, huh. Maybe Lucy is obsessed with you too."

And like clockwork, my phone began to ring. I saw Lucy's name flash on the screen and I instinctively answered.

"Hey girl, so we still on for tonight?" she said, her voice echoing into the room. I looked at Pat, and he frowned. I shook my head.

"Luce, I'm with Pat tonight. Sorry." I hated myself for apologising to her, but I couldn't help it. There was still a part of me that wanted to please her.

"Oh my god, Ava. Were you not listening to anything I said earlier?" I could hear her chewing her gum loudly. Pat signalled for me to hang up, but I couldn't.

"Sorry Luce. We'll do tomorrow," I told her. She went silent for a second.

Then, "I'm good thanks." And the line beeped. Pat looked at me in shock, and I was sure that my face reflected his.

*   *   *

Pat and I decided to go out for dinner. It was our three-month anniversary. *We think.* We never really decided when we were official, but we still wanted to celebrate.

Pat and I clinked our glasses of champagne together, and all of a sudden and I saw Lucy walk in. She was with a boy I didn't recognise.

"Hey Luce," I called as she walked past, but she simply cast a bored look over me before looking to her date and pointing at me. He chuckled before pulling a chair out for her to sit down.

168

"What the hell?" Pat reached over and stroked my hand. "What is she doing here?"

"I have no idea." I glanced over at Lucy and saw her smirking at me. I suddenly heard my name mentioned so I tried to listen.

"So that's the ex-best friend, is it?" the boy asked Lucy.

"Yeah. She's so obsessed with me. It's like she followed me here. She's literally stalking me," she said loudly as if she wanted me to hear.

"Shall we go? We can eat somewhere else," the boy asks.

"No, it's fine. I can't let her control my life," Lucy said and I felt sick. She was acting as if the roles are reversed. I could barely believe what I was hearing.

"Babe, are you okay?" Pat said in a low voice. I nodded quickly. "I'm going to say something to her. She's full on crazy."

I put my hand on his to stop him. "No, please don't. It'll make it worse."

"I can't let her treat you like this," he murmured. I glanced over to see Lucy looking at me again. She tilted her head to one side before lifting her hand and making a shooing gesture. Pat stood up. "That's it."

"Please Pat, don't." But it was too late to stop him. He stormed over to their table and stood over Lucy.

"You need to remove yourself from Ava's life. Go to a psychologist because you are messed up, Lucy. Stop telling lies to this poor boy," he said aggressively. Lucy put her hand to her chest in fake shock.

"Mate, calm down," said the boy. "I think Ava is the one that needs to go to see someone."

And before I knew it, Lucy's date was on the floor, and Pat was throwing punches to his face. I stood there, unsure of what to do. Finally, a waiter managed to get Pat off Lucy's date, and we were asked to leave.

"You need to stop harassing me," Lucy told me when we got outside. Her date was mopping up his bloodied nose whilst Pat paced in order to calm himself down.

"Are you kidding me?" I hissed, all control lost. "Lucy, you need to stop harassing me. It's embarrassing, and frankly, you do need to go to see someone. I'm your only friend, and this is how you want to treat me?" I shook my head. "Leave me alone. This friendship is over."

THIRTY-THREE

Louise was shocked by the events at the funeral, but that wasn't what shocked her the most. What shocked her the most was Ava's behaviour. It was as if she didn't care that she was—most likely—going to be put behind bars for Patrick's murder.

If Louise was in her position, she would have hired a lawyer. Or she would be researching every route to her salvation. Louise knew in her heart that Ava hadn't done it, so why was she acting as if she had?

Unless . . .

A thought crossed Louise's mind and it was so far-fetched that she was surprised that she had conjured it.

Unless.

Unless Ava was being framed. And she was being blackmailed so she couldn't say anything.

It was crazy. But could it be possible?

She rubbed her temples before walking to the counter and popping the kettle on. El walked through the door yawning. Louise gave her a smile.

"How you doing, cuz?" El asked as she sat down at the table. Louise shrugged.

"I don't know. My friend, Ava . . . I just feel so hopeless." Louise poured two mugs of tea for her and El. El frowned and pushed a strand of hair behind her ear.

"Is that the one . . . who killed her husband?" she asked, and her words shocked Louise. Louise shook her head quickly.

"She didn't, that's the thing," Louise said. "Well, at least I think so." She moved to the fridge and grabbed some skimmed milk.

"Oh really?" El asked. "And why is that?"

"I just know. I think someone has framed her." Louise shrugged and brought the two steaming mugs to the table. El frowned at her and chuckled.

"Alright detective." She took a sip of her tea. "So, have they arrested her?"

"Yeah. She's out on bail until her trial." Louise took a long sip of her drink, burning her tongue. "So, I need to help her find the person who framed her."

El laughed in disbelief. "You go, girlfriend."

*   *   *

Ava felt somewhat triumphant the morning after the funeral. She had figured out how her stalker was hearing everything she said. Now, she just needed to be careful about what she said around her phone.

"Mummy's taking you to school today, Mia!" Ava told her little girl, who was sitting at the table and shovelling her cereal into her mouth. Mia beamed.

"Yay, mama!" Mia exclaimed happily. Ava smiled and felt a surge of a new feeling—or one that hadn't come her way for a very long time. And she immediately knew what it was; hope.

She hurried Mia into the car, a smile on her face. She remembered the press from the other day crowding at the school, and silently hoped they'd given up.

Mia chatted non-stop on the way to school. She told Ava about her upcoming projects, and her friendship with Kai. Ava almost slammed on the breaks at the mention of Kai.

Jake.

Christ, what a mess. With him turning up at the funeral, and just being around in general. Right guy, wrong time.

She prayed that he wasn't at drop-off because she couldn't face the wrath of the mothers eyeballing her. Although, the alternative would be a hundred times worse.

As she pulled up to the front gates, her happiness began to dwindle. She tried to cast away her doubts and attempted to regain the confidence that had surged within her in the morning.

"I can see Kai!" Mia exclaimed as they pulled into a parking space. "Hurry up, mama!" Ava felt her stomach plummet, following Mia's gaze to where little Kai stood. A rush of nausea swept over her as she saw him holding Nancy's hand.

Yes, the alternative was a million times worse.

As Ava and Mia made their way over to the school entrance, Ava took deep breaths to keep herself calm. Mia was oblivious, pulling at Ava's hand to make her move faster. Ava just wanted to rewind.

Mia finally unlatched herself from Ava's hand and ran over to Kai. Nancy looked down to Mia before looking up and locking eyes with Ava.

Jesus Christ. Never mind her stalker, Nancy might be the one to seal her coffin.

Ava lifted her hand up to give Nancy a timid wave. Nancy narrowed her eyes and walked over to Ava in her high heels.

"Hi, Nancy. I've been meaning to . . ." She began as Nancy approached her. She could hear the hushed voices of other mothers, relishing in the gossip.

"Let's not tell fibs, shall we now?" Nancy said before holding her hand out to Ava. Ava looked at the outstretched hand in confusion. "Look, I'm not your biggest fan, Ava, but for the sake of the children and the school community, I think we should call a truce." Ava was speechless, silently taking Nancy's hand.

"I just want to apologise, Nancy," Ava said when she finally regained her voice. "I fully take responsibility—" Nancy cut her off.

"Don't take responsibility, dear. Jake is certainly not one to let go of things that he wants. He becomes . . . fixated. I was once something he wanted." She shrugged and Ava was again speechless. "And now it's you. He's always liked blondes. I think it stemmed from a blonde girl from his youth who broke his heart. Now, he just pines after girls that look like her." Nancy was oversharing, and Ava wanted her to stop. She felt uncomfortable.

"Nancy, I—" she tried to speak, but Nancy wasn't listening.

"Just a little warning, Ava. Neither of us will ever be enough. Neither of us will ever be her." She shrugged. Ava didn't know what to say. Was what she was saying true? Did Jake have some sort of . . . complex about blonde girls? It could just be a coincidence that she and Nancy had the same hair colour.

But why would Nancy lie?

*   *   *

Zoe wasn't sure what to expect when Louise had sent her an ominous text reading, 'Meet me at the White Horse in one hour. Don't tell anyone.'

When she arrived, Louise was sitting in the corner of pub wearing dark clothes. Zoe's confusion deepened.

She sat down slowly, eyeing her friend with awe. "Louise, what the frig is going on?"

"Shhh." Louise hushed her friend. "You need to hear me out."

Zoe narrowed her eyes in suspicion. "Ookay . . ."

"I think Ava is being framed," Louise said in a quiet voice, and Zoe rolled her eyes. Really? Louise put her hand up to stop her friend from speaking.

174

"Just listen, okay?" she said, and Zoe nodded. "It came to me when I was thinking about what I would do in that situation. I would be doing everything I could to prove my innocence. Any normal person would."

"Yeah, you're right," Zoe agreed, but she was unsure of what Louise was saying. Part of Zoe still thought that Ava could have done it.

"Exactly. She's being framed. And I think the reason she hasn't told anyone is that she's being blackmailed," Louise stated, and Zoe frowned.

"Is that all your evidence?" Zoe said, and Louise nodded. "Christ, Louise. That's nothing," Louise threw her hands up in exasperation.

"I know, but I'm convinced. Plus, there's no harm in looking into it, is there? If I'm wrong, there's no harm done. But if I'm right . . . " Louise looked at Zoe meaningfully. For the first time, Zoe put herself in Ava's shoes.

Louise was right, they had to at least try.

THIRTY-FOUR

My books were almost tumbling from my arms by the time I was back in halls from my lecture. As I turned the corner, I saw Matt on his way back to his room.

"Matt!" I called out, and he turned around. I shrugged my shoulders, my books fell to the floor. I bent over to pick them up and he rushed over to help me.

"Thank you. I was carrying my friend's books back for her and overestimated my strength," I said as Matt carried most of the books into my room.

"I was hoping to catch you, Ava," he said, holding my door open. I placed the books on the desk and took the pile from his arms.

"Oh yeah?" I sat down on my bed, out of breath. "What did you want?"

"I was just thinking about the other day," he said. "And I wanted to check that you're okay."

"Yeah. I mean no. But yeah," I mumbled awkwardly, twisting my hands in my lap. He sat down next to me.

"I also just . . . need to get something off my chest." He nodded slowly. I gave him a confused look.

"Everything okay?"

Suddenly, Matt leaned towards me, his lips puckered, and eyes closed. Before his lips could touch mine, I stood up like a shot.

"Woah Matt, I have a boyfriend," I said, putting my hands up. "I don't know what you think is going on here, but I'm taken." Matt looked shocked at my reaction, his face was so close to mine I could smell the cigarette smoke on his breath.

"A boyfriend who doesn't even like you. A boyfriend who is cheating on you." He tucked a strand of hair behind my ear, and I recoiled. My stomach dropped. My week really wasn't going well. First Lucy, now this? I couldn't believe him; he was lying. Of course, he was.

"Pat's not cheating on me." I shook my head and took a step back. Matt shrugged.

"Why don't you ask him? Or better yet, why don't you go to his room when he's 'hanging out with the boys'?" He sucked a breath in. "I would treat you so much better than that." I flinched away from his finger that trailed down my cheek. He was just saying this to make me hate Patrick, wasn't he? There couldn't be any truth in it.

"Matt, you're being really inappropriate. I know you like me, but seriously back off. We got together once. You really need to get over yourself." I rolled my eyes at him. "It's embarrassing." I turned away from him and strode towards the door.

"It's funny how you think that the world worships you. Maybe I should call you your majesty. You'd like that. But it would be a façade; just like your personality and your relationship. In reality, you're just a manipulative slut," he said to my back, trying to get a reaction. But I ignored his words and slammed the door behind me.

*   *   *

It had been nearly a week since I last saw Lucy. I was scared that she was hiding out, starving herself like last time. It didn't matter how many times Pat told me to not worry, I still did. Even after that crazy stint last week, I couldn't help but worry about her. She was a parasite.

We finished lectures yesterday, so at least I was packing to go home for the Christmas holidays. Pat and I planned to go skiing together; our first holiday. The thought of that was at least taking my mind of Lucy.

But a friend of mine in second year was having a house party tonight. And Lucy was invited. Part of me was expecting her to not show, which would probably be the better outcome. I had even thought about not going, but Pat insisted that we go. He hated how much she controlled me.

So did I.

I glanced down at the text Pat had sent me, informing me that he would arrive in ten minutes. I glanced at the mirror, almost disgusted at my appearance. The house party theme was naughty Christmas list, so Pat and I dressed up as matching elves. My tutu barely covered my underwear, and my boobs were pushed up to my chest. Pat's outfit wasn't any better, though. He was not even wearing a top.

I sighed. I had just finished my look with a bright red lip when I heard a knocking on my door. Confused, I made my way over to the door, the bells on my outfit ringing as I did. I opened the door. Shock ran through me as I saw Lucy standing in front of me, dressed up as a tarty Mrs. Claus. And she was smiling.

"Nice outfit, Ava!" she exclaimed as she let herself into my room. "What do you think of mine?" She twirled in front of me and I frowned at her.

"What? You don't like it?" she asked, her smile falling from her face. I rolled my lips into my mouth and stared at her. She was acting as if nothing ever happened.

"No, it's lovely, it's just . . ." I started, but Lucy cut me off.

"Tonight is going to be so fun. I can't wait! Plus, now that you're single and all . . ." She wiggled her eyebrows. "Matt is especially looking forward to seeing you." She bumped her hip to mine, and I stared at her some more.

"Lucy, I'm not single. Pat and I are still very much together," I told her, folding my arms. "Plus, aren't you forgetting about last weekend? We aren't exactly on speaking terms." Lucy didn't even register my words; she kept a complete poker face.

"You're not together." She shook her head, frowning. "He told me that you broke up. Oh Ava, I'm so sorry. You're in denial." She ran her hand down my arm before taking my hand in hers. I felt anger boil inside me, but I suppressed it.

"I'm not in denial. Patrick and I are still together, and you and I are no longer friends," I spoke in a calm voice, but I did not feel calm. Lucy stepped back and put a hand to her chest in shock.

"What do you mean?" she asked. "But you're my best friend."

"Oh my god, Lucy. Are you deluded? Do you not remember last weekend? You showed up at the restaurant and pulled that stint?" I explained with wide eyes. I needed to keep my anger down, otherwise who knew what I would do.

"You're still mad about that?" She waved her hand and giggled. "That was just a little joke, Ava. Lighten up a little." She moved to my side and wound her arm through mine. "Let's go to the party." I pulled my arm away from hers and took a couple of steps away from her.

"Lucy, I can't be friends with you anymore," I told her, and her face fell. "I'm sorry."

"Don't be. I don't even like you, anyway. No one does. Not even Pat," she snarled before leaving the room and slamming the door behind her.

*   *   *

I didn't tell Pat about Lucy's outburst. It was unnecessary stress considering that we were both leaving tomorrow. There was an air of tension between us though. Or maybe it was just me overthinking things.

As we entered the party, we were immediately hit by the smell of smoke and alcohol. I silently regretted not drinking more before we left. Pat spotted a group of his med friends and excused himself. Feeling isolated, I made my way to the bar and poured myself a drink.

"Hey, Ava." Annabelle's voice came from behind me. I spun around, leaving my drink on the side. I gave her a small smile, unsure of what to say. Last time I saw her, she slapped me. Clearly, she was not my biggest fan.

"Hey Annabelle." I fiddled with my fingers. "I'm really sorry about the other week. You were right about Lucy. She does manipulate me, and I'm pretty sure she's batshit crazy. So . . ." I said, trying to make my apology seem sincere. I really was sorry but being Lucy's best friend was hard work. I was the victim here.

"I forgive you, Ava. But I can't be friends with you." She shrugged her shoulders. "I'll be civil, for the sake of Pat, but I really can't be friends with someone like you." She cocked her head to one side, almost condescendingly.

"Okay, Annabelle." I didn't have the energy to fight. "I'm sorry again." Annabelle glanced behind her and gave me a small smile before turning around and walking away.

I spent the next hour or so wandering around the party, looking for Pat. *Where the hell was he?* It was not a big house, so he couldn't have gone far.

Unless . . .

Lucy's words rang in my ears, and I cast away the voices. She was a liar. I knew she was. It was then when I heard voices from a room to my right.

"Perfect. Yes, just like that." It was Lucy's voice. I peered my head into the room. My stomach dropped in horror; Pat was laid on the bed and a girl was straddling him. She was kissing his neck, and he didn't seem to be objecting at all. I brought my hand to my mouth, tears brimming my eyes. Lucy stood in the corner, watching.

"What the hell?" I screamed, and the girl barely even noticed me. Lucy looked up, confusion in her eyes. I didn't hang around to hear what she had to say; I was out of the room before she or Pat could even utter a single syllable.

*   *   *

I was four or five drinks down now, my misery consuming me. After finding Pat, I stormed out of the room. I didn't want to see anyone.

"Ava." A familiar voice interrupted my misery, and I knew who it was before I looked up. Matt grinned at me and sat down next to me.

"Hey, Matt," I spoke cautiously, remembering the way he spoke to me the other day. Calling me a manipulative slut. Trying to kiss me.

I needed to get out of this university, I swear.

"Can we have a chat?" he said, and I glanced around uncomfortably. I didn't want to talk to him. I was depressed, and in all honesty, part of me was scared of him. But I guess I was single now, and I really wanted Pat to feel how I was feeling right now. So, I nodded.

"How are you?" he asked, his tone seemed genuine. I tried to look past our conversation from the other day; maybe he was just butt hurt. I chuckled ironically.

"I've had better days. Yourself?" I asked, trying to keep tears from my eyes.

"Yeah, good. I just wanted to apologise for the other day. It was super weird of me to do that, and really wrong of me to speak to you like that. So, I'm really sorry," he told me, nodding slowly. I heard his words, but they seemed fuzzy.

"It's okay," I told him, but my words were slurred and came out as muffled. Matt frowned at me in concern and looked at my drink. My world began to spin

"Are you okay, Ava?" he asked, and I felt my body become limp. This was not alcohol. *God. Have I been spiked?* I looked at him with wide eyes, my mouth incapable of moving. He put his arm around me and got me to my feet, and I wanted to run away. Matt led me along a corridor, my feet falling behind me. I tried to resist but my body was not responding. I was led into a bedroom, and I felt horror ran through me.

He placed me down on the bed before going to the door and locking it. He turned back to me and his eyes locked on mine.

"Time for some royal treatment, Your Majesty."

THIRTY-FIVE

Louise wasn't sure where to start her detective work. She had never done this sort of thing before, and her experience was limited to watching all those detective tv shows, which—let's face it—are far from accurate.

"We need to look for anyone that might not like Ava," Zoe asked, thanking the waitress who brought her a coffee. Louise nodded, and her mind flickered back to the woman at the funeral.

"That woman; the one who made a scene at the funeral," Louise started, "She could have something to do with it, right? She clearly hates Ava."

Zoe nodded. "You're right. But surely she wouldn't want to draw attention to herself if she had done it?" Louise pondered this and found herself agreeing.

"I don't know. She could have done it to draw more attention to Ava though, not herself." Louise sighed and pulled her laptop out of her bag. "I think we should do some digging."

"What was her name? The girl? And how did she know Ava?" Zoe asked, and Louise racked her brain. She remembered a man trying to calm her down, and if her memory served her correctly, she remembered him calling her Annabelle.

"Annabelle, I think. And she must have been from Ava's university, right? If she knew Patrick too," Louise guessed, and Zoe nodded. At least they had a starting point. Louise opened google and hovered her hands over the keyboard. She could hardly type in Annabelle and expect to find an answer.

"What university did Ava go to again? Was it Bristol?" Zoe asked, and Louise nodded. But still, there must be thousands of Annabelle's who went to Bristol. How on earth were they going to narrow it down?

"We've barely started and my brain already hurts," Zoe complained. "It's a good thing we've got all day, because I think this is going to take longer than we think." Louise nodded and put her head in her hands.

"We need to figure out her last name. But we can't exactly ask Ava, I don't want her to know that we're looking into this." Louise hesitated. "We can't let her know we're investigating, or else whoever did this might find out too."

"It's far-fetched, but I agree. We'll have to figure out the last name another way." Zoe rolled her shoulders and took a sip of coffee. Louise needed one too if she wanted to be productive. She called the waiter over and ordered herself a cappuccino.

"I have an idea." Zoe put her finger in the air. "The funeral director. Surely, they would have the guest list."

"Yes!" Louise beamed. "That's a good idea. But how would we get it? Surely they'd think that was a bit odd." The waiter returned with a steaming cup of coffee, and Louise thanked him.

"We could ask to meet him or her, and say we need it for personal reasons. No one messes with personal reasons," Zoe said in that sassy way of hers, but Louise wasn't convinced. It had to be a legitimate excuse, one that wasn't going to raise eyebrows.

"Unless we don't use an excuse," Louise said thoughtfully. "We could steal it." Zoe's mouth dropped open and she shook her head.

"No, that's a bad idea, Louise," Zoe said, and Louise did agree with her. But it seemed to be the only way that was going to work.

184

"Look, we could ask to meet up with them, and one of us could sneak into the office and take it from the computer. It would be easy," Louise explained, but she wasn't entirely convinced herself.

"Are you serious?" Zoe asked, clearly shocked at the idea. "You want to stray from the straight and narrow?" Louise shrugged her shoulders. What other choice did they have?

*   *   *

Ava was still in shock from Nancy's comments about Jake. Did he have a blonde complex? Or was he just a normal man who had a type? When she returned home from school, she had tried to get her mind off it by getting back to work, but it lingered in her mind. Why was it bothering her so much?

She knew she had feelings for Jake, that much was obvious. But she knew that pursuing him would be more trouble than it was worth. An affair would just add fuel to the fire.

Ava placed her head in her hands in frustration. Her trial was approaching quickly, and she had no way of escaping her murder sentence. It would likely be for life. Jesus. She knew she needed a lawyer. Or better yet, to find the person who was framing her.

Was it Annabelle? It might make sense, but she loved Pat. Why would she kill someone she loved? She understood that Annabelle hated her, but would she still be holding a grudge? Ava remembered her last conversation with her at university. Annabelle said that she had forgiven her. That was the same night that . . . nausea pooled in her stomach as memories haunted her.

She shook her head as if to expel the bad memories. She couldn't let those memories engulf her again. She just couldn't.

She racked her brain to think of who else could be framing her. Her university days were her darkest—with that toxic friendship with Lucy. And then she sat bolt upright.

Lucy.

It couldn't be Lucy, could it? Thinking about her ex-best friend brought back unpleasant memories, and she wondered how she hadn't crossed her mind before.

But last Ava heard, Lucy had been seeing a therapist to deal with her problems, and then she had moved away. Pat had been extremely relieved.

But that was ages ago, Ava thought. Lucy couldn't have done it. Right?

*   *   *

After two hours of planning on how to get the guestlist, Louise and Zoe decided to hedge their bets and simply ask the funeral director for it. The plan to steal it was too risky, and neither of them wanted to end up in the same position as Ava.

Louise pulled her phone out of her pocket and opened the e-invite from the funeral—Ava was going paperless; she was a hippie type trying to save the planet. Louise admired that about her—and looked at the bottom of the invite. In small writing, the name *Abby Funeral Services* was written with an email address and phone number next to it.

"I guess I should just call then," Louise said timidly, suddenly feeling nervous. She wasn't worried about the funeral director; she was worried what the person who killed Ava's husband would do if they found out about the investigation. She had to remind herself that this was real life—not something out of a movie. Lives were on the line here.

Slowly, she dialled the number. It rung a couple of times before someone picked up the phone.

"Abby Patridge funeral services, how can I help?" said the cheery voice on the other end of the phone.

"Hi there, I attended one of your funerals recently . . . Patrick Jules?" Louise said slowly, diving straight into the deep end. Zoe gave her a thumbs up. The woman sighed.

"Are you from the press? Because I'm not answering any questions." The woman suddenly seemed a lot less friendly.

"No, um, I attended. My name is Louise Jones," Louise said, praying that the woman wouldn't hang up. She heard some rustling around on the other end of the line.

"Okay, you are on the list. What do you want?" the woman asked, her tone becoming harsher by the second. Although Louise didn't blame her; she wasn't sure how cheery she would be as a funeral director.

"I'd just like a copy of the guestlist," Louise blurted before adding, "For personal reasons." Zoe shook her head at her friend slowly, and Louise rolled her eyes. The line was silent for a few moments, and Louise was worried they'd messed it up.

"Look, if this is about that crazy woman, you can tell me. I would be interested to know who she is too if I was in your boat," the woman said.

"What's her name?" Louise answered, crossing her fingers under the table. The rustling continued on the other side of the phone, and Louise hoped that it was because she was searching for her name.

"Annabelle Brown. Her name was Annabelle Brown." And then the woman hung up the phone. Louise looked to Zoe with a triumphant smile on her face.

"We have a name!" She high fived her friend. Zoe chuckled and nodded her head. Then, "I told you. No one messes with personal reasons."

THIRTY-SIX

24th December 2009

I walked into the room slowly before sitting down on the chair opposite Doctor Simmons. She gave me a smile, her clipboard resting on her lap.

"It's lovely to meet you, Ava," she told me as she shook my hand. I nodded and knotted my hands together in my lap. They were clammy and trembling. I held them to stop them from shaking.

"How are you feeling today?" she asked softly. I could tell she was treading carefully. I nodded slowly.

"Better." I didn't know what else to say. I didn't have anything else to say. She nodded and gave me a small smile.

"Would you feel comfortable telling me about yourself? Your life and experiences before the incident," she asked, her voice soft. It angered me that she referred to it as the incident. Just call it what it really was.

"Um." I wrapped my fingers tighter around themselves, and I saw them turn white. "I've had a simple life. I went to an all-girls school, did well in my exams. And then I went to university." I sighed, my hands becoming shakier.

"And university wasn't so simple?" Doctor Simmons prompted, and I shrugged my shoulders.

"University has ruined my life," I said, looking at her right in the eyes. My eyes filled with tears and I looked away.

"University or the incident?" she asked me, and anger bubbled inside me again. I slammed my hands down on my legs, leaving a sting on my thighs.

"It wasn't an incident; it was rape!" I shouted, and Doctor Simmons wasn't fazed by my outburst. I ran my hands through my hair, my nails scraping against my scalp. "I'm sorry. I didn't mean to . . ."

"Ava, don't ever apologise. I didn't want to use the word rape in case it upset you. I will refer to it in any way you'd like me to." She nodded, and I felt a tear trickle down my cheek.

"It wasn't just the rape," I began. "It started off fine. I thought I was in a cool friendship group. I had a nice boyfriend. I loved it."

"What changed?" Doctor Simmons asked, a curious frown on her face. I take a deep breath.

"One of my friends, my best friend, she started acting a little crazy. She was possessive and manipulative. I let her control me." I shook my head. "She hatched a plan to make me want to break up with Pat. Made it look like he was cheating on me. She sedated him. Paid some random girl to pretend to hook up with him, so it looked like he was . . ." Anger seeped through my body.

"And this was the same night as the . . . rape?" she asked me, concern etched in her features.

"Yeah. I had no idea that he was sedated. I blindly believed my eyes and walked straight into the arms of a rapist." I brought my hands to my face and let out a sob.

"Ava, Matthew Riley is going to go to prison for a very long time. You will never see him again." Doctor Simmons said, anger lacing her tone too. I nodded.

"What are they going to do about Lucy, though?" I asked. "She drugged my boyfriend. She's a head case. Aren't they going to put her away too?" I sounded desperate. *Well, I was.* I was back

189

home now, but when the winter term arrived, I would have to see her again. And quite frankly, I was terrified of her.

"I'm no police officer, Ava. I agree that your friend should receive some help, but I do not know the circumstances of the event," she told me officially, and I rolled my eyes. The police already gave me my answer about Lucy. There was no evidence that she sedated Patrick, and she did nothing to him. She walked away free.

"I'm wondering if you would feel comfortable opening up about the rape, Ava. Of course, if you are not comfortable, we can talk about something else," she asked me, and I sat back in my chair. Pain rippled up my back and I shook my head. Tears rolled down my cheeks.

"No. I can't talk about that yet."

Patrick was waiting for me when I left the meeting. He greeted me with soft eyes and wrapped his arms around me. I cried into his shoulder.

"Let's go back and have some tea," he told me, taking my hand and leading me to his car. He was staying with my family and I before Christmas. I felt safer having him around. I was too scared to sleep alone.

"How was it?" he asked me as he turned the car on. I let tears trickle down my cheek, turning to lock eyes with him. He reached up and brushed his thumb over my cheek. I shrugged my shoulders.

"It was fine. I just . . . I'm scared," I told him, and that was the truth. It was not only Matt I'm scared of. It was Lucy too. I couldn't help thinking that it was not over.

THIRTY-SEVEN

"It's the weekend!" screamed Mia as she ran down the stairs into Ava's arms. Ava smiled and hugged her daughter.

"Exciting, right? Are you excited to go to Legoland?" Ava had asked Louise to take Mia out for the day. Ever since her memories of Lucy had come back to haunt her, she couldn't help herself from thinking that it was her. It had been years since university, but Lucy was unstable. Crazy.

"I am *so* excited mummy. Issie said that El is coming too! And she is *so* fun." Mia gave Ava a gap-toothed grin. Ava had heard multiple stories about Louise's cousin, El, yet hadn't had the pleasure of meeting her yet. She made a mental note to ask Louise to introduce them.

"Well, you better eat your breakfast because Louise will be here soon." Ava placed a bowl of warm porridge in front of her daughter, who eyed it suspiciously.

"Momma, where's the choc?" she asked, staring into the bowl. Ava rolled her eyes; she was trying to cut down the amount of chocolate Mia was eating. But with everything that was going on, chocolate consumption wasn't at the top of her priority list. So, she sourced some chocolate chips from the cupboard and sprinkled a couple on top.

"That's the last time, okay Mia? You shouldn't have chocolate for breakfast." Mia wasn't listening and happily tucked into her food. For a moment, Ava felt as if she were back in her old life. Where simple dramas felt like the ultimate war. She could almost hear Pat making his way down the stairs, cursing because he was going to be late to the hospital *again*. She would shake her head at him, because she *had* reminded him to set alarm. He would kiss Mia on the head before kissing Ava. He would grab a banana and run out the door, screaming 'I love you' as he did. Mia would giggle at her father and Ava would chuckle in disbelief.

But that was her old life.

The doorbell rung, snapping Ava out of her trance. Louise let herself in, looking flustered. Ava smiled at her friend and welcomed her with a hug.

"God, sorry I'm late. Issie and El have left, they're going to meet us there. Mia, are you ready?" Louise asked, and Mia nodded.

"Have a nice time, Mia!" Ava told her daughter as she gave her a kiss on the head. Mia nodded and ran to the door, and just like that they were gone.

Ava hated it when Mia wasn't in her line of sight, but she needed some time alone. She needed to figure out if Lucy was behind this.

It shocked her that Lucy hadn't crossed her mind before now. It was as if Ava had placed those memories so far in the back of her mind that she'd never let them resurface. But now they're back at the forefront of her mind and she was cursing herself that she hadn't thought it before. Lucy was unstable and unpredictable. But surely she wouldn't still hold a grudge? Either way, Ava had to look into it. If it turned out that Lucy lived miles away, then at least Ava's mind would be put at ease.

She turned to her laptop and opened it. She was unsure of where to start; if she Googled Lucy Miles, she'd probably be overwhelmed with thousands of results. Instead, she turned to Facebook. She couldn't remember the last time she had even used the platform, but it was worth a shot. At least, she'd be able to identify her from her profile picture.

Ava slowly typed the letters in. Her heart was pounding, terrified of what she was going to find. The page loaded. Results filled the page—Lucy Miles was a popular name. There was a range of profile pictures; from selfies to dogs to action shots. And none of them resembled Lucy.

Ava put her head in her hand and sighed. She knew she'd been foolish to assume that Facebook could answer her problems. She turned back to the page and begun to scroll, hoping to catch a glimpse of Lucy's brilliant red hair. But there was nothing.

Frustrated, Ava refreshed the page and looked at her own profile. Her profile picture was still of Patrick and she almost laughed. She really needed to update this. In the corner, she spotted a few notifications, so she opened them to see a couple of friend requests. She smiled; they were from Louise, Zoe, and a couple of other mothers from the school. Accepting them all, Ava turned to her profile and changed her picture to a new one.

Ava sighed and glanced at the time. She immediately regretted sending Mia away for the day; she felt immensely lonely. She was angry at herself for giving up on Lucy so easily, but she knew that it would be impossible to find her.

So, she turned back to her laptop and began scrolling through Facebook. It was going to be a long day.

*   *   *

The kids were excited to be at the theme park. So was Louise, and El was looking pretty happy too. Louise was glad, because amongst all the drama, she needed to make sure her kids were happy. And she had really begun to care about Mia too.

"Let's go on the duck ride!" screamed Issie in delight, looking back to Louise. Issie was extremely over excited, her gregarious personality placing little Mia in the shadows. Mia was a very quiet girl, with a personality very similar to her mother's. Issie absolutely adored Mia, and Louise treasured Ava in the same way.

Louise's mind briefly flashed back to the trial. She hoped that Ava would somehow be saved from being locked away. Zoe had said she was doing some more research into Annabelle today, giving Louise the day off being a detective. So far, they'd discovered that Annabelle was a doctor, working at a very prestigious hospital. They had gotten as far as assuming that Annabelle knew Patrick through medicine. They were proud of their work so far.

"El, will you come on the duck ride with me?" Mia turned to El with big bright eyes. El smiled down at Mia and held her hand out.

"I would love to, Mia." El grinned at Louise and Louise felt jealousy sprout in her stomach. Mia had taken a particular liking to her cousin. She was glad that they got along well, but her cousin always ended up being the favourite. Yes, she was glamorous. Yes, she was cool. But it often knocked Louise's confidence.

"Lou, you want to join?" El said as she swung Mia's arm back and forth. Mia looked to El with admiration. Louise let her jealousy cool and shook her head.

"No, I'm good. You guys go. I'll pick up some sweets for the kids or something," she told her cousin, reminding herself that not everything was a competition. El and the kids ran off, handing their tokens to the bored teen who solemnly wished them a happy ride.

Louise made her way over to the brightly coloured sweet stand, picking a variety of chocolates and lollies for the children to enjoy. Her phone buzzed into her pocket, and she opened it to see Zoe's name on the screen. She accepted the call.

"Hello?" She picked at one of the white chocolate mice, popping it into her mouth. It was much too sweet, and she grimaced.

"Louise, you're not going to believe what I've found out." Zoe sounded almost exasperated. Louise turned and walked away from the sweet stand, suddenly on full alert.

194

"What? Something about Annabelle?" Louise asked anxiously.

"No. I typed in Ava's name on a whim and scrolled until I saw something in relation to Bristol." Zoe hesitated; her voice quiet. "In her first year of university, Ava was raped. She was raped, Louise." Zoe swore, and Louise almost dropped her phone. Anger filled her and she ran her hand through her hair. She didn't know what to say.

"Jesus." Louise swore. *Poor Ava. Poor, poor Ava.* "Who . . ." Louise shook her head. She had not been expecting this.

"The guy was a friend of hers. From university. Matthew Riley. He was sent to prison for ten years." Zoe sounded close to tears. "Poor Ava."

"Would he be out by now?" Louise did mental maths in her head. Ava was twenty-nine if she remembered correctly. First year, she must have been eighteen . . . Christ. Her and Zoe came to the conclusion at the same time, swearing once more.

"He would have been released last year," Louise said with a gasp, her stomach recoiling.

*   *   *

Ava got nowhere with her search for Lucy, and she was beginning to give up hope. Her trial was quickly approaching, and she had nothing. She placed her head in her hands and sighed. She hadn't heard from her stalker for a while. Maybe they'd given up.

Her phone buzzed, removing her from her trance. She unlocked her phone to see a text from Jake. Christ. Part of her wanted to just ignore the message, because he was causing more trouble than he was worth. But the butterflies in her stomach couldn't be ignored.

Jake: Hey. Sorry about the funeral. I hope you're okay, would love to see you soon.

Ava sent a reply before she could stop herself.

195

Ava: Are you around now?

Jake came over pretty quickly after Ava's text, and Ava half wanted to tell him to leave. But the other half of her wanted him to stay.

"Hey," he said, his nose red from the cold. He looked unsure of how to greet Ava, so Ava took the first step and wrapped her arms around him. It was nice to be touched. Ava wordlessly lead him into the sitting room, where she sat down. He sat down next to her, looking at her carefully.

"How are you?" he asked, placing his hand on her arm. His fingertips left fireworks going up her arm. She smiled at him.

"I'm alright. I don't know. I just don't know what to do." She shrugged her shoulders. Jake looked at her with soft eyes and took his hand in hers.

"Whatever happens, you know I'll be here for you, right?" He rubbed the pad of his thumb in circles on her hand. For the first time in ages, she felt comfortable. She felt loved.

"Thank you." A tear fell down her cheek. "I can't believe that amidst all this craziness, I've met you. Bad timing." Jake chuckled, before frowning.

"I really like you, Ava. I wish we didn't have these circumstances. I've been wanting to kiss you ever since the gala." He looked down bashfully, taking his hand out of hers as if embarrassed. "But I would never want to make you feel uncomfortable, so I took a step back."

Ava felt a warmth in her that she hadn't felt in a long time. She looked into Jake's beautiful eyes before reaching up to touch his face.

"I like you too, Jake." She smiled; the movement foreign on her face. He smiled back before bringing his face to her face. And then Jake's lips were on hers, and she couldn't help herself. She kissed him back.

*   *   *

Ten minutes later, they were both sweaty and confused. Ava could hardly believe what she had just done.

"You're amazing, you know that right?" Jake told her, taking her hand and kissing her fingertips. Ava put her head in her hands. She shouldn't have done that. She'd just got carried away in the moment.

"I can't let you go to prison, Ava," he said. Ava sighed before wrapping his arms around his torso.

"It's not at the top of my priority list, either," she tried to joke. But really, it wasn't funny at all.

THIRTY-EIGHT

It took a while, but Christmas break had given me the time and energy to forget about that night with Matt. Therapy really helped, and Patrick had been amazing. I also felt safe in the fact that Matt went to prison for ten years pending appeal. I just hoped that I would never see him again.

The university had been very understanding of my circumstances. They had moved me from my halls to a self-catered flat. Pat was going to stay with me for most of the time.

I hadn't heard from Lucy for the entirety of the Christmas holidays. I was glad because I might go crazy if I saw her. Pat and I had vowed to stay away from my toxic friendship group. Hopefully, this term would give me a chance to grow and meet new people.

After the last box had been emptied, Mum looked like she was about to cry. I felt emotional too, scared to be away from parental protection. But I couldn't live in fear my whole life.

"We're going to stay in Bristol this week, darling. Just as you adjust," she told me, and I was glad. It would help me adjust. Pat walked in, placing a box of my textbooks next to my desk. He wrapped his arm around me and kissed my head.

"I'll be here 24/7, Carol," he said to reassure mum. She nodded before taking me in her arms and saying goodbye.

Pat and I decided to have a relaxing afternoon as I got settled into the flat. My therapist advised that I should gradually immerse myself back into my social life, and that house parties were a no-go for at least a couple of weeks. She didn't have to tell me that though. I wouldn't go to a house party even if I was paid one million pounds.

The knock on the door interrupted Pat and I's viewing of the latest Harry Potter film. I stood up, assuming it was my mum and dad. Maybe I forgot something.

I opened the door and my heart stopped.

Lucy stood before me, her face solemn. I was frozen in my spot.

"Before you slam the door on my face, I want to tell you I'm sorry," she said, and I still couldn't move. "I'm in love with you, Ava. It's made me crazy, I'm not proud of it. I'm here to tell you that I'm going to get some help."

"Pat!" I managed to scream out, tears rolling down my cheeks. Lucy nodded slowly, her eyes sad. Pat came up behind me, wrapping his arms around me and pulling me behind him.

"You need to leave us alone, Lucy. Or I swear to God, I will kill you," Pat seethed. Tears continued to fall down my cheeks, my heart booming in my chest. Lucy nodded at Pat's harsh words and turned to leave. She gave me one last look and sighed

"It's not me that you should be scared of."

THIRTY-NINE

The day at the amusement park was a success, but Louise couldn't keep her mind off the news she'd received earlier. Matthew Riley had the perfect motive for Ava. And the fact that he got out a year ago couldn't be a coincidence. Louise was convinced that she'd worked it out.

But how could she prove it? Clearly, the guy was clever; he was managing to frame Ava very well. It was almost too much for Louise do deal with. She felt so hopeless.

"We've got to drop Mia off at Ava's on the way home," Louise told her cousin as they made their way to the cars. Issie and Mia were looking a little ill after all the sweets they'd consumed. "I'd like to introduce you to Ava. I think you'd get along really well." El frowned and shook her head.

"Sorry, Lou. I've got to get back. Gotta make a call." El shrugged her shoulders. "Another time though. She sounds really cool." Louise wanted to roll her eyes. El was always busy, surely she could make some time for Ava? She had been so interested in the murder, so why didn't she want to meet Ava? Unless she was scared of her. Louise didn't blame her.

"Okay. I'll see you back at home then." Louise tried to keep the disappointment from her voice, but she failed miserably. El didn't pick up on it though. She effortlessly slid into her car without any further words and drove off.

"Right, time to head home kids!" Louise switched her mummy voice back on and ushered the children into the car. A message flashed up on her screen as she plugged Ava's address into the sat nav. It was from Zoe.

Zoe: We need to talk. ASAP.

The message was enough to get any thoughts of El out of Louise's brain, and onto the motorway. She had to know what Zoe needed to tell her.

*   *   *

Zoe wasn't expecting Louise to show up as quickly as she had. Although, the text she sent had been urgent, and it was.

"Dave, could you take Issie and Luca through to the Wii room and keep them entertained, please?" Zoe asked her husband, who was hoovering the sitting room. He looked up with a frown on his face.

"Louise is coming over?" he asked, turning the hoover off. Zoe nodded.

"Please. I'll be extra nice to you later." She winked, trying to keep her tone light. She didn't want him suspecting anything. He still thought that Ava was the killer. The doorbell went, and Dave obediently opened it before ushering the kids away into the Wii room. Louise walked into the sitting room with rosy cheeks and unwrapped the scarf from her neck.

"Christ." She sat down on the sofa next to Zoe. Zoe looked at her friend, unsure of where to start. Sure, she'd sprung some pretty big news on her earlier. But there was more.

"So." Louise turned to Zoe with curious eyes. Zoe took a deep breath and reached for her laptop. She opened it and showed the page to Louise.

"The guy, Matthew Riley, did go to prison for raping Ava. But I found out that he didn't get out last year. Somehow, he was released after only three years. Probably because of a very rich

201

family member." Zoe scrolled down the article on the case. Louise put her hand to her mouth.

"That doesn't mean that he didn't do it, right? If anything, it means he's had more time to plan it." Louise's heart was thumping. It had made so much sense. Why would Matthew have waited until now?

"That's the thing." Zoe moved to the other tab, where the headline read: *University rapist goes missing three days after release.*

"He went missing. And he's never been found." Zoe shrugged her shoulders. "I don't know if that means anything to us. But it's weird. Too weird."

Louise nodded. "You're right. All these weird occurrences must be linked. Right?" She knew she was reaching. But it was too odd. A rape, a prison sentence that ended early, followed by a murder? And they're all connected, somehow. They must be.

"Definitely. Poor Ava. I feel bad for suspecting her," Zoe said, and Louise sent her daggers. Zoe put her arms up. "Hey, it made sense at the time." Louise nodded. Zoe sighed.

"The police will think we're idiots. Yeah, it's weird, but we have no actual evidence," Zoe said, stumped. They could hardly turn up to the police station with this. They'd laugh and tell them to leave.

"I don't know what to do." Louise put her head in her hands. "It's pretty clear that Ava didn't do it. And she was being framed." Zoe agreed. Was the killer still in their midst? Had Matthew Riley come to haunt Ava? There were so many questions, and so little time.

"Let's look up the university newsletter. They must have had one," Zoe said, grasping for straws. "If the local newspaper covered the story, the university must have also. Maybe there will be some coverage on that night. It might even mention some of Ava's friends. We could find them, and then ask them about it." Louise nodded with a small smile. It was a reach, but they had to give it a go.

202

It took Zoe a while to find the Bristol university letter from 2009, but when she found it, it didn't take long to find an article on the night Ava was raped.

Student, 18, raped at house party

Last night, a student was raped at a house party in Clifton. The girl was sedated using the date rape drug, rendering her unconscious for the assault. The offender, Matthew Riley, was a fellow student at the university.

Whilst in he was in the first year of his course, Riley was a few years older than the victim, who will remain unnamed.

A friend of the victim has spoken to Clifton News to provide some insight on the night.

"It all happened so quickly. I was dancing when I'd realised she had been gone for a long time. I decided to look for her, and there she was, unconscious on the bed. Completely naked. She had bruises all over her body . . . She's my best friend. I can't believe what happened to her. I hope Matthew goes away for a long time."

The friend, who will also remain unnamed, informed us that Matthew had made several sexual attempts on her as well.

More news on this to follow.

By Anna Meadows

Louise and Zoe looked to each other. They knew what they needed to do. They needed to find Anna Meadows.

*   *   *

Ava felt guilty all afternoon. Jake had left shortly before Louise had dropped Mia off. Ava felt dirty and stupid. How could she do that when her trial was so soon? She was so foolish.

As she prepared the food, she let her mind wander back to Lucy. Could it really be her? Coming back to get her revenge after all this time?

But Lucy was . . . in love with her. That's what she said, anyway. Ava cast her toxic friend from her brain and turned to the fridge. She needed some comfort food, so she put some chips in the oven. When they were ready, she almost engulfed them, burning the inside of her mouth.

And then her phone beeped. She knew what that meant immediately. She hadn't heard from her stalker in a while, she'd wondered what he was up to.

Subject: Your Majesty.

That looked like some royal treatment, Your Majesty.

Her stomach turned over and the fell to the floor. Your Majesty. The exact words that Matthew Riley had used before he raped her.

FORTY

"This is crazy." Zoe looked to Louise as they drove along the motorway. Louise changed lanes and turned to her friend, nodding.

"I know. But I'm determined to help Ava." Louise checked the sat nav and saw that they were close. They had found Anna Meadows, now a journalist working in London. They'd asked to meet her to give her an exclusive on Ava's story. They felt bad using Ava as bait, but they knew that Anna wouldn't be able to turn down such a good opportunity. Little did she know, they were getting information from her.

Louise took the junction off the motorway before following the directions into a suburb of London. The coffee shop where they were meeting appeared on the side of the road, so Louise pulled into a bay to park. She looked to Zoe, who looked as scared as Louise felt.

"Let's go."

The two friends walked into the coffee shop, and spotted Anna immediately. She had dark hair and round glasses that were popular in the 70s. She had an emo look to her, and with her laptop in front of her, it was clear that she was a journalist.

Louise, ever the confident one, marched up to the table and stuck her hand out. Anna looked up, her glasses magnifying her eyes. She gave Louise a smile.

"Louise." She had an American accent. Louise shook her hand firmly before sitting opposite her. Zoe closely followed.

"Thank you for meeting us, Anna," Louise said, smiling at the woman. Anna shook her head, her shiny hair swaying.

"It's no bother. It's actually crazy you asked, because I was writing a story on this case anyway. I went to university with Ava." She nodded, looking smug. "You don't look surprised though, so I guess you knew that." Anna smiled. "You've done your research."

Louise nodded. "We have. We're friends with Ava." Anna looked surprised at this, nodding her head slowly.

"The police have already spoken to me, you know." She blinked her long eyelashes. "About the rape." It was Louise's turn to be surprised. It had seemed like the police had been doing nothing about it. They just arrested Ava and that was that.

"What did they ask?" Zoe pressed, speaking for the first time. Anna turned to Zoe.

"They asked about Matthew Riley. If I knew him. Blah blah. I told them all I know." Anna shrugged her shoulders. "Which is that he disappeared." Her eyes darted between the two women, pursing her lips. "Anyway, I'm the journalist here, so I should be asking the questions." Louise rubbed her forehead and looked to Anna.

"I'm going to be honest with you, Anna. We're not here to give you an exclusive," she said, fearing Anna's response. The dark-haired woman narrowed her eyes.

"What do you want then? To hear about Ava's deep dark secrets?" Anna said, her tone frustrated. She slammed her laptop shut. "I wasn't friends with her at uni. You know, I wasted an afternoon on this." She stood up, and Louise panicked.

"We think she's being framed," Louise blurted out, and she could feel Zoe's eyes burning on the side of her head. But they couldn't lose Anna now. Anna frowned and sat back down.

"You have thirty seconds to explain yourselves."

*   *   *

Ava was left in fear after the message she'd received yesterday. All her past memories from university were flooding back in. She thought she'd never had to worry about Matthew Riley ever again. He had been locked away.

But she'd been naïve. After dropping Mia at school, she'd gone to the library to do some research. Her fears were confirmed when she'd searched his name. Not only had he been released early, but he had gone missing.

It must have been him. Getting revenge on her for putting him in prison. It all made sense now. It was always going to be about revenge. She put her head in her hands, tears falling down her cheeks.

A hand touched her back and she jumped, but to her relief it was the librarian, who had a soft smile on her face.

"Are you alright, dear?" She had sweet eyes, and Ava almost felt like sobbing like a little girl. Instead, Ava just nodded and wiped her tears from her face.

"I'm fine." She closed her webpages and thanked the librarian, before walking out into the rain. She slid into her car and looked to her phone. Somehow, Matthew had got into her house. Somehow, he'd bugged her phone. The thought made her feel sick. But why kill Patrick? Why not just kill Ava?

Ava couldn't be alone right now. She needed to be with someone. So, she drove to Louise's house. She pulled up on the side of the road and ran to the door.

Ava rang on the doorbell, before noticing that Louise's car wasn't in the driveway. But the lights were on in the house, and Ava remembered that Louise's cousin was staying with her. She heard some rustling around, and then footsteps coming closer to the door.

The door swung open, revealing a woman standing behind it. Ava's stomach dropped and her legs nearly collapsed from underneath her.

"Well, I was hoping for a slightly more dramatic reunion, but I guess this will do." The woman smiled, pulling Ava into a hug.

"I've missed you, Ava."

*   *   *

"We think that Matthew Riley has come back to get revenge on Ava. There's no way that she killed her husband," Louise explained, talking as quickly as she could. Anna folded her arms and nodded.

"Go on."

"If you can help us prove that it wasn't Ava that did it, think about the story you could write. I think that would equal a promotion, don't you?" Louise fumbled over her words, but this perked Anna's interest.

"How are you going to prove it, then? I know nothing about Ava. I just interviewed some of her friends who were at the party." Anna shrugged, but Louise knew that she was invested now.

"Exactly. We're hoping that if we can find the friend that you interviewed, we can find out more from her. She said that Matthew had made several sexual assaults on her too." Louise pulled the article out of her bag and pointed to the quote. "This girl. Do you remember her?"

Anna looked at the article and nodded. "Oh, I remember her. She's a loose end, though. One screw loose, that one."

Louise frowned. "What do you mean?"

"She *was* Ava's best friend. But shortly after the rape, she got sent to a mental hospital. Ava claimed that she sedated her boyfriend, Patrick. I always thought she was a bit odd." Anna shrugged her shoulders. Louise looked to Zoe, who had the same shocked expression on her face. Ava's life was turning out to be far from ordinary.

"What was her name?" Zoe asked. "She might still be of use to us."

Anna sighed. "This is really supposed to be confidential."

"Please, Anna," Louise begged. Anna looked between the two friends and rolled her lips into her mouth.

"Her name was Lucy Miles," Anna said, and Louise's blood ran cold. "But really, she won't be any use to you."

"Are you sure her name was Lucy Miles?" Louise asked, her voice strained. Anna nodded, looking confused. Louise put her hand to her mouth.

"What's wrong, Louise?" Zoe asked, putting her hand on her friend's arm. Louise turned to Zoe, shock running through her body.

"That's my cousins name." She ran her hand through her hair. "I forgot that she went to Bristol university."

Zoe frowned. "I thought your cousin was called El."

"El, like the letter L. My nickname was Lou, so she couldn't have the same. We settled for El." Louise turned back to Anna. "Do you have any pictures of her?"

"Lou, I'm sure it's not the same Lucy. Lucy Miles is a common name," Zoe said in attempt to calm Louise down. Louise shook her head, her eyes brimming with tears.

"Do you have a picture?" Louise asked Anna again, and Anna nodded slowly. She turned the laptop around to face the two women. Louise almost couldn't face looking at it. But as the picture loaded, Louise's fears were confirmed. The image was of a very young Ava, with her arms wrapped around Louise's very own cousin, El.

*   *   *

"Lucy," Ava croaked, pushing the woman off her. She had aged, yes, but it was her. Lucy pushed her bright ginger hair behind her shoulder and frowned at Ava.

"You don't look very happy to see me." She reached out and touched Ava's cheek. "I have missed you *so* much." Ava stepped back, tears filling her eyes. Her heart was racing.

"It was you, wasn't it?" Ava shook her head. "You killed Patrick, didn't you!" She ran her hands through her hair. Lucy's smile didn't drop from her face. She shook her head.

"Ava, why would I do that? I love you." Lucy reached out to touch Ava again, but Ava smacked her away. Lucy stuck her lip out in mock sadness.

"Yes, you did. You've been sending me those texts, you sent me that picture of my daughter." Ava screamed, terror running through her. Mia had been in the house with this lunatic. How could Ava not realise?

"Mia is so sweet, by the way. Just like her mummy. We get on *so* well." Lucy smiled. "But it wasn't me. I would never hurt you, Ava." She took a couple of steps towards Ava, holding her hand out.

"Stay away from me, Lucy," Ava shouted, feeling helpless.

"Come inside. I'll explain everything." She nodded. "I promise."

Ava looked at Lucy, her heart in her chest. It was almost the end of the school day; Ava needed to collect Mia. She needed to protect her. The thought that Mia had been in the same house as Lucy made her sick to her stomach.

"How are you Louise's cousin?" Ava asked, confusion rushing through her body. It was too much of a coincidence.

"I'll explain everything, Ava. Just come inside." Lucy ran her hand down Ava's arm. Ava shrugged her arm and took a step back.

"Get away from me, Lucy. Get out of this town. If I see you again, I swear . . ." Ava began, but her voice trailed off and her threat diminished. Lucy cocked her head to one side, and she smirked.

"You'll what, Ava. You'll kill me?" Lucy twirled a strand of hair around her finger. "Come inside. We have so much to catch up on."

"I'd rather pull my eyes out," Ava spat before turning away and rushing to her car. She didn't look to see if Lucy was watching her, because she knew the answer. She'd been watching her this whole time.

FORTY-ONE

Louise couldn't believe her eyes. El and Ava had been best friends at university. How could that be? And Anna had said that she was crazy . . . how did Louise not know about that? Louise had thought El had taken a gap year after university.

"Are you okay, Lou?" Zoe asked. Louise couldn't remove her eyes from the photo. El looked so happy in the photo, her arms wrapped tightly around Ava. Louise felt a tinge of jealousy.

"Are you sure she went to a hospital?" Louise croaked, barely finding her voice. "The mental hospital?" She felt tears gather in her eyes. How well did she really know her cousin?

Anna looked uncomfortable. "One hundred percent. It was the talk of the town. We called her kooky Lucy." Anna paused. "Sorry."

"It's fine. I had no idea." Louise brushed a tear from her cheek. "She never mentioned Ava." Zoe shuffled next to Louise and put her hand on her arm.

"You don't think . . ." Zoe begun, but Louise knew what she was thinking. The thought had crossed her mind as soon as she'd seen the picture. Could Lucy have killed Patrick?

"I don't know." Louise bit her lip. "I have no idea."

"Look, if it helps, Lucy was a good friend to Ava. I always saw them together." Anna spoke up, clearly trying to ease the tension. "It's just that Lucy was a little obsessed with Ava. Hated it when Ava spent time with other people. She especially didn't like

212

Patrick. I think that Lucy might have been in love with her." Anna's voice was not sympathetic, it was curious. She was clearly thinking the same thing as Louise and Zoe.

And the more Anna spoke, the more Louise feared it.

Maybe Lucy killed Patrick because he divorced Ava. Maybe she'd been angry at Patrick. Maybe she'd been angry enough to kill him.

*   *   *

Ava was left in fear after her confrontation with Lucy. She anxiously awaited at the school gates for Mia to come out. Her mind was reeling. Lucy was Louise's cousin. Matthew Riley was missing. It couldn't be a coincidence. Lucy was back in town immediately after Patrick's death. But was Matthew playing a part too?

Her mind was so preoccupied that she didn't notice Jake coming up to her. He gave her an easy grin and pulled her into a hug. Ava wanted to pull away; she could feel the eyes of the other mothers on her.

"How are you?" he asked her, his eyes boring into hers. She nodded, trying to look positive. Regret was flooding through her veins.

"I'm fine." She fought the tears. "You?"

"I'm good. Kai has been demanding to have Mia over for a playdate. We could make an evening of it." Jake bumped his shoulders into Ava's in a flirty way. Ava's immediate answer was no, but then she remembered her afternoon. Lucy was in town, and potentially dangerous. Ava knew that she and Mia would be safer with Jake. Lucy wouldn't try anything at someone else's house.

"Sure." Ava nodded. "Why not?" Jake beamed at her, and Ava felt a little relieved. The school bell rang, and Mia ran out of the doors, shortly followed by Kai. It was sweet that they were getting on so well. Ava was looking forward to spending the evening at Jake's.

"We're going to go to Kai's for a playdate," Ava told her daughter as she wrapped her arms around her legs. Mia smiled happily and turned to Kai.

"Can we play that ship game?" Mia squealed, and Kai nodded. Jake put his arm around Ava and squeezed her slightly. It was comforting.

Mia was excited on the way to Jake's house. Her and Kai had been planning their playdate all day. Ava almost forgot about Lucy. As they pulled up to Jake's house, Ava remembered Nancy. Were they still living together? Ava knew Nancy would be at work, but she felt a little uneasy. But then she remembered that Mia's safety was the most important thing.

Jake and Nancy's house was a mansion, but that didn't surprise Ava. She knew how successful Nancy was. Jake led them into the open plan kitchen, and Mia and Kai immediately ran over to the corner where a mountain of toys laid.

"Drink?" Jake asked, and Ava nodded. After her day, she certainly needed one. Jake grinned and grabbed two glasses from the cupboard.

"Dare I ask about the trial?" Jake asked, his tone unsure. He poured red wine into each glass and passed one to Ava. She took a long sip.

"It's still happening, if that's what you mean." Ava ran her hand through her hair. "I don't have anything to prove that I'm innocent." She shrugged her shoulders, unsure if she should mention Lucy to Jake. He was trustworthy and had been supportive through the whole situation.

"I see." He narrowed his eyes, and something about the expression reminded Ava of someone. She took another long sip of her wine.

"Anyway, enough about that." Ava waved her hand dismissively. Her phone was in her pocket, so she needed to be careful about what she said. "How are you?"

"Divorces are not fun experiences. But I guess you know that." Jake lowered his voice so the kids couldn't hear. "Nancy and I can't speak to each other without wanting to rip each other's heads off."

"Ah." Ava nodded slowly. "Patrick and I were actually pretty civil about it." She remembered those interactions clearly. She wished she could go back in time to save him. Maybe they could have worked through their issues. Maybe she could have saved him.

*   *   *

Zoe was grateful that Dave had taken the day off to collect the kids from school because her and Louise's trip had lasted longer than they anticipated. Zoe couldn't believe what they had discovered. El—or Lucy—was Ava's best friend at university. A best friend who was obsessed with her. El had turned up shortly after Patrick's murder. Was it a coincidence?

"Lou, are you okay?" Zoe asked carefully. Louise had barely spoken a word since they'd left their meeting with Anna. Louise kept her eyes on the road.

"I'm angry," she said in a low voice. "I'm so freaking angry with El."

"It could just be a coincidence, Lou," Zoe tried, but she knew that she didn't sound convincing. "Let's not jump to any conclusions until you speak to her, okay?"

"That's where we're going. I'm going to confront her." Louise paused, malice in her voice. "And you're coming with me."

Zoe frowned. "It's not my place. This is between you and her."

"I'm scared of her, Zoe." Louise's voice was weak, shocking Zoe. "I need you there." Zoe wanted to say no. Louise was right to be scared of El; from what Zoe had heard, she seemed unstable.

"Fine. I'll come with you. But if she tries anything, I'm out." Zoe couldn't believe her own words. Tansbury was supposed to be a quiet town, when the biggest piece of drama is a kid falling over at school. Now, they had a murder case on their hands.

When they arrived at Louise's house, Zoe felt a surge of nerves rush through her. She had no idea how El was going to react to their revelations. Louise stormed into the house ahead of Zoe, heading straight for the kitchen.

"Hey, cuz!" El's voice appeared, and Zoe cautiously followed her friend into the kitchen. El was blissfully unaware, twirling a stand of her red hair around her finger. "Good day?"

"Why didn't you tell me you knew Ava?" Louise spluttered; her voice angry. Zoe was shocked at her outburst; she thought Louise might have eased into it. But she knew how angry she was. El rolled her red lips into her mouth and hopped off the bar stool.

"I think we better sit down." El sat down on the sofa and patted the spot next to her. "I can explain."

"Explain what? That you lied to me? That you're crazy?" Louise shouted, making Zoe wince. She felt out of place. El sighed and shook her head.

"I withheld the truth, Lou. I didn't lie." El shrugged her shoulders. "Just sit down. I'll explain."

"You killed him, didn't you?" Louise shouted, tears now streaming down her face. Zoe wanted to tell her to calm down; they didn't know what El was capable of. She looked calm, though. Too calm.

"I didn't kill him." El shook her head. "I would never do that to Ava."

"Explain it to me, then. It's a bit too much of a coincidence that you arrived in town shortly after Patrick was killed." Louise

216

stood over her cousin, her face screwed up. Zoe had never seen her like this.

"Sit down, Louise," El said, her tone sterner this time. Louise reluctantly sat down next to her cousin. "I didn't kill Patrick. But I know who did."

*   *   *

"Another glass?" Jake asked Ava, and Ava was shocked to see her glass empty. She must have been drinking more quickly than she realised.

"I'm good, thank you. I'll need to drive Mia back later." She looked at the clock, realising they needed to head home soon. It was getting late.

"Can I use your bathroom?" Ava asked; the wine had gone right through her. Jake nodded and pointed down the corridor. As Ava made her way down the corridor, she couldn't help but look at the photos on the walls. They were happy memories; Jake and Nancy looked happy. Ava walked past a study, presumably Jake's. Her nosiness got the best of her, and she tip toed in.

She wondered what Jake did before Kai came around. Accounting, maybe? His desk was cluttered with papers and files, and Ava rolled her eyes. Messy guy.

But then she spotted a file that made her heart falter. The file in the middle of the desk had Ava's name on it. Her breath caught in her throat. Why would Jake have a file with her name on it? She glanced back at the door, checking that Jake wasn't there. Her heart in her mouth, she opened the file.

The first document was a picture. A picture of Ava from university. She frowned, turning the photo over. In pencil, it said: 'Ava, 2010." Ava's heart began to race, and she flicked to the next document. It was a picture of her and Patrick at their wedding. Ava put her hand to her mouth. Why did Jake have these photos? Had he been stalking her?

217

Terrified, she turned to his computer. Wiggling the mouse awoke the screen, and the homepage was scattered with files. Her stomach recoiled when she saw one with her name on it. She opened it, and as the contents loaded, she felt her legs weaken. The first video in the folder read:

'Ava sex tape.'

FORTY-TWO

"You know who did it?" Louise shrieked, covering her mouth with her hand. "Why haven't you gone to the police?" She couldn't believe her ears. El rolled her eyes, and Louise felt the urge to slap her.

"This is why I didn't tell you, Louise. You're so dramatic." El sighed. "If we go to the police, we're putting Ava and Mia's lives at risk." Louise's stomach dropped. What madness had El got involved in?

"We need to do something!" Louise shrieked, looking to Zoe. She shared the same shocked expression as Louise.

"Will you just listen to me, Louise?" El's voice was louder this time, and Louise nodded. "You're right, Lou. I did lie to you. I went to university with Ava. We were best friends."

"Until you went crazy." Louise narrowed her eyes. El frowned and shook her head.

"You could call it that, I guess. Borderline personality disorder to be precise," El said, and Louise's stomach dropped once more. How could she have never known?

"I have it under control, by the way. Psychotherapy. My saving grace." El gave a small smile. "I was in love with her, Louise. Have you ever wondered why I've never settled down? I've never gotten over her." El paused. "But I was young, naïve. I couldn't comprehend why she didn't feel the same way. She loved Patrick, not me. So yeah, that made me pretty crazy. Impulsivity plus a broken heart? Not a good combo.

"I did anything to get her attention. I starved myself. I made up lies about Patrick. I'm not proud of it, but I can't take it back now." El looked at Louise, who was staring at her in surprise. Louise had no idea that El was into women. She used to come back bragging about all the men in her life.

"But one night, I took it too far," El continued, "I knew that Matthew Riley was into Ava, so he and I hatched a plan," El said, and Louise felt her heart lurch. Matthew Riley was the one who raped Ava.

"You were friends with him?" Zoe was the one to speak now, an expression of disgust on her face. El shrugged her shoulders.

"I didn't know what he was going to do. We both wanted to get into Ava's good graces, so I used him. The plan was simple. Matthew kept Ava occupied while I sedated Patrick. I had paid some girl to pretend to be hooking up with him." Louise looked at her cousin in horror. She had sedated Patrick?

"You are crazy," Louise spat.

"Just listen, okay? The plan was in place. Ava would walk in to see Patrick hooking up with a random girl, pushing her into my arms. But Matthew got too drunk. He didn't follow the plan. When Ava saw the girl 'hooking up' with Patrick, I was still in the room. It looked like a . . . threesome. So, she went to Matthew instead of seeking comfort with me. And we all know how that ended." El exhaled. "If I had known that Matthew had his own plan, I never would have done it. I was stupid."

"He raped her, El. That's more than stupid," Louise shouted. "And you're no better. Patrick would have told her the truth. She would have never loved you." El looked stung by Louise's words, but she eventually nodded.

"You're right. But I was in love, Louise. I was willing to try anything." El combed her hair back. "I wish I hadn't. When

220

Matthew was sent to prison, I admitted myself to a hospital. I knew that there was something wrong with me."

"Just tell us who killed Patrick, El," Zoe hissed. "If Ava is in danger, you need to hurry up."

"I'm getting to that." El narrowed her eyes at Zoe. "I moved away, tried to forget about Ava. Of course, I couldn't. I kept tabs on her life, made sure that she was okay. And that's when he came to me." El lowered her eyes, as if embarrassed to tell them more.

"Who came to you?" Louise asked, dreading the answer. El looked up, her eyes filled with tears.

"Matthew Riley. He'd been released from prison. He wanted me to help him fake his disappearance." A tear dripped down El's cheek. "He told me that if I didn't help him, he'd go after Ava. I didn't have a choice."

Louise had no words. El had helped a rapist disappear?

"Why did he want to disappear? Why not move on with his life?" Zoe asked, staring at El with disgust.

"I know people who specialise in new identities. There's only so many career paths you can pick when you're discharged from a psychiatric hospital. Surprisingly enough, no one wants to hire a crazy woman," El laughed, but Louise kept her face stern.

"My friends fixed him up with a new identity," El continued, "I thought that he wanted to move on so that he could escape his past. I was wrong." El looked to Louise, who felt her body shaking.

"It was him, wasn't it?" Louise asked. "He's framing Ava to get revenge." El nodded slowly, and Louise felt sick. They had worked it out.

"But what was his new identity, then?" Zoe asked. "What was the identity that you gave him?" And as El spoke the name, the world came to a halt. Louise barely made it to the sink before she threw up.

                    *   *   *

Ava held a sob in as she stared at the video contents. Jake
was not who she thought he was. She needed to get out of the
house. She started to make her way out of the room, when she
heard footsteps. She froze in her place.

"Ava?" Jake's voice called, before looking into the study,
surprise on his face. He sighed and frowned. "You weren't
supposed to be in here." Ava's eyes widened and she looked around
to see if she could find something she could use to defend herself.

"Why do you have a file on me, Jake?" she spat, reaching
for the letter opener on the desk. She held it out in front of her, her
heart racing.

"Damn. I was hoping this would turn out differently. Even
so, I think this change of events will do just nicely." Jake rubbed his
hands together and took a step towards Ava. "I guess I better
explain myself." Jake's voice deepened, and a smirk grew on his
face. "But to be honest with you, I'm surprised you didn't work it
out for yourself."

"Work what out? That you're a psycho?" Ava hissed, terror
running through her veins. Jake laughed.

"Don't hurt my feelings, Ava. I thought that you were
cleverer than that." He raised his eyes to the ceiling. "Come on,
wrack your brain. Don't I look familiar at all?" He narrowed his
eyes, and Ava felt sick.

"I don't know what you mean," Ava muttered, but she
knew she was lying to herself. She knew that he'd looked familiar.

"Okay, okay. I'll give you a hint." Jake cleared his voice.
"Time for some royal treatment, Your Majesty." Ava's legs
weakened and she dropped to the floor. It couldn't be . . . she
would have recognised him. She looked up, and past the changed
nose and hair, she saw it.

It was him.

"Matthew," she spat, pushing herself off the carpet. He grinned and shook his hands either side of him.

"Ta da!" He chuckled. "Changing your identity is *so* much easier than I thought. One nose job and a hair change and I look like a different person." Jake pushed his hair back to reveal more of his face. How could she have not realised it before?

"You disgust me." Ava felt sick to her stomach. She'd slept with this man. She'd slept with her rapist. Her insides were on fire. Matthew put his hands up in mock surrender.

"I'll admit it, the sex was better when you were enjoying it." He narrowed his eyes. Ava's stomach recoiled and she held her stomach to stop herself from throwing up. None of it made sense. How could Matthew had known that Ava was going to move to Tansbury? Was it a coincidence?

"You killed Patrick, didn't you?" Ava spat, too angry to cry. Matthew shrugged his shoulders and nodded.

"A low blow from me. But you ruined my life, Ava. I'm only returning the favour." He grinned, and Ava realised. Matthew, Jake, whatever she should call him, was deluded. She needed to get away from him. She needed to save Mia.

Mia.

Oh God.

It was as if Matthew could read the fear in her eyes.

"Don't you worry about your precious daughter." Matthew cocked his head to one side. "Kai is only doing what he's told." Ava didn't let him finish his sentence before she was upon him. She ran at him with the letter opener, thrusting her entire body weight on to him. She was successful at pinning him down for a couple of seconds, stabbing blindly at his chest barely making contact.

He grunted, before pushing her slight frame off him and pinning her arms down by her sides. Ava squirmed under his grip but to no avail. His contorted face was above her, a thick vein throbbing from his forehead.

"You try that again, and Mia is dead," he spat at her, droplets hitting her face. She stopped squirming, panic rising within her. He smiled in triumph before pulling her up by her arms and pushing her backwards into a chair.

"I think it's time for a story," Matthew said in a singsong voice, pulling a draw open. He took out some ropes from it and shook it in his hand. "Don't want you trying anything now, do I?"

Wrapping the rope tightly around Ava's hands and feet, he secured her to the chair. She felt an anger in her that she had never felt before. Not even after he raped her.

"Where to start?" Matthew pulled his desk chair so he was sat facing Ava. She wanted to spit in his face. "I guess at the beginning."

Ava sat silently, resenting him.

"I'm sure you're aware by now that lovely Lucy is in town. Such a character, Lucy. So crazily in love with you that she was willing to do anything to gain your affections and save your life. She even helped me rape you. I guess there is a fine line between love and hate." Matthew chuckled and looked at Ava as she flinched.

"Of course, Lucy didn't realise what I was planning to do. She thought I was just a lovesick fool who wanted you for myself. You hurt my feelings, Ava. I just wanted to hurt yours.

"I didn't think the police would find me as soon as they did, you know. I thought I'd be able to skip town easily. But you tattled on me. Sending me to prison. And guess what, sweetheart? Prison is not fun."

"I don't think it's supposed to be," Ava growled at him, wishing he was still locked up. He deserved to be. He deserved to be there *for life*. A slap hit her hard across the face.

"No interrupting," Matthew seethed, twitching his neck to one side. "Anyway, a friend of mine got me out after three years. But three years gives you a long time to think, Ava. And in that time, I'd come up with a plan.

"I wanted to ruin your life. Step one: new identity. That part was easy enough. Lucy Miles had gotten herself involved with the wrong crowd, which luckily for me meant she knew the right people that could sort me out. I threatened your life, you see. She couldn't say no to that. And so, after my nose job and hair change, I became Jake Gilbert. Step two of the plan was simple enough: find a lovely wife. After realising the lengths Lucy would do to save you, I decided to blackmail her some more.

"She was living with her cousin, Louise. Ah, lovely Louise. I thought that it would be easier to get into a town that I knew. So, I got Lucy to report everything about Tansbury's residents to me. That way, I could pick the perfect woman to be my wife. That's when lovely Nancy came in." Matthew winked. Ava felt repulsed. Poor, poor Nancy.

"Nancy was easy seduce. Rich and insecure, I nestled my way into her life, and within six months, we were married. To be honest, the kids weren't part of the plan. But I needed to keep Nancy happy, so we did.

"My eyes were always on you, Ava. I kept tabs on your marriage, little Mia. I needed to find the right time to strike. But the issue was you and Patrick were happy. I needed you to leave him. If my plan was to work, you needed to be here, in Tansbury." Matthew ran his tongue over his teeth and grinned. "So, I threatened Patrick. I went to the hospital and told him if he didn't divorce you, then I'd kill both you and Mia." He laughed. "It's funny how much people are willing to do when you blackmail them. So easy!"

Ava's stomach dropped and her eyes filled with tears. The divorce had felt so real.

"I bet you didn't see that coming, did you?" Matthew laughed. "I was very impressed at the haste he managed to get rid of you. Maybe he was grateful to me for pushing his hand. That led me onto step four. I planted Tansbury brochures in your post. I hacked into your email preferences and subscribed you to a mailing list with Tansbury offers. It was a gamble, but it worked. I got the landlady to reach out to you with an *amazing* offer. I needed you to be here."

Ava's cloud of confusion deepened. She'd thought that she'd picked Tansbury on a whim. She thought that it was her decision. How wrong she was.

"Of course, I asked Lucy to move away from Louise months back. I couldn't risk you bumping into her, could I? And once you moved in, it was time to make my move. The mothers loved me already, and I relied on Louise to talk me up. That's when I started causing problems with Nancy. I know you're a moral girl, Ava. I knew you wouldn't go for me unless I was available.

"Then it was time for the main event. I want you to suffer what I suffered. I want you in prison, Ava. So I killed Patrick. I killed Patrick with your baseball bat and planted it in your home. Called in anonymously, told the police that I saw you wandering around in a disorderly fashion. It was easy. Too easy." Matthew leaned forward, placing his head in his hands. "Well, are you impressed?"

FORTY-THREE

Louise wiped her mouth as she lifted her head from the sink. El's words echoed in her ears, ringing, deafening her.

Jake Gilbert.

Jake Gilbert was Matthew Riley.

Lovely Jake. The perfect husband. Ava's shot at moving on.

"How?" Louise stuttered, her eyes landing on Zoe. Her eyes were glazed with tears and her hand was covering her mouth. She was as shocked as Louise was. El looked at her cousin sadly.

"It was all me. Helping him change his identity. That's why I've come back, Lou. I need to save her." El stood up from her chair. "But there's no more time. We have to get to Ava and Mia before it's too late."

Louise copied El's movements, her heart in her mouth. This was dangerous. Very dangerous. Jake Gilbert was not a good man. He was a *very* dangerous man.

"Zoe, I don't want you coming. I've already put you in too much danger." Louise put her hand on Zoe's shoulder. Zoe shook her head, tears tumbling down her cheeks.

"I'm in too deep now, Lou. I couldn't live with myself if something happened to you," Zoe said before turning towards El.

"Why can't we just call the police? You could explain everything." Zoe asked, desperation in her eyes. El shook her head.

"He'd see it from a mile coming. He had years to plan his revenge. He's ready," El said. "We've just got to do something he won't see coming."

Zoe threw her hands up in frustration. "And how exactly will we do that? We're not exactly criminal masterminds."

"We use the one thing he didn't anticipate in his plan." El's lips curled into a smirk. "Falling in love with Nancy."

*   *   *

"If you wanted me to go to prison, why keep me here? Why tell me everything?" Ava asked, grasping for a way out. Surely someone would notice her absence. Louise was intelligent, she must have worked it out by now.

Matthew laughed. "I haven't told you everything yet. Aren't you curious about the calls? The emails? How I knew about your every move?"

"You bugged my phone. I figured that much out," Ava said. "I assume you bugged my house too when you brought Kai over. The break in too; you took a key." A slow clap came from Matthew.

"Correct! Suggesting that play date was what put the plan in motion. I bugged the house, took a key. I broke in, placed the baseball bat. Took it back again once you realised it was there. And the photo of Mia . . . that was all Lucy. I got her back into town when I realised how easy it was to get her to do my dirty work. Honestly, when your life was on the line, she would do *anything.*" Matthew was so pleased with himself that it made Ava sick. The planning, the lying. All for this. All to get revenge on her.

"And you really shouldn't leave your email password by your computer, Ava. That allowed me to delete all record of the emails I sent to you. Your carelessness just made life easier for me." He shrugged and looked towards Ava with narrowed eyes. "And aren't you wondering about the calls? The breathing down the phone? Why would he do that? I hear you ask. Well, Ava. I have an answer for you; the more unhinged you were, the more it was easy to pin it on you. Imagining emails, running to your friends about spooky calls, calling the police about a break in that 'never happened'." He sighed. "An unhinged Ava was much better use to me that a sane one."

"You won't get away with this," Ava spat. Matthew simply laughed.

"But I will. Nancy and I's divorce will go through, I'll leave town. Disappear. I've done it before. I can do it again."

"What are you going to do with me, then?" Ava asked weakly, rage and nerves rinsing every bone of her body.

"It wasn't part of the plan for you to find out that it was me. I was hoping you'd just go to prison. But then I found you snooping. That's . . . changed things. So, I'm going to need you to write a suicide note for me."

Ava's stomach dropped. "A what?" Her insides coiled up. Her worst nightmares were being confirmed. He wanted to kill her.

"See, I can't have you blabbing my secret out. You'll write a suicide note confessing to your husband's death. Your parents will be given custody of Mia. The end." Matthew shook his hands as if to say, 'ta da'. Ava pulled at her restraints.

"Go to hell, you bastard," Ava spat, pulling at the ropes with every will in her body. She needed to get out. Matthew simply chuckled, leaning over to his desk and sourcing a pen and a sheet of paper.

"If you don't do it, I'll kill Mia. It's you or her, Ava." Matthew shrugged his shoulders. "I roll like that."

"You're disgusting," Ava cried, tears filling her eyes. "Won't people find it a little suspicious that I committed suicide in your house?"

Matthew smirked. "I'll move your body, duh." He rolled his eyes. "Now do you want me to do this the easy way, or the hard way?"

It was then when the sound of hope entered Ava's ears. She heard the front door unlock. Matthew's eyes filled with surprise, glancing towards the door.

"Make a sound, and you're dead." Matthew pulled a gun from his jacket pocket and pointed it at Ava's head.

"Jake?" the voice called, and it was distinctively Nancy's. This was Ava's only opportunity. She needed Nancy to find her.

"One second, Nancy," Matthew called back before grabbing a roll of duct tape and covering Ava's mouth with a strip. He looked back at her with hatred, before leaving his study and shutting the door.

Ava wiggled in her seat, gaining a rocking action. She moved her body faster, before the seat fell on its side. Pain shot up her side, but she ignored it. She needed to get out to save Mia.

"What's that?" she heard Nancy say, and Ava felt hope spring in her stomach. Come on, Nancy.

"Nothing. My window is open, the wind must have knocked something over," Matthew said, his voice calm. *He really is a sociopath*, Ava thought.

"Okay." Nancy sounded concerned but accepted his answer. Ava pulled at the ropes, but they were too tight. She needed to find something sharp. She looked around, but on the ground, she was too far from his desk. She wiggled around some more, but Matthew had really secured her.

"Okay, well, I'll pick Kai up tomorrow then. I'll be in the city tonight, just call me if you need anything," Nancy said, and it sounded like she was making her way towards the door. Panic rippled inside Ava's stomach. She needed more time.

"See you tomorrow," Matthew called, and then the door slammed shut. Ava's eyes filled with tears. It was over. She tried to escape the bonds one last time, but there was no hope.

The door swung open, revealing Matthew's looming figure. He shook his head.

"I guess we're doing this the hard way then." He took a step closer, before his body tumbled forward, hitting the floor in a slump. Behind him stood Nancy, holding a smashed bottle over her head.

Ava's eyes widened in surprise, and Nancy ran over to her.

"Ava, oh my God." She pulled at the knots, untying Ava's hands. "I am so sorry." Once Ava was free, she threw her arms around Nancy's neck, tears falling down her face.

"Thank you. Thank you thank you thank you," she cried into her shoulder. Nancy stroked Ava's hair.

"Don't thank me yet. We need to get out of here before he wakes up," Nancy said. Ava nodded, glancing at Matthew's slumped figure. Nancy took Ava's hand and they ran from the room.

"I need to find Mia," Ava told Nancy as they ran towards the door.

"She's fine. Louise and her cousin have her," Nancy said, pulling Ava up and ushering her into the hallway and to the door. Ava's stomach dropped once more. Mia would not be safe with Lucy.

"Where are they?" Ava said, panic in her voice. "Lucy is dangerous, Nancy."

"She's not, Ava. I promise you." Nancy pulled at Ava's hand, taking them out of the house and into the driveway.

It was then when the gun fired. Ava turned back and saw Matthew running at them, his gun posed to shoot again. He had missed the first time, but he was gaining ground.

"Run, Ava!" Nancy screamed. Ava did not need to be told twice, but the second gun shot was loud in her ears. Pain rocketed up her sides, the bullet hitting her her lower back. She fell to the floor, screaming in agony. A third gunshot sounded, but she was already unconscious.

* * *

231

She runs towards me, fear in her eyes. I know what I need to do.
I do what I should have done all along.
I lift my gun and I pull the trigger.
Death is a small price to pay for happiness.
And now I finally am free.

*   *   *

Ava knew where she was before she opened her eyes. The smell, the lights, the atmosphere—she was in hospital.

Her eyes flickered open to see her mother sitting on the visitor's chairs.

"Mum?" she said, her voice croaky. As she spoke, pain blossomed from the wound in her back. Her midsection was restricted, presumably from a bandage. Carol Milberry sat up and rushed to her daughter's side.

"Darling, thank goodness you're awake." Tears trickled down her cheeks and she kissed Ava's forehead.

"Careful, I'm sore," Ava said, laughing slightly. "What happened?"

"Matthew shot you, darling. In the back." Carol wiped her cheeks. "But your friends have explained everything. The police have withdrawn the arrest. You're free, Ava. And Matthew is going to prison. For life this time."

Ava's eyes filled with tears, and for the first time in a long time, they were happy tears. She was free.

"How did they get him?" Ava asked, confused. She'd thought she was dead when she'd heard that third gunshot.

"It was Lucy, honey. Lucy shot him in the stomach." Carol shrugged her shoulders. "His injury was severe, but he'll live. As soon as he recovers, he'll be locked up for good."

Lucy shot him?

232

Ava had been wrong before. Lucy was in town because she needed to save Ava, not ruin her life.

She had been wrong.

"Where's Mia?" Ava asked. "Is she okay?"

"She's at home with Dad. We didn't want her to know about Matthew. All she knows is that mummy fell down the stairs at Kai's house." Carol stroked Ava's arm. "I'll let everyone know that you're awake."

"Everyone?" Ava questioned. Carol gave her daughter a small smile.

"Your friends. Lucy, Louise, Zoe, and Nancy. They're very worried about you. I'll go get them." Carol stood up and left the room.

Ava's head was spinning. *Lucy had saved her life.*

How wrong she had been.

EPILOGUE

Ava Milberry did not like to consider herself a widower. It was something that had never appealed to her, and as much as her seventeen-year-old self had believed in happily ever after, it had happened anyway. Her story was dramatic, sad, and surprising. A complicated murder.

But Ava was no longer lonely. She had a fantastic group of friends, including Lucy.

Lucy was slightly unstable, and a little bit dangerous.

But so was Ava.

As she pulled up to the school gates, Mia cried out in happiness, "Last day of school!"

"You excited for Christmas, Mia?" Ava said, mocking surprise. Mia nodded, before climbing out of her car seat.

As they made their way towards the school gates, Ava spotted Louise, Zoe and Nancy chatting. Mia ran over to her school friends, and Ava greeted hers.

"Morning," she said, wrapping her arms around each of her friends.

"We were just thinking, we should do a joint Christmas this year," Louise said, folding her arms. "It would be really fun."

"I could host. I have a lot of space now," Nancy joked, but there was still sadness in her eyes. Ava put her hand on Nancy's arm and squeezed it reassuringly.

"That sounds lovely," Ava said. "Really lovely." She put her arm around Louise, wincing slightly as the skin around her wound stretched. It was healing, slowly but surely.

It just needed time. All wounds need time to heal.

But slowly, they would heal.

And whilst the scar would remain, the pain would be gone.

And soon, they'd forget.

Nancy would forget her ex-husbands darker side.

Louise would forget that her cousin lied to her.

And Ava would forget about the man who tried to ruin her life.

So . . . let the healing begin.

The End

FREE DOWNLOAD

Can't get enough of the story?
Get these two bonus chapters when you sign up at
typewriterpub.com/author/flora-mcconnell

Do you like thriller stories?
Here are samples of other stories
you might enjoy!

CHAPTER ONE

I hated riding the subway. Not just any subway either. The subways in New York City, to be exact. I hated those things with an unyielding passion. There were no ifs, ands, or buts about it.

Who wanted to ride in an underground train that smelled like stale play dough and old people? Maybe it was just me, maybe I was over exaggerating, or maybe I was losing my sense of smell, but that was definitely the smell that aggressively assaulted my nose whenever I stepped foot in a subway car.

I hated how crowded they were too. I would receive an elbow to the ribs or a hard shove from someone's shoulder almost every time I was forced to ride that thing. At the end of my ride, I always walked out looking like I just went ten rounds with a mildly ferocious ten-year-old.

There was never anywhere to sit. If all the seats were taken by the time I got on—and they usually were—then I would be forced to stand among the crowd of swaying bodies, where perverts would "accidentally" rub up against me. It was like a game of musical chairs where the loser would get felt up by a bunch of strange old men as a punishment.

As if all that wasn't bad enough, the ride itself took at least twenty minutes and I had to ride the damn thing twice.

Why did I have to ride it twice?

Well, that's because I lived right outside my school's district. So *technically*, the school bus couldn't pick me up from my house, but we lived close enough that I could walk to the subway station in the city and get a ride closer to school and walk the rest of the way every single day.

I was eighteen. I should have been riding back and forth in my own car but no. My parents, who were definitely using their parent logic on this, thought it would be better if I rode the subway every day, despite the fact that I kept reminding them that I was bound to be kidnapped, robbed, shot, or a mix of all three by doing so. I did live in New York after all. Worse things had happened.

I made it my job to constantly remind them that when they saw me on the news with the caption "Missing Girl" above my hideous high school ID picture, it was going to be all their fault. With all the money I spent riding the subway, I could have bought my own car by now, but did I? No. Apparently, I wasn't ready for that big of a responsibility yet.

This is where you insert the eye roll and dramatic sigh.

Basically, they trusted me to venture into a crowd of people that could easily be hiding serial killers and knife-wielding maniacs—I really needed to quit watching so much *Law and Order*—but they didn't trust me with my own car.

Parent logic.

However, what happened on that one day I rode the subway, that one day that was supposed to be just like any other, I don't think anyone saw it coming.

Not me, not my parents, not the unsuspecting passengers on the subway.

No one.

The day where I would really be in my very own episode of *Law and Order*, and unfortunately, I'd end up being the victim.

Lucky me.

*   *   *

Whoever decided to make an alarm clock sound like the siren for the end of the world was an idiot. If I didn't die from the small heart attack the stupid thing gave me, then I'd end up smashing Satan's creation against my nightstand.

I'm currently on alarm clock number three.

Lucky for my current alarm clock, I wasn't in a *complete* hostile mood when it abruptly woke me this time.

Groaning, I blindly slammed my hand down, knocking various items off my nightstand until I found the snooze button and rolled out of my warm bed, blankets and all.

I landed on the hardwood floor with a loud *thud*.

My mom's voice rang from downstairs not even two seconds after.

"Gemma, what was that?! You better not have broken anything!"

Yeah, Mom, don't ask if I was the *thing* that fell and possibly broke.

I didn't even bother getting up or untangling myself from my blanket to answer her. I just rolled over to the door like some sort of deformed giant baked potato and yelled, "It was just a shirt!"

"What kind of shirt makes that sound when it falls?!" she yelled back. I could almost picture the deadpan look on her face.

Did I leave out the part where I was *in* the shirt when it fell?

"Well, I'm fine anyway! Thanks for asking!" I yelled back down.

"Just hurry up! You're going to be late!"

There was a slight pause before she added, "Again!"

Groaning again, I sat up and threw off my blanket, making goose bumps instantly rise against my skin as I slowly made my way across the hall to the bathroom.

I even made an extra effort to drag my feet.

Who cared if I was late? Was I really missing out on something important?

Lord forbid I miss out on my science teacher teaching us that the nucleus was the powerhouse of the cell.

Or was it the mitochondria?

See? I couldn't even bother to remember.

And don't even get me started on the whole y=mx+b thing.

I'd *definitely* need that information later in life.

After showering and doing my basic morning routine, I brushed out my hair so it no longer looked like a bird had made a nest in it, and it fell in its usual lifeless sheet down to my shoulders.

I got dressed in a simple white long-sleeved shirt, black zip-up hoodie, and jeans that my mother had bought me for Christmas last year, claiming that they hugged the curves I had, but I was pretty sure they were nonexistent.

I'm sure she only said it to try and make me feel better.

She got an A for effort.

After slipping into a pair of Converse, I did a once-over in the mirror to make sure I passed the 'Acceptable to be seen by society today' test, which really just consisted of me making sure I didn't look like I had been living in a cave for the last three months before I went outside.

Satisfied with my look, I grabbed my backpack off the desk in the corner of my room and bounded down the stairs one at a time. I tried the whole taking two steps at a time thing once, and let's just say my face paid the price.

As soon as I reached the bottom step, the smell of bacon assaulted my nose, making my mouth water. Stepping into the kitchen, I saw my mom—her dark and slightly graying hair pulled into a messy bun—still in her pajamas, leaning over a frying pan full of bacon.

My dad, with his also graying black hair, was sitting in a chair at the kitchen table with a newspaper in one hand and a white "World's #1 Dad" mug—one of the many I had gotten him for three Christmases in a row—filled with coffee in the other. He looked like a dad straight out of a TV series. Who even still reads newspapers these days?

He was dressed in a white button-up shirt and a black tie with purple polka dots—another Christmas gift from me—black slacks, and a pair of glasses was sitting on the bridge of his nose.

Walking over, I plucked two pieces of bacon off his plate and smiled sweetly at him as he looked up from his newspaper with his eyebrows raised.

"You weren't going to eat it anyway," I said in response to his look as I shoved a piece into my mouth.

I walked over to my baby brother, Aiden, who was sitting in his highchair with a bowl full of, for lack of a better word, slop. I hope he hadn't been eating that.

I ruffled his fluffy brown hair before I leaned down and whispered in his ear, making sure I was still loud enough so that my parents could hear me clearly. "If you want live to see three, I wouldn't eat that," I said, gesturing to the unidentifiable contents that I'm pretty sure had just moved in his bowl.

In response to my whispered warning, Aiden smiled up at me like he knew exactly what I was talking about. My dad chuckled and my mom turned around to glare at me.

I shrugged and kissed her on the cheek before heading towards the front door.

Before I opened the front door, I yelled over my shoulder, unable to stop myself, "Only eat the bacon, anything else and you have two options: hospital or the grave!"

I quickly ran out the door before my mom could throw the frying pan at me. I could hear my dad's laughter echoing outside before I shut the door.

My mom would swear up and down that she was a good cook, but after last Thanksgiving, I beg to differ. That year, we had pizza for Thanksgiving, so I think that pretty much explained itself.

I couldn't help but laugh, then instantly checked to make sure none of my neighbors were out and saw me laughing by myself. I continued munching on my last piece of bacon before I made my way down the sidewalk, the chilly air stinging my cheeks, and toward the subway, not knowing what exactly would be in store for me when I got there.

If you enjoyed this sample, look for
The Subway
on Amazon.

PSYCHO BILLIONAIRE

KASHMIRA KAMAT

CHAPTER ONE

KIARA

The first time I ever saw him was during a long rainy night. The clock ticked 11 PM, which was cutting close to the restaurant closing time. Since it was a weekday, the restaurant barely had any customers.

I worked at a small Chinese restaurant called *Sea Dragon,* where we served the best chicken dumplings and roast egg rolls in town—at least that's what the restaurant was popular for, and people loved visiting here all the time.

My coworker, Kathy, had left early tonight because she had a date. She had requested me to cover for her, begging me with her puppy eyes, and I eventually gave in since Kathy usually did favors for me too.

Thus, I was left me alone with Diego who seemed to be mopping a puddle of Coke that a kid had spilled a few minutes back off the floor. He gave me a tired smile, a smile that indicated the impending doom of Friday, knowing full well that it was going to be hella crowded. We barely had time to breathe on a weekend.

We were almost done cleaning all the tables when suddenly, Sam, the chef walked out of the kitchen frantically. Worry was written all over his face. He had never seemed so agitated before, so this was clearly something serious.

"What's wrong, Sam?" I inquired.

"It's my daughter," he replied. "My wife was telling me on the phone that Lily is being rushed to the hospital because she's running a high fever. I . . . I need to go."

"You can't!" Diego interrupted. "It's still an hour before closing. What if there's another customer?" He threw me a look.

"Can't you guys just manage for one hour? Please." Sam's pleading eyes turned towards me. "I need to be with my daughter."

I nodded. "We will manage." I placed my hand on his back, giving it a reassuring pat. "You can go."

"What? Are you nuts?" Diego shrieked. "If Manager Jeff finds out, we are going to get our asses handed back to us. And we could get fired!"

"Jeff doesn't need to know," I said. "It's just one hour. No one's going to walk in at this time"

Diego sighed and resumed his work. His face was going red. It looked like he was going to burst a vein or two. Sam packed his stuff and stormed out of the door, thanking me for the millionth time.

I watched from the window as he settled into his old Honda Civic and pulled out of the parking lot.

Fifteen minutes after Sam left, the little restaurant bell dinged, indicating there was a customer. I knew that if it was just one person or perhaps a couple, I could manage, but in walked three men in suits and occupied a table near the window. One of them was Asian, the other was a lanky redhead, and the third, by the window, looked younger than the two.

I approached their table with a smile, and they probably noticed I didn't have a menu card in my hand.

"Gentlemen, actually we closed early tonight because the chef had to leave due to an emergency. We wouldn't be able to serve anything at the moment," I said. "I apologize."

"Maybe you haven't noticed, but the weather's bad outside, and there aren't many restaurants in this area, and most of them are closed," the attractive Asian explained. "Isn't there anything you can serve us?"

"Chicken fried rice and Wonton soup," I suggested. "That's the best I can make."

The group of men agreed to the suggestion. Feeling motivated to become the evening's chef for once; I rushed back into the kitchen, tied the apron around my waist, and began dicing the veggies.

Diego was nowhere in sight, probably sulking in the staff room at the back, having wanted nothing to do with my little adventure of serving the customers in the restaurant without a chef. He clearly did not trust my cooking skills.

I, for one, had always been observant of what Sam cooked and had tried his recipes at home a few times, and it had turned out good. Although I just knew a few things off the menu, it was enough to serve someone during desperate times like these.

A few minutes later, I served them their dinner. "Enjoy your meal," I said and resumed my work.

I noticed another man seated alone a few booths down. Diego had served him coffee and turned the *"Open"* sign to *"Closed"*

I could feel a pair of eyes boring into my back as I wiped the counter with a rag. I turned to look, and the young man from the trio was staring at me. He smiled, so I smiled back at him and looked away.

Something about his attitude gave me the creeps. I didn't dress sexy because I appreciated predators staring at my ass. It was part of my job. They told me putting on makeup usually earned a lot of tips, and yes, my coworkers were right. I knew it was appealing to some men to see women serving around dressed in a Chinese *Qipao*, and I received more compliments for it, but some men were downright pervy. That was what bothered me about this job.

The three men seemed to be enjoying the meal, and when it was time to pay, one of the men pushed his American Express card towards me, along with numerous hundred dollar bills.

"You're pretty good at cooking for someone who doesn't work as a chef," the dark-haired man said.

"Thanks," I said with a smile and then noticed the tip he had given me.

Four hundred dollars as tip? Either he hadn't noticed how much he'd given me or he was totally insane. The two men stared at him incredulously, and my jaw was probably on the floor too.

"It's for you. Don't be so surprised," he added.

"Are you sure?"

"Of course," he said.

A few seconds later, I gained my composure, and I knew that my face had lit up by then.

"Thank you so much, sir. I really appreciate it."

I was desperate, alright. I had bills to pay, my father's debts to clear, and a whole bag filled with responsibilities. It didn't help that my salary wasn't much, so the tips helped me a lot.

I pushed the money in my pocket and went as far as to see the customers out of the door as a polite gesture for their generosity.

After the coffee-drinking customer had paid and walked out, Diego and I were left to close the restaurant. He stayed at the cash counter to settle the bills while I took the trash out of the back door.

The storm had come to a halt. I placed some leftover fish and water for the stray cat that I had been feeding for over the past few months and started to make my way back inside the restaurant when a strong hand reached for the doorknob first and slammed the door shut.

I looked up to see who it was. The darkness made it quite difficult, but a flash of lightning allowed me to see that it was the same man as before. The man who'd generously tipped me.

I fidgeted. "Do you need anything?"

He straightened his blazer jacket and turned to look at his watch and smiled at me. "I can give you an extra two hundred," he suggested, smiling coyly. "What do you say?"

"I don't understand."

He sighed, took my hand in his, and placed it on the crotch of his pants, rubbing on it slightly, and groaned.

"I have my car parked just around the parking lot. We'll make it quick."

I snatched my hand out of his grasp, feeling disgusted. "I'm not a whore."

"Oh c'mon. I saw how you were smiling at me," he said as if that explained anything.

"I smile at all my customers. It doesn't mean anything." My voice was shaky by now.

"Just a quick fuck. You can do some exceptions for extra tips, right?"

I reached for my pocket and thrust the dollar bills in his face. "Here. I don't need your money. Now, move out of my way."

I should have known he was one of those creepy men who lured women by showing them the power of money. I shouldn't even have accepted such a hefty tip.

Stupid. Stupid. Stupid.

He let go of the door handle, so I opened the door and started walking in when he grabbed me out of nowhere, slammed the door, and locked it behind him. Next, he grabbed me and pushed me against the wall, ripping the top button off the dress.

I struggled, screaming for someone to help me when he covered my mouth with his palm. I heard my own muffled cries over the sound of thunder. I tried to knee his groin, and I may have scratched his cheek because it was now bleeding.

I smacked him, and he smacked me hard in return, muttering, *"stupid bitch"* under his breath. I was resisting so hard, but

I felt like I was going to lose the fight. I had this gut feeling that something bad was going to happen.

I realized this was the end; an ugly one where I would probably end up sexually assaulted and dead somewhere near the dumpster. They said you should never beg for mercy at the person causing an assault because begging usually fed their fantasy and made their experience even more fun, but I wasn't even in the state to think of all that.

I continued to repeat the words *"please"*. My dress was tattered and dirty from struggling on the ground. He had my wrists pinned down. His knee was nudging between my thighs as his hand made its way towards my panties when suddenly, he stopped.

I was brawling, trying to pull myself to a sitting position, covering myself and I dared to look towards him to see what had stopped the assault.

A man was standing in the alley. I couldn't see his face properly, but at that moment, I knew that he was my knight in shining armor.

If you enjoyed this sample, look for
Psycho Billionaire
on Amazon.

THE STRANGE DISAPPEARANCE OF CALLA RIVERS

ANNE MARSHALL

Before

There was a chill in the night air as the leaves falling from the first changing trees of the season scattered along the sidewalk. They blew past house after house before settling in a pile against a thicket of bushes that the homeowner neglected. With the warmth of the clicking heater that needed tossing out years ago, the homeowner with the shaggy bushes sat among his deep thoughts with corn nuts scattered over his chest. Seemingly without a care in the world, he grunted and coughed up a few nuts before grabbing aimlessly for the remote stuck between him and the tattered leather armrest.

Flipping through the static-filled cable channels, the grimy homeowner breathed a deep sigh of relief. He didn't see any reporting on the abduction last night. His luck and attitude changed when the channels stopped on the twenty-four-hour news. He turned the volume up when he saw a familiar face plastered in the upper right corner that he wished he hadn't. Pausing and sitting forward, letting the nuts fall to the floor, he paid as much attention to the news as he could. Clicking the remote a few more times for the volume, he listened to what they had to say about the girl on his screen.

"Reports about a young coed that's been missing since last night have come in. Her parents called in a report that she ran away, but a witness might be able to shed some new light on the subject. More on the story at eleven. Until then, if you see a young woman, five feet eight, long brown hair, hazel eyes, and pale skin, please call your local police department. Her photo provided by her

parents is on the screen now. Any information is helpful. Now, onto the latest traffic report—"

He cut the TV off seconds after they changed the subject. He might not have been as careful as he thought. Cursing, he thought about the lies he would need to tell to get out of this situation. He couldn't run, not yet. He needed to bide his time until the coast was clear. This wasn't like the times before; they didn't have anyone looking for them. Why had he accepted this tempting offer? He knew it was too good to be true when he was given the information, but he took it anyway. One look at her and he fell harder than he ever fell before. He was promised that no one would be looking for her, that she was no one from a nothing family. The added information settled sourly in his stomach. He could hear the conversation with his supplier now. Pushing his fingers into his eyes until he saw only purple, he tried to think of something else.

No more than five minutes after the news report, a telltale sound came from the back bedroom. Clicking the TV back on, he turned the volume up until it drowned out the new noise. If his nosy neighbors reported him again, he would have to leave sooner, exposing himself and his project to the town—something he very much did not want to happen. The muffled sounds coming from the room started rising above the sound of the three stooges smacking each other on the television. Thinking on his feet, he decided to silence the noise the only way he knew how, without having to start the fun plans he had planned later.

Changing pace, he stood up from the ratty recliner and headed for the back room. Taking long strides down the short hall, the oily man threw the back bedroom door open and set his sights on the closet.

He stood at the front of the closet door while he listened to the pathetic moans and whimpers of the new project, the young lady that set his soul on fire when he looked into her begging eyes. He stood there for a moment and thought about that night. He thought of her pleading eyes, the ones swimming with wantoning need as her hands reached out for him, barely able to stand on her own feet without his help. The memory of her perfume engulfed him as it did that night. The scent of her sweat just under it—she had been dancing that night. He could even smell the vodka on her breath, remembering the drink he had spiced up for her at the club. It was only something to help her into his rough arms, nothing that would hurt her. He hated the idea of her being harmed in any way.

Breaking out of his memories when the sounds didn't stop, he banged on the door three times. When it finally died with a yelp, he turned to leave the room, but a sharp, piercing screech brought him to a full stop.

Turning back and making quick work of the small lock, he threw it on the bed behind him and slid the other locks out of place before pulling the door open.

Reaching for the lightbulb's string, he pulled on it until the yellow light was cast around the small room. Crouching down, he came face to face with his beloved new project.

"You're going to have to keep quiet. We wouldn't want to wake the neighbors, would we?" Lowering himself more, he reached out to touch the side of her face through the kennel bars, but she backed away as far as the metal cage would allow her to. He hummed to himself as he caught her hair between his rough fingers. His eyes lingered on the strands of deep brown hair as he curled them around his index finger. With the space of the walk-in closet, he had plenty of room to sit and stare at her all night, if he wanted. However, seeing the tears, dirt, and sweat on her face infuriated him. He wanted to clean her up and make her smile like he'd seen weeks ago when they first met. She didn't know him then, but when she smiled at him from across the room, he was consumed. It wasn't even just the tip about her existence from his buddy; she was truly a beauty, one that shouldn't be forgotten or wasted too quickly.

Tilting his head to the side, he opened the door to the kennel, just enough for him to reach in and hold her dirty face in his thick hand. Her eyes didn't meet his as they stayed stuck on the wall behind him. He shook her head until she squeaked and moved her eyes to look at his. "Good girl," he whispered as she flinched. He loved seeing the terror on her face. She was such a good actress, he believed. "Stay quiet and I'll give you a little treat." He twirled her hair again once his hand fell from her face.

"We're going to change a few things, dear. Don't worry, it won't hurt. I would never hurt you." With his unsettling grin, the fear that bloomed in her chest seeped into her soul. This wasn't a situation she was going to walk away from, that much she knew. Worse than that, she saw the empty void behind the man's eyes. Telling her every word that came out of his mouth would happen despite any effort she made to turn them into lies—to not believe in them. Hearing the news before told her everything she needed to know.

Breathing deeply, she closed her eyes as the kennel door closed and locked with a thick click. The last bit of hope that someone would come for her disappeared as she swallowed back the fear stuck in her throat. The light died around her as her mind searched for something to hold onto. With fuzzy thoughts, she reached for any sort of light still lingering inside her but found herself as dark as the closet. Her hope for survival was stuck in the room with her, hanging by a string of hope that frayed with every passing day.

If you enjoyed this sample, look for
The Strange Disappearance of Calla Rivers
on Amazon.

AUTHOR'S NOTE

Thank you so much for reading *Her Final Sorrow*! I can't express how grateful I am for reading something that was once just a thought inside my head.

I'd love to hear your thoughts on the book. Please leave a review on Amazon or Goodreads because I just love reading your comments and getting to know you!

Can't wait to hear from you!

Flora McConnell

ABOUT THE AUTHOR

Flora McConnell is a Psychology graduate who currently lives in London. She works at an advertising agency as a Creative, where she uses her writing skills to come up with cool ads you see on TV. She has enjoyed writing since she was a child, and is the author of the book 'Sweet Revenge', which gained its popularity via the writing platform Wattpad.